Gods and Guardians
CHRONICLES
Book 1

The Reaping

Gods and Guardians
CHRONICLES
Book 1

The Reaping

by

Alana Wells

XIERE'S
DOMINION
PUBLISHING

Library of Congress Control Number: TXu 1-874-407

This novel is entirely a work of fiction. The names, characters and incidents portrayed in it are the work of the author's imagination. Any resemblance to actual persons, living or dead, events or localities is entirely coincidental.

Alana Wells asserts the moral right to be identified as the author of this work.

Alana Wells has no responsibility for the persistence or accuracy of URLs for external or third-party Internet Websites referred to in this publication and does not guarantee that any content on such Websites is, or will remain, accurate or appropriate.

Designations used by companies to distinguish their products are often claimed as trademarks. All brand names and product names used in this book and on its cover are trade names, service marks, trademarks and registered trademarks of their respective owners. The publishers and the book are not associated with any product or vendor mentioned in this book. None of the companies referenced within the book have endorsed the book.

Editing by Kathryn Hastings
Front cover art by Lindsay Hayes
Back cover art Kathryn Hastings
Graphic design by Brian Hill
Typesetting by Natasha Combs

www.xieresdominion.com

Contents

Special thanks to Kathryn Hastings
who without her love and support this
book would have not been possible.

Prologue

Nadia awoke with a start. She had been dreaming of the darkness again. Cold and evil things with glittery eyes lived in the shadows, lusting for her soul. She tried to change her dreams repeatedly but, she returned to a vast land of nothingness. Her screams echoed as they ripped her open and tore her apart. She watched as her soul was sucked from her flesh like a greedy aspirator.

Her life was different before … before they came. She couldn't even remember the last time she had a good dream. She wanted to give into them … it would have been easier. She would finally be free from their torment. Her strength was waning, but still, she resisted … and with her resistance came pain.

Even worse was when she woke and saw their glittery eyes above her and their laughter ringing in her ears.

The Dark Visitor

Chapter One

Nadia was a different sort of child. She learned new things at an extraordinary rate. Within a year of being born, she could string together full sentences. She went from sitting up to walking, skipping the crawling stage altogether. She was easily frustrated, however. When she didn't learn something immediately, she would scream to high heaven. At the age of four she learned to read, but they weren't books for her age group. Nadia called Dr. Seuss books "baby books." Instead, she insisted on reading something more compelling and on a fifth-grade level.

Her parents knew she was gifted but couldn't afford to place her into a special program. They supplemented with constant trips to the library where Nadia scoured the place for interesting material. Some of the books she selected were over 700 pages long. She never asked anyone to explain the words she didn't understand, opting to look them up in a dictionary. School was dull because she aced all her tests without studying. Homework only took her minutes. Her parents, like most parents of a gifted child, envisioned her working for NASA or the White House.

Nadia and her family lived outside a small town called Ravens Wood in New Hampshire. As she aged, everyone told her she looked exactly like her mother. She had dark brown hair with hazel eyes. Her little face was oval-shaped, and her eyes crinkled when she laughed. Nadia had a slender build, but she was strong for her size, often getting into scraps with the neighborhood boys. Bashing one of them in the head with a metal bucket didn't help matters. He had called her a name she didn't like so she responded with action rather than words. Nadia often responded with action, and she was quick on her feet. Her father chastised her for the event, but Nadia knew he was secretly proud.

Their house was perched on top of a little hill surrounded by trees. It was painted green with brown shutters. Her parents told her they picked the house because it blended so well with the foliage. Their home was at the edge of a small forest which Nadia like to explore with her mother. The house was a two story, with an attic and a cellar. The upper floor had her bedroom next to her brother's, while the downstairs consisted of a kitchen, family room, and bedroom. There was also a den her father called his 'man cave.'

The staircase leading upstairs had an elaborate banister which Travis, her only sibling, slid down daily when he was supposed to be watching her after school. Nadia always wanted to slide too but Travis wouldn't allow it. He insisted it was too dangerous. She liked the danger and slid down it a few times when he wasn't looking anyway.

Travis was 5 years older than Nadia and resembled their father. He was a tall, bulky blond with brown eyes. He hunched while he walked which earned him the nickname Ogre … a name he thoroughly despised. Travis teased her constantly, making her scream at the top of her lungs. When he took things too far, she punched him as hard as her little fists could. One time she stabbed him in the leg with a pencil, which earned her a spanking from their father. Nadia loved her brother despite his incessant teasing and constant reminders that he was older and far wiser.

Travis was a baseball fanatic. He collected cards, which he kept in pristine condition in a large binder by his desk. He brought them out frequently to show Nadia. She pretended to be interested but had no idea who any of the players were. Travis knew everyone by heart and could easily recite their stats without looking. Nadia never understood the appeal of baseball or any other sport for that matter. It just wasn't interesting to her.

Nadia wasn't attached to material things except for one item her mother bought for her. It was a small, red, plastic dragon that could fit in the palm of her hand. Nadia spent hours examining it, turning it over and over. Its little wings jutted out from either side like it was going to launch into the air. Its mouth was open in a silent roar. She didn't know why she was so attached to a piece of plastic, but it was her favorite.

Her parents Robert and Sarah were high school sweethearts, marrying immediately after high school. Robert became a plumber and Sarah worked at the town's only daycare. They weren't rich by any means, but they made enough to pay the bills and keep the family happy. They only had one car which Sarah drove most of the time. The plumbing company allowed Robert to use their van for transportation. They were the typical middle-class, American family.

Her father was stern but fair with Nadia and her brother. While Nadia loved her father, she had a stronger connection with her mother. Sarah spent any extra time she had with Nadia even if she was exhausted from work. Evenings with her mother were Nadia's favorite time. The two of them would sit and talk while Sarah brushed Nadia's hair. On warm weekends, Sarah would wake Nadia early in the morning. They would creep silently out of the house and head into the woods. It was their special time. Sarah knew the names of every plant and taught her daughter medicinal uses of many of them. Nadia soaked up everything, like a sponge. Her mother made her feel extraordinary.

When Sarah was busy, Nadia would occupy her time playing in the attic. It was Nadia's favorite place in the house. A long set of narrow stairs on the second floor led to a pink door. The attic was huge, and it was filled with many 'treasures.' The solid wood floor led to two large round windows at either end of the room. Light bulbs hung on long wires from the rafters. It was bright and happy, unlike many attics she had seen in movies. It felt magical.

Her parents encouraged her to hang her drawings on the walls which gave her a private art gallery. Sarah bought her some plants, which she kept near the window to breathe life into her secret hideaway. She had a table, chairs, a desk and an old bean bag chair she loved to flop into. Nadia, having a vivid imagination held many tea parties in the attic with her stuffed animals. Once she even got Travis to attend, but he left before the party ended. Nadia suspected it was because she made him wear a frilly bonnet while serving her tea. She preferred the attic to her own room and later when the darkness came, it became her only sanctuary.

As bright and cheerful as the attic was, the cellar was the opposite. It smelled dank and musty. The walls and floor were made of stones and seemed to weep moisture. There were only two lights for the entire basement which cast shadows everywhere. The floor was made of broken concrete and dirt which made it even creepier. It had a low ceiling making it impossible to escape the cobwebs sinewy strands.

Nadia hated the cellar. She refused to go down there unless someone was with her. Once when she was seven, her brother thought it would be funny to lock her inside. Her screams caused the neighbors to come rushing over. Travis was punished for his stunt, but the incident gave her nightmares for a week. He apologized profusely and promised never to do it again. He seemed nicer to her afterwards even though he still refused to partake in her tea parties.

Nadia had a best friend who lived across the street. She was an African American girl named Tasha. She was thin as a rail and taller than Nadia. Tasha had a pile of brown curly hair and light brown eyes. They were inseparable during school, and after school, they spent hours chasing each other. Their favorite thing to do was annoy Travis by threatening to pour water over his baseball cards. Travis would lock himself in his room to protect his precious cards while screaming at them to go away. During the summer, they slept over at each other's houses.

Nadia was happy … until *it* came … when darkness infected their lives. Her whole life changed when she turned ten. Shadows and whispers crept close to her as she was playing with her dolls. It told her things … bad things. It made her feel hopeless and dead inside which was ironic since her name meant 'hope.' The assaults usually came at night. She would have horrific nightmares and often awoke screaming.

The nightmares weren't the worst part though. The worst part was opening her eyes and seeing the tall, shadow man standing at the end of her bed. She couldn't see his face except for his eyes … eyes that glittered red. It never said anything, but on occasion, it would laugh at her. The sound of its gravelly voice sent chills down her spine. Nadia was so terrified she couldn't move. He always disappeared when her parents burst through the door. They continually dismissed her fears as bad dreams.

Her parents expressed their concern for her fears, but they couldn't fathom what was happening. They didn't know why … and Nadia couldn't tell them. She tried to tell them once when she was 11, but it only made the situation worse. They whisked her to the doctor, worried there was something wrong with her brain. The doctor told her parents she was hallucinating and if the situation became worse, he would put her on medicine. Nadia knew there was nothing wrong with her. What she was seeing was real. She knew what was haunting her. It was a demon.

The first time she saw it, it flitted in and out of her sight. After a year of the cat and mouse game, it began appearing, showing more of itself. It terrified her because she didn't know what to do about it. She couldn't talk to anyone. Her father was an atheist and her mother simply believed in a 'higher power.' Her family wouldn't understand, and so she was alone. It never stayed for a long time, just long enough to make her worry. Nadia learned to mask her fear from her parents, so they never knew how tormented she was inside.

After her incident with the doctor, Nadia decided to speak

with the demon to find out what it wanted. No one else saw it, so she knew it wanted something from her. Nadia sensed when it was in the house even before it showed itself. She felt its dark energy. Nadia knew exactly where it stayed when it was visiting … in the cellar. It took her a long time to develop enough courage to creep down there by herself.

She collected her nerves one crisp April day while her parents were still at work and Travis was playing outside. She grabbed a flashlight and inched downstairs. It was a little after her 12th birthday, and that made her feel a little braver. Each stair creaked in protest as she slipped further and further into its domain. Her flashlight seemed to dim as she stepped further into the abyss. It felt like a crypt, emanating with evil. Nadia sniffed the air. It smelled like mold and rotting meat. She didn't want to be here by herself but was determined to carry out her plan.

"I know you're down here. What do you want?" Nadia asked, her voice trembling.

Out of the furthest corner, she saw it approach. She directed her light in its direction and froze as her flashlight suddenly extinguished. The main light flickered, threatening to go out. She wanted to run. She wanted to scream. She wanted to be anywhere but here in the cellar … with it.

"Ah, my sweet little Nadia," it cooed in a raspy voice. "come to visit me in my home, have you? Do not worry my child. You will always be welcome here … with me … in the dark."

Nadia didn't feel welcome. She felt afraid and a little insane for confronting it. It floated closer until it towered over her. She knew it was a male by his stature and voice. He was shrouded in darkness, but its red eyes glowed, crinkling in amusement.

"Wh … What do you want?" She stammered.

"Do not be afraid, my child. I won't hurt you. I am your friend."

Inside, she knew he was lying.

"You are a demon," she said flatly.

"Why yes, I am. Thank you very much for noticing," he chuckled.

"What do you want!" she repeated more forcefully.

She felt her fear turn to anger. Nadia hated being afraid.

"Ahhhhh, yes. Become angry my child," he almost seemed to sing. "I like your fear, but your anger is much tastier."

Nadia didn't know what to say. She knew he wouldn't give her the answers she wanted, so she turned to leave.

"Do not leave me, my child," it pleaded, suddenly changing its tone. "I am all alone in the dark."

"I don't care," Nadia said, finding her courage. "you're not welcome here. You need to leave!"

He began to laugh a kind of throaty chuckle, making the hair on the back of her neck rise. Shivers ran down her spine.

Nadia sprinted up the stairs and didn't stop until she reached her bedroom. She slammed the door and clamped her hand over her mouth to stop herself from screaming.

"You didn't think you could get away from me that easily, did you?" a raspy voice asked behind her.

Nadia screeched and spun around, backing away from him. Her small room made his stench unbearable. She could see his full form in the light. He was tall, almost reaching the ceiling. His body was black and mottled with grey streaks. He wore a shadow cloak. The hood itself covered most of his head, but she could still see his eyes … those horrible evil eyes.

"It has just occurred to me I never answered your question. How very rude of me." he confessed, redirecting his tone once again. "you wish to know what I want, don't you?"

Nadia's words escaped her. She nodded her head slowly.

He grasped her face with its long fingers and pulled her to him, locking her eyes with his. His touch repulsed her. She felt a piercing chill course through her body.

"I want you, Nadia," he said, his putrid breath coating her face "I know what you are capable of, dearie and it is great indeed. I have seen your power. My master has a great, let's say, interest in you. Therefore, he sent me to convince you to join his cause."

Nadia reacted instinctively. Without realizing what she was doing, she summoned energy and shoved him across the room. He spilled backward onto the floor.

"I will *never* join you!" she shouted, feeling a little like Luke Skywalker.

"Oh, I think I might be able to change your mind," he chuckled softly. "I will give you a year to think about it and mull things over. I will leave … for now but I will be back, and I will bring my friends."

"GO!" she shouted, stomping her foot.

"Very well, but before I leave, let me give you a little reminder of our conversation. I would hate to think you would forget about me in a year."

He reached out and grasped her arm, tightly wrapping his long fingers. She tried summoning her energy, but a sharp pain raced through her body, making it impossible to concentrate. She struggled but couldn't break free from its grasp. Nadia squealed in pain, as fire coursed through her body. He released her after a few moments. She slumped to the ground, her arm pulsing in agony. His handprint was burned into her arm.

"Goodbye, sweet Nadia. I look forward to seeing you in a year."

He disappeared, his laughter hanging in the air. Travis burst through the door after he heard her screams.

"What's wrong?" he asked, concerned.

She held her arm out to him.

"Yea? It's an arm. Why are you screaming?"

"My *arm!* Look at it!" she shouted.

"What about it?"

Nadia looked at him with disbelief. He couldn't see it. Once again, the feeling of isolation blanketed her.

"Nothing," she mumbled. "I thought I saw a spider."

"You're a dork!" Travis laughed, closing her door.

He left her alone … with her thoughts.

The next year flew in a blur. She tried to put the demon out of her thoughts, but she couldn't. The mark on her arm never faded, but no one else could see it. As the months progressed, she felt the need to do something … anything to fight it. She insisted her parents take her to the library every weekend. She read every book she found about demons although, there weren't many. She found a better selection when they went to Manchester to see a baseball game during their summer vacation.

After the game her parents told Nadia she could go anywhere she wanted within reason. Most girls her age would want to go to the mall, but Nadia wasn't like most girls. The only place she wanted to go was the bookstore. Her choice made Travis happy because he knew he could buy more baseball cards. Nadia felt like she walked into the promise land when she arrived at the metaphysical section in Barnes and Noble. She could have stayed for days pouring over the books, but her parents insisted they leave after an hour. When her time was up, she met them at the front counter with fifteen books overflowing in her arms. Her parents looked surprised.

"I said you could buy *one* book, Nadia," Sarah huffed.

"I need these books Mom," Nadia protested.

"What are these anyway?" her father asked, taking the books from her arms.

He was shocked when he perused through her selection. He was used to her abnormal tastes, but he didn't expect every book to be about demons.

"Nadia! All of these books are about demons," he clucked, disapprovingly.

"I know," she said quietly.

She didn't know how to explain it to them. She didn't know how to make them understand.

"These books aren't meant for you. I don't want you reading this dark stuff," her father scowled.

"But I *need* these books Dad!" she protested, her voice rising.

"Why? Why do you need books about demons?" her mother asked, concerned.

Nadia didn't know what to say. She wanted to tell them their lives would be changed forever unless she knew how to fight against the darkness. If she told them, her parents would take her back to the doctor, who would only put her on pills. She felt helpless and knew she had to lie.

"Cuz I find it interesting. Can I get some horror movies too?"

Her parents looked at each other and shook their heads. They found her new interest disturbing.

"Fine," her mother finally agreed, "you can have one book, and we have to approve of it."

"What kind of horror movie?" her father asked.

"Can I have the Exorcist?"

"Absolutely *not!*" her father grunted. "pick your book so we can get out of here."

Nadia put the books on the floor in a secluded corner and tried to pick the best one. In the distance, she could hear Travis complaining about wanting to leave. She ignored him and read the description of each book once again.

After twenty minutes she picked a book about fighting demons. Her father rolled his eyes and paid for it. She held it tightly, hoping the book would give her the answers she so desperately needed.

During the ride back, she began reading it. Nadia felt somewhat disappointed. The author spoke a lot about God and praying to angels for help. There wasn't anything in it about defending yourself against demons. It was more based upon faith which was something she didn't really know anything about. Nadia believed in God but didn't feel any kind of connection with him. She decided to ask her parents to take her to church on a Sunday. Maybe a priest could give her the answers she needed.

When they got home, Travis immediately ran upstairs to file his new baseball cards in their proper place. Nadia went into the attic and thumbed through the rest of her book. It was basically useless. She knew the author had never encountered a demon and was just spouting recycled garbage. Nadia wished she had a good source of information. A thought crept into her head. Her father had a laptop in the den, and he allowed her to occasionally play games. Her favorite game was The Sims, but she hadn't played it in over six months. She felt like kicking herself for not remembering it earlier. She glanced down at her arm, scratching it absentmindedly. Nadia felt like it had marked her but for what … she didn't know.

The next day she got up as soon as her parents left for work. She knew her brother wouldn't slither out of bed for at least three more hours. He was paid as her babysitter during the summer, but she didn't need him. She could fend for herself. She got on the computer and typed 'demons.' Nadia was amazed at the endless selection of demon information on the internet. Hours flew by like seconds. Before long, she heard her brother moving around upstairs. She quickly shut down the computer and went into the living room to turn on the TV.

Nadia kept the same routine for the rest of the summer and well into the school year. Any chance she had, she was on the computer. She had a special notebook she kept under her dresser which held her notes. There were lots of websites about demons but not as much information about actually fighting against them. Many websites she found were faith-based. Nadia wondered if that's why the demon came to her ... because she had no faith. At night, Nadia got down on her knees and prayed for help. She didn't know if anyone heard her, but she desperately hoped so.

Towards the end of the year, she asked her parents to drop her off at a church. Nadia wanted to talk to the priest ... alone. Her father was immediately skeptical about her request. It took a lot of persuading, but he finally agreed to allow her to see one at the Holy Trinity Catholic Church. She didn't understand his reluctance though.

"We will walk you in, but we'll be waiting for you in the entrance," Sarah informed her.

"OK," Nadia agreed

"I still don't understand why you want to do this," her father said, exasperated.

"Robert, just let her." Sarah pleaded. "It's something she wants to do."

She briefly listened to her parents arguing behind her.

22

"I thought we agreed to raise our kids to be free thinkers and not believe in this superstitious nonsense!" her father barked.

"Oh my god, Rob! Just let her do it. If we don't, she will continue to bug us about it. Let her just get it out of her system. You know she has always been different. She wants to learn. What's the harm in her talking to a priest?" Her mother asked, defending Nadia.

Nadia increased her pace, till their voices dimmed to heated murmurs. She hurried before her father changed his mind. The priest was waiting for her in his office. He was short, squat, and partially bald. He had a ruddy complexion as if he had just finished running. He smiled and beckoned to her.

"Yes, my child. What can I do for you today?" he asked kindly.

Nadia sat across from him wearing her most serious expression. She didn't like being referred to as 'my child.' It reminded her too much of the demon.

"I need to know about demons," Nadia stated.

"What do you wish to know?" he asked, cocking his head to the side.

"How does a person fight one?"

"Through the power of prayer and faith in God, but I'm sure you have nothing to worry about my child."

Nadia expected his canned response. After all, no one really came out and said there was another way to fight against demons.

"There has to be another way," she insisted.

"But there isn't. That is the only way to fight demons. Now, why on earth are you troubled by this?" He asked.

"Because I had one in my house and he's coming back in less than a year. I have to figure out how to get rid of him … it … whatever," she blurted.

"I see. And how do you know he's coming back?"

"He told me he would be back and make my life miserable. He wanted me to join him. I won't! I won't join him," Nadia swore.

"I see. You spoke with this entity?" he probed.

Nadia knew he didn't believe her. She could tell by his tone.

"Yea! And he's coming back!" Nadia shrilled, trying to make him understand.

"Calm down my child. I'm sure you have nothing to worry about," he uttered, trying to placate her.

"Do you at least have holy water or a crucifix that you can give me?" she asked, frantically.

The priest shook his head in bewilderment. He reached back and took a large, wooden crucifix off the wall, handing it to her. It was a gift from a friend in Italy. He didn't believe her tale, but he wanted to make her feel better. She needed the crucifix more than he did.

"Here," he said. "you can have mine. I can't give you any holy water though."

"Th … thank you," she stammered, grateful for his generosity.

24

"Maybe you should come to church on Sunday. It might make you feel better."

"No. That's not a good idea," she said, firmly.

"Why not?"

"My parents … my father wouldn't allow it. I have to go," she said, clutching his gift to her chest.

"That is unfortunate. You're always welcome to come back and see me if you need to."

She thanked him once again and raced to her parents. Her father wasn't thrilled when he saw the crucifix but didn't feel like pressing the issue. Nadia hung it next to her bed, so she could easily reach it if needed. Before she went to sleep that night, she plucked it off the wall and examined it. It should have put her mind at ease, but it didn't. It felt as foreign to her as French. She thought about everything she learned so far about demons.

They were liars, but she knew that already. They liked to twist words and use them against a person. When he had been around her, she felt hopeless and alone. Without hope, Nadia felt defenseless. It was hard to fight against something like that especially when she didn't know how. She remembered when the demon had touched her. It felt so cold and … burning. She shuddered, recalling the terrible sensation.

"What did it mean when it said I had power?" she wondered silently.

Nadia remembered pushing the demon away, but she didn't know how it happened.

"Why does his master want me?" she asked aloud to a silent room.

She fell asleep not knowing the answer.

"NADIA! Get down here!"

Her father's voice startled her from her slumber. Sunlight was streaming through the curtains. She rubbed her eyes and blinked, wondering if she had been dreaming.

"NADIA!" her father screamed again.

She raced downstairs in her PJ's. They stood as a united front by the computer. Her father's eyes turned into slits and her mom looked bewildered. She was busted.

"What's this?" Her father asked, pointing to the screen.

"What?" Nadia asked, sheepishly.

"Nadia don't play games with me! How long have you been using my computer?" he demanded.

"I dunno," she mumbled.

"Well, I can tell by a history search it's been at least a month," he said, pointing to the screen.

Nadia felt stupid. She forgot to erase the history.

"Six months. I've been using your computer for six months," Nadia blurted.

"Look at these sites!" he yelled. "every one of them is about demons … summoning demons, killing demons, avoiding demons! Here's a site about everything you wanted to know about demons but were afraid to ask. What the heck are you doing, Nadia?"

26

"I just wanted to …," she began before her dad erupted.

"NO! No more! I'm putting a password on the computer and you are grounded from using it. There will be no more talk about demons or priests or anything supernatural. Do I make myself clear!"

"But …,"

"NO MORE! You are done with this demon stuff!" her father bellowed.

Nadia turned and ran up to her room, tears springing from her eyes. She didn't know what to do. Her parents were hindering her ability to fight. As she stormed around her room, she felt more helpless than ever. She didn't have nearly enough information to fight them, and now she was restricted from learning more. Fear enveloped her.

The rest of the year went by too quickly for Nadia. She couldn't even enjoy Christmas because she knew April was right around the corner. She managed to do some research on Tasha's computer and at the library, but she still couldn't find anything useful. She began praying regularly at night. As much as she prayed, however, it didn't feel right. It was almost as if she knew he couldn't help her. She didn't know what else to do.

On the anniversary of the demon's departure, Nadia didn't sleep a wink. She stayed up all night waiting for it, but it never made an appearance. In the morning, she went into the cellar, but it wasn't there either. After a week, Nadia felt relief wash over her. After a month she started to forget about it. Normality returned to her life. Her parents commented that she had found her smile again. For the first time in a long time, she slept without fear … until a familiar voice woke her from her slumber.

"Hello my sweet Nadia."

The Return
Chapter Two

Nadia couldn't move, gripped by the icy tentacles of fear. The demon had returned, and this time he wasn't alone. He stood at the end of her bed, flanked on either side by his 'friends'. The stench of three demons in such a tight space was overwhelming. As her eyes adjusted to the darkness, she began to see their forms and hideous faces. The demon on the right was the shortest of the three. It was hunched and seemed to have a limp. The demon on the left was the same height as the middle one, but thicker around the middle. It had a long white scar running from the top of its skull to its chin. There was an angry empty socket where its eye had once been. She saw its hatred in that lone eye. The scarred one frightened her even more than the other two, but she refused to give in to her fear.

Her mouth was as dry as ash. She didn't know what to say to the trio, but after gulping a few times, she made a joke.

"You're late," she quipped.

"Ah, my dear little Nadia missed me. Isn't that sweet boys?" the middle demon laughed.

The two other demons began laughing with him. The raspy sound sent chills down her spine. She hugged herself tightly.

"There is a reason I delayed my return," he announced.

"And what was that?" she asked, dreading the answer.

"I simply wanted you to feel hope. It will be much more fun when I take it from you once again."

Nadia reached for her crucifix, plucked it from the wall and held it out in front of her with both hands. She felt a little ridiculous.

"Begone!" Nadia said, forcefully.

The three demons looked at each other and laughed hysterically. Nadia felt confused and wondered why they weren't affected by it.

"You are funny, my child," the lead demon chuckled. "did you really think that would work?"

"But I thought …," she whispered before her voice faltered.

"Do you know why it doesn't work?" he asked softly, creeping closer to her. "it is a symbol of something you don't believe. You have to believe for it to work."

Nadia looked at the crucifix and let it fall to the ground. It hit the floor with a deathly thud. She knew in her heart the demon was right. They were known for their twisted lies, but they did tell the truth occasionally. Humans were easier to fool if they were told the truth occasionally.

"So here I am again and as I promised I brought my friends. I have waited a long time for your answer. I do not wish to wait much longer."

"What answer?" Nadia asked, knowing exactly what it wanted.

"Will you join our side, sweet child, or do you prefer to suffer?" he asked.

Nadia grew angry. She hated facing such a dilemma.

"What have I done to deserve this?" she wondered to

30

herself. "I haven't done anything bad. I'm a good person. Why are they bothering me?"

"Well princess?" the demon mocked.

"I choose to suffer," she said quietly.

The demons began laughing with delight.

"And suffer you shall, my child. We were hoping you would say that. After all, if you had folded too quickly, you would have spoiled our fun. We knew you weren't that weak. In the end, you will join us, or we will take everything from you. The choice is yours," he revealed.

They disappeared in front of her eyes, their laughter still clinging to the air. Nadia put her face into her hands and closed her eyes. The entire atmosphere of the house changed with their arrival. The house felt creepy, and the air was heavy. She knew they were nesting in the cellar. Nadia worried she didn't have the strength to resist them. Not knowing what they had planned was the worst. She grabbed the crucifix and shoved it into a drawer. It brought her no comfort or peace.

The countless articles she read about demons were informative, but she felt ill prepared. She read if a person ordered a demon away, it would have to leave, but that didn't work at all. They only laughed at her. An interesting thought came to Nadia. She knew they preferred the cellar because it was dark and creepy. Maybe she could make them uncomfortable, forcing them to leave. A hidden memory unexpectedly floated into her consciousness. These particular type of demons hated cinnamon.

"How do I know that?" she wondered to herself.

She read nothing about cinnamon in her studies. The thought just came to her like she had always known it. Her mother kept a big container of it in the spice cabinet. She planned to pour it around the cellar after school. Nadia hoped it would force them out of their nest, not that she wanted them to move upstairs.

"Maybe I could put cinnamon in all the rooms to stop them from nesting anywhere else," she said softly to herself.

She flopped back down and fell into a troubled sleep.

That night she dreamed of a sword with a red hilt. The blade was glowing brilliantly. It was so bright she had to squint. Nadia could see words etched into the metal. They were in a language she didn't understand but seemed eerily familiar. Suddenly, the sword began to pulse, becoming brighter and brighter with each wave. It filled the entire room with light. Nadia awoke as the morning sun streamed through the windows. When she opened her eyes, she saw the sword suspended in mid-air in the middle of the room. It wavered a few seconds before disappearing. Nadia rubbed her eyes and wondered if she had seen it at all.

Lucifer sat upon his throne and waited for his messenger. He drummed his fingers on the armrest, growing impatient. Patience … was never his virtue. His throne room exhibited what anyone would expect, walls made of black stone and a lone symbol of authority. He fashioned a magnificent chair for himself from a dragon serving his enemy. Lucifer molded the dragon itself to suit his purpose. The dragon's feet were the legs of this throne. He sat roughly on the

32

lower stomach. The dragon's head rose high above him and curved toward the front. The tail curled around the chair and the wings were extended on either side.

This dragon was blood red. While alive, it was a fierce beast named FlameEater. He was a protector of his enemy. It was unfortunate FlameEater was easily distracted. Lucifer's demons lured him away one day with a horse carcass. While he was eating, they cast an immobilizing spell and carried him to the netherworld. Lucifer twisted him into his throne while he was still living. His bones cracked and snapped as they were put into unnatural positions. His mouth remained open, forever in a silent scream. FlameEater died shortly after, and Lucifer sealed the dragon's flesh so it would never decay. This throne was the one thing that gave Lucifer joy.

He shouted again for his messenger. He hated waiting. It seemed Lucifer's whole life consisted of waiting. Finally, things were beginning to align, but his many plans could easily go awry if his watcher demons failed their missions. It would be most disastrous ... for them because he would rip them to shreds. He quickly rose and strode to the balcony directly behind his throne. Stepping onto the terrace, he surveyed the scene below. Most new arrivals were surprised by the realm. It was divided into two sections with vastly different temperatures.

The old legends were true ... relatively. There was a scorching side of hell, but it wasn't the kind of heat a human soul could handle. It was like stepping onto the sun and quite miserable for those not born of fire. The landscape on this side was black and charred with craggy rocks. Steam rose from putrid pools of stagnant black water, filling the air with a sulfurous smell. Vicious, sinewy creatures swirled in the water snatching unsuspecting souls from the surface. They crushed and mutilated their victims, allowing them a brief moment of regeneration so they could be slashed again. It was a brutal never-ending cycle of agony.

The other side of his domain was bitterly cold. It was so cold it burned, mutilating victims as easily as fire. Icy wind howled across windswept mountainous peaks. Deep, grey snow covered the ground making it near impossible for the damned to travel. They were forced to trudge through the deep drifts, climbing the never-ending mountains. The unyielding cold region had its own share of monstrosities. Black serpentine monsters hunted beneath the surface of the snow. They would charge upwards through the deep drifts, snatching a victim like a killer whale hunting an unsuspecting seal. Unable to die, a soul would writhe in agony as it was masticated.

Far above him was the dark sky. It was bruised and purplish black, extending throughout the reaches of the dominion. When Lucifer was particularly angry, blue lightning streaked across the sky, followed by deafening thunderclaps. Strange beasts, resembling harpies, swooped down to capture their prey in their cruel talons. They were impossible to see as they hid in the darkness, waiting for a chance to attack. They shrieked shrilly as they hunted. They were terrifying, but they weren't the most terrifying entities in Lucifer's kingdom.

The damned entered his kingdom through a massive granite door. They were immediately whisked away by one of his demons. He had spent many years attempting to create the perfect nightmare for his home … and his 'guests.' After numerous redesigns, he chose to divide his realm to achieve optimum pain. He would move souls frequently from one section to another to keep them in a constant state of despair and hopelessness. The sound of their anguish was deafening, filling all corners of his realm. Their cries were sweet music to his ears.

A high wall made of bleeding flesh divided the two sections with Lucifer's castle between them. His demons could travel freely between the sides without being affected by the temperatures. Lucifer's castle could be seen from anywhere in Hell. It was dark, menacing, and made entirely of blood-red stones. It had two entrances which opened to either side. Demons were constantly seen moving in and out of the castle to attend their various duties.

Evil *human* souls received another delightful surprise upon arrival. Humans were the most arrogant and obtuse creatures ever created. They foolishly thought they were the only beings in the universe. His realm however, housed an infinite number of souls and many were not human. Souls of every being imaginable inhabited Hell. Creatures such as elves, trolls and even a few gods from other realms were punished here. Lucifer took all evil and used it to his advantage. Above all, he hated humans and their flawed existence. Of his vast collection it was the pure souls he truly coveted. He loved corrupting them and punishing them for their choice.

Lucifer wasn't permitted to travel to the human realm lest his presence tip the balance, so his demons did the work for him. He could however, travel to other realms, but it took a significant amount of energy. There were two gateways available to his demons which allowed travel to the human territory. One was immediately in front of the castle, and the other was inside the castle's central chamber. Both gates were heavily secured by two colossal guards, preventing demons from taking it upon themselves to travel freely between the realms. Demons were ambitious, impetuous creatures and needed constant control. He couldn't allow them to disappear and create chaos without strict authorization. Everything he did was for a reason, and he couldn't allow any of his subjects to interfere with his long-range plans.

A sudden knock on the door quickly interrupted his thoughts. He smoothly glided to his throne and sat down.

"ENTER!" he shouted.

A scaly, orange demon with five horns and a humped back entered quickly. He moved with the grace unbefitting a hideous creature. He bowed deeply until he was addressed. It was Lucifer's strictest rule. Those who stood before him needed to bow until he allowed otherwise. Sometimes Lucifer would keep demons bowing at his feet for hours just to see them grovel. He was impatient for information this time however, and quickly gave approval.

"Yes, Araphel? What is the news?"

Araphel, having been granted permission rose to his feet and spoke quickly. His voice was soft and ethereal.

"My lord," he began, "Nezatel, Ieckisht, and Tyrient have begun the process. They are firmly entrenched."

36

"Most excellent." Lucifer beamed, clapping his hands. "inform Nezatel to begin slowly. I sense something special about this one. I am certain she is one of the warrior angels. I want her to suffer as they have made *me* suffer."

"Yes, my lord," Araphel bowed.

Despite his long years of service, Araphel still had trouble looking at Lucifer. Lucifer didn't appear as one might expect him too. He wasn't hideous with massive horns protruding from his head. Lucifer was quite becoming. Only his arrogance matched his looks. He purposely twisted his fallen to appear ugly so he could be the 'shining star'. Lucifer refused to look at his own reflection, however. He had been given a scar during a battle, and every time he saw it he flew into a rage. Even though it didn't hinder his looks, he felt it marred him.

Lucifer had long, brown hair which fell to his shoulders. His piercing, dark eyes glinted with malice. He was tall with a muscular build. He often wore a simple pair of red pants and shirt with a set of grey leathery wings against his pale skin. Coldness seeped from him and touched anyone nearby. He was powerful, evil, and had a lust to claim his rightful place.

"You are dismissed," Lucifer snapped, waving his hand.

His messenger bowed and retreated quickly. No demon wanted to spend any amount of time with their master. His mood changed rapidly, and it was far too dangerous. Many of his greatest warriors were destroyed because they said something inappropriate. Lucifer didn't have an aptitude for patience so when things weren't accomplished in a timely fashion, his punishment came swiftly.

Humans knew very little about the truth, believing Lucifer was weary of his prison and desired his freedom. They were visionless, foolish creatures stuck upon their own pride. In Heaven, he was merely a slave sent to do the bidding of its ruler. He was nothing there, but in Hell, he was a god with billions of servants eager to please him. What Lucifer desired most was revenge.

Humans called the realms leader a 'god' because they were too stupid to learn otherwise. Lucifer only knew him by his true name, Zavier. Zavier was enamored with his little creations, and he couldn't see them for what they were … a plague upon the Earth. Lucifer would make him see. He actively influenced humans to force Zavier to recognize how wretched his creations were. They needed to be wiped again from existence and he was more than eager to help. After Lucifer destroyed them, he would unleash his army against Zavier. It would be glorious.

Zavier always had time for his pets but never for him. At one time, Lucifer held a high position and had control of Zavier's armies, but he was quickly demoted to servant. Zavier expected him to watch over and guide his little toys. Lucifer believed he finally had a chance to prove himself worthy when Zavier departed for an extended vacation. Zavier placed Lucifer in charge of the entire realm. Apparently, he didn't live up to Zavier's expectations and was banished. Lucifer took his own army of angels and revolted. They stormed the gates of Zavier's palace.

In retrospect, he had been a little overzealous in his ploy. He should have waited and gathered information first. When he arrived on the palace grounds, it was teeming with Red Wing warrior angels. They quickly defeated Lucifer's army, and Zavier cast him out to live with the disgraced. Zavier claimed to be 'all forgiving,' but Zavier never forgave him. Lucifer didn't want or need Zavier's forgiveness … not anymore. Lucifer saw Zavier for what he truly was … a hypocrite.

Humans were so selfish and self-serving, they actually believed Zavier should answer all of their requests. Zavier's worst mistake was giving his pets free will. Humans took advantage of it incessantly which made it easier to corrupt them. Zavier didn't interfere very often. In actuality, the last time he put his hands-on Earth was several thousand years ago. Zavier lost his temper and destroyed his pets in one quick flash of flame. After that incident, Zavier refused to intercede directly. Instead, he created his soldiers who did most of the battling for him. Zavier now spent most of his time away at his home and relied on his spies to keep him informed. Zavier's idleness would make it easy to move his plan into action.

It was Zavier's warriors who interested Lucifer more than anything. They were an elite group of angels and often, many of them were reborn as humans. It was their job to help people and hunt his minions. They would become valuable assets if they were corrupted. So, while they were hunting his demons, Lucifer was hunting *them*. He played a continual game of chess, and the victor was the one with the most pieces.

Lucifer chuckled softly, toying absentmindedly with his hair. He learned how to use situations to his advantage. When Hell was sealed, he learned the art of terrorism, sabotage, and subversion. He had spies everywhere. Nothing happened on Earth without him knowing about it. He even had a few angels under his thumb while his demons were always hard at work. Contrary to popular belief demons and angels were not former humans. They were a class of creatures all by themselves.

Many of his demons were former angels which he had corrupted. It wasn't hard to do since most angels despised being babysitters as well. Lucifer offered them the chance to torture instead. He would sweeten the deal by reminding them they could do anything they wanted … even things considered forbidden for an angel. These corruptible angels fell when they were touched by Lucifer.

Their wings burst into flames and burned away, leaving long scars down their backs. Often, they screamed in agony as the change occurred. Damnation was a painful process, but relatively quick. Once their wings were gone, their flesh would blacken with deep blotchy patterns. Their fingers and nails would elongate into vicious claws.

Angel eyes were normally white or blue, but when the process initiated their eyes would begin to glow red. All demons had red eyes except for an elite legion of soldier demons called the Varafe. The Varafe were the only demons with black eyes. They were the vilest of the vile and the evilest of the evil. The rest of his demons found the Varafe unnerving and avoided them at all costs. Their savagery was attributed to the fact they were all females.

There was a common misconception all female demons were beautiful succubi who seduced humans with a flip of their hair. Lucifer wasn't interested in beautiful demons.

He only wanted warriors. Their skin was gray and stippled. They had huge black eyes which could see into the very depths of a soul. Their noses were nothing more than vertical slits, and their mouths were filled with sharp, jagged teeth. They were over 10-foot-tall with shaved heads. Their armor was black and red with their symbol ♈ etched into the breastplate.

Most demons didn't dare confront the Varafe since they would likely lose their heads. Lucifer wanted his elite army to be female. In every battle, females fought harder and more viciously. They enjoyed killing and drinking the blood of their victims like tea. They were completely fearless, riding towards their own deaths if needed. They were so powerful Zavier made it exceedingly difficult for them to be summoned to the upper realm. Once they were free, a Varafe had to work quickly.

Zavier implemented an annoying failsafe a long time ago. Powerful demons like the Varafe began losing their power when they were away from Hell. If a Varafe didn't make it back before her powers were completely diminished, she was stuck on Earth as a powerless entity. She would be an easy target. Lucifer had lost a great number of his elite army in the past. He avoided using them excessively at all costs and only used them when the benefit outweighed the price.

The rest of the demons were ranked in a hierarchy like any other military establishment. Lucifer only allowed certain positions to live inside the castle. The rest either had sleeping quarters inside the Great Hall or they slept outside. The Great Hall was a huge building adjacent to the castle and housed the majority of his demons. It consisted of a large central room flanked on either side by individual rooms. As a demon rose up the ranks, he was allowed to have upgraded quarters and more privileges. It wasn't easy to achieve higher positions. It took thousands of years of hard work. He insisted his demons work hard or they were immediately dispatched.

The lowliest of all demons were called Kerbals. They slept outside and had no personal space to call their own. Kerbals were the most heavily abused demons and did the worst jobs. Most demons began as a Kerbal. They had to prove themselves worthy to be promoted to the next rank. Kerbals could be found working on all levels of the castle. They cleaned Lucifer's stronghold constantly, including the dungeons. Lucifer had a number of beasts, and their pens always needed cleaning, a disgusting job for any demon. Kerbals had limited resources to eat or drink with very little sleep time. Fallen angels often began as Kerbals. Lucifer sought to punish them for serving his enemy.

The next rank of demons was called the Urburkas. This rank had a few more privileges but not many. They were given sleeping rugs, so they didn't have to sleep directly on the jagged ground. They also had an hour of free time and slightly better food. Urburkas were the first rank allowed to punish wicked souls … a job they did quite splendidly. Oddly enough, Urburkas abused the Kerbals more than any other rank. There were degrees of sordidness even among demons. Once an Urburka received his first taste of power, it didn't take him long to begin abusing it.

The largest group was called the Nifuwas. They slept

inside the Great Hall in the central chamber. The one big room held many beds and offered little chance of privacy, but it was better than sleeping outside. There was plenty of fresh food and drink for them. Nifuwas were given more leisure and sleeping time. Their duties mostly involved supervising the ranks below and torturing the damned.

The following class of demons was called the Waru. They were a special group of warrior demons and held the highest number. They were large and muscular, standing close to seven foot. Their fierce armor was permanently stained with blood. They were not as powerful as the Varafe, but they didn't lose their powers either. Lucifer used them the most on the upper realm. Each had his own quarters in the Great Hall. When they weren't battling, they spent their time drinking and squabbling amongst themselves. The Waru were the only demons with wings. They were widely respected and feared by all demons, apart from the Varafe.

On more than one occasion, a Waru would pick a fight with a Varafe. The fight usually ended badly for the Waru. There was only one Waru who had ever defeated a Varafe. His name was Mortoc and he was their leader. A Varafe named Jurisatel pushed him while he was gathering his troops for a battle. Mortoc wasn't stupid or impatient. She thought he would rush to confront her blinded by his anger. Instead, he just laughed and brushed himself off, turning his back to her.

Enraged, she charged him, raising her mighty sword to cleave him in two. Mortoc simply stepped to the side and quickly brought his ax upward, removing her head.

Thunderous cheers rang out among the Waru. Lucifer stopped the fighting before it became a bloodbath. The Varafe craved revenge … and they were willing to wipe out every Waru to get it, but Lucifer forbade it. Mortoc became the most admired demon among his kind and the most hated by the Varafe. He fueled their hatred by tying Jurisatel's head to a staff and brandishing it in their faces. Lucifer only tolerated their hostilities for so long. When their squabbles became riotous, he immediately put a stop to it. He understood their lust for power, but he would not have chaos in his own realm.

There were several other classes of demons, who served Lucifer in various capacities. Imps were a class entirely separate from the rest. They were small and relatively weak but highly useful in many situations, especially when they banded together. Lucifer preferred to use them to influence children. Children had powerful psychic abilities but often lost their gifts as their reality changed. Their size made them seemingly harmless and easy to trust. It was their job to corrupt children before they lost their abilities and control them to hurt others. It was a grand game Lucifer played.

Lucifer promoted Nucaira, a short, squat demon with black skin, as his historian. Her position of power was mighty. She oversaw the collecting of Hell's history, and Lucifer often relied on her to predict future events. Nucaira had access to multitudes of information and could travel anywhere she chose. She lived close to Lucifer in a plush room. She was hated by most demons on the council because of her undying arrogance.

44

Lucifer's head demon and messenger also lived near him. His head demon, Yarish was the highest-ranking demon in Hell. He was given all the comforts of the castle but carried a huge responsibility. Lucifer expected much from his head demons and were often 'replaced' when they didn't fulfill his expectations. Yarish was his twenty-third head demon and a vast improvement from the others.

Araphel, his messenger had once been a guardian angel. Lucifer claimed Araphel's soul after he fell into despair. Araphel's favorite human had died, and his soul crumbled into ash. Zavier deemed the soul unworthy and destroyed it so it could never be reborn again. Araphel lost hope and fell from grace. Lucifer took him under his wing giving him a position close to him, but it wasn't because Lucifer liked him. It was because deep down Araphel missed being an angel. Lucifer wanted to give him a constant reminder of what he gave up.

Lucifer's dark priests and mediums came next in the hierarchy. They had large circular rooms in the middle of the castle. Their chambers surrounded a wide-open space used to conduct their rituals. It was filled with various alters and mystic tools to help Lucifer see beyond Hell. They rarely left their area unless it was to speak with their master. They felt associating with other demons would taint their sight.

Only demons in special positions had horns. It was a mark of their rank. Lower-class demons didn't deserve horns, and those who fought in battle found them to be a major inconvenience. Lucifer didn't bother with horns for himself, finding them to be quite ugly. The largest set of horns belonged to his head demon. He had large, curled horns, similar to a ram. The smallest set, barely horns at all, belonged to his watchers.

His watchers were in a class all their own. These were his spies he sent to the upper realm to watch and report. Most of the time they observed others, but Lucifer made a special class of watchers who could directly influence people. They could even possess weaker souls. Watchers were greatly envied by most of the other demons because they came and went as they pleased. As long as they satisfied Lucifer, they could essentially do what they wanted. They answered to Lucifer and no other.

Finally, there was Lucifer's council which was made up of his generals and trusted counselors. They advised and fought with him in battle. He called a meeting every time he suspected there was an opportunity to strike. Mortoc and the replaced Varafe leader, Elistax were important members of the council. They only put their differences aside when Lucifer was in the room. Otherwise, they insulted each other, often coming close to blows.

Mortoc only missed a council meeting if he was in a skirmish. Most humans never realized a battle was raging around them … a battle between good and evil. Very few humans could see angels or demons and if they did, they didn't understand what they were seeing. Many were driven mad by the mere sight of a demon. Humans never knew how demon's battles changed their world either. Their war tainted the land, making it almost impossible for vegetation to grow. It took thousands of years for the land to cleanse itself. Deserts were just accepted as natural

46

occurrences. Blinded by fear, most humans never looked beyond normal explanations.

It was human ignorance which caused the most damage … to themselves. Many wanted power and purposely summoned his demons. They had no idea the suffering they unleashed … onto themselves. Making a contract with a dark force tainted the soul. Although a soul could be purified, it took work and dedication, something humans weren't exactly known for. His demons knew how to find a loophole in any contract. They made sure everything backfired onto the stakeholder.

Demons could be summoned accidentally, which is how they preferred it. The accidental summoner typically had no idea a demon was living with them. Since there was no contract to negotiate, the demon could influence without interferences. If a human was weak, their life would quickly spiral out of control as they made one bad decision after another. If a soul was particularly vulnerable, the demon could possess it, and that's where the real fun began.

People often wondered why a perfectly happy and normal person would commit horrific crimes. Humans became their puppets. Parents killed their children and children murdered their parents. Teenagers turned rifles onto their classmates. Unsuspecting neighbors were arrested for a variety of heinous murders. People never learned. They always meddled with things they didn't understand. When they finally came to Hell, Lucifer punished them severely. He despised their weakness.

War was brewing, even if the humans were blissfully unaware. Soon he would eradicate the vermin from the Earth.

The Strange Vision
Chapter Three

"Mom, can I have some cinnamon?" Nadia asked, stuffing a pop-tart into her mouth.

Her mother reached into the spice cabinet and handed her the spice. She didn't say anything. A pained expression crossed her face.

"You OK, Mom?" Nadia asked, concerned.

"Yeah, I think I'm getting a migraine. I slept terrible last night. When I was able to sleep, I dreamed about … well, I had nightmares," Sarah said, scowling.

Nadia shook the jar of cinnamon.

"Mom, can we get another one of these? I want to do an experiment, and I need a lot more."

"I will pick you up some after work," Sarah agreed, rubbing her temple.

"Can we go for a hike in the woods this weekend?"

"Maybe," Sarah replied. "if I'm not so tired."

Sarah kissed her daughter and headed out the door for work. Nadia loved it when her mother showed her affection. It made her feel warm and special. As the year progressed however, her mother would grow increasingly distant.

Nadia, now 13, hiked often by herself in the woods. She felt at peace among the trees. It was the only place she could think without being influenced. In the forest, her thoughts were her own. The demons tried to follow her, but they couldn't enter. They snarled and pleaded for her to return.

She usually went deep into the woods until she could no longer hear their voices.

After her parents left for work, she headed outside. The days were becoming hot although the mornings were still quite pleasant. Her brother was still asleep, opting to waste his summer vacation by sleeping it away. Nadia sat down on the ground with her back against an old pine tree. The sunlight filtered through the branches, casting shadows among the trees. She inhaled deeply, enjoying the earthy aroma. She knew she couldn't stay for long. Eventually, someone would come looking for her. Nadia headed home after she felt her inner tranquility return.

Friday night, Nadia woke up at three AM, the time when the demons were their strongest. They stood around her, laughing. When they had first returned, she asked them what their names were, but they wouldn't tell her. She made up her own names for them. Nadia called them Larry, Curly, and Moe. Moe, the leader, was the original demon and the only one who spoke. Curly was the shorter one, and Larry was the one who seemed to hate her the most.

"You cannot hide in the forest forever, sweet child," Moe cooed. "we will find a way to flush you out."

They didn't stay long, just long enough to let her know the game was afoot. She tossed and turned unable to fall asleep for several hours. After a while, sunlight streaming through her window shades woke her. She grabbed the new cinnamon jars her mother bought for her and quietly slipped from her room. It was early, and everyone was still asleep.

Nadia was overcome by a sense of empowerment. She

50

crept down to their vile lair. She sensed the demons hiding in the shadows. Surprised by her boldness, they drifted closer. Nadia popped the top on each bottle and began pouring the powder around the room. The demons were immediately affected by it. They hissed in their guttural language and scrambled away. The leader cocked his head and chuckled after a few moments.

"Ah, so our sweet little Nadia has come to play with us, has she?" Moe chuckled.

"I want you to leave!" She snarled at them.

"Do you now? It will take a little more than that vile dust to make us leave," Moe crowed.

"I know you hate it. I will fill up the entire cellar with cinnamon!"

Larry growled something to Moe.

"But sweet Nadia, how will you acquire it? I will personally make it, so your parents won't allow you to buy it. In fact, I think I shall make them hate the very smell of it. No sweet child. You won't do anything of the sort."

She stomped her foot, refusing to give into fear.

"If you don't mind me asking, who told you we hated cinnamon?" Moe inquired, nonchalantly.

Nadia wanted to lie to them. The words, 'it's none of your business', lingered on her tongue. In the end, however, she told them the truth. She was hoping they might give her some small hint about how she knew. Unfortunately, they rewarded her with nothing.

"No one. I just knew."

"Ah," Moe replied, turning his back to her.

He began quickly conversing with his companions before disappearing. Nadia slunk back to her room feeling confused but a little triumphant. She had found something they didn't like. She suspected they hated other things as well. It would only be a matter of time until she discovered the answer and when she did ... she would force them out.

The demons were true to their word. Later, when she asked her mother for more cinnamon, she refused, claiming it smelled bad. Nadia was able to get some from Tasha, but she needed vast amounts. When her mother found her with cinnamon, she scolded her for bringing it into the house. After a while, Nadia gave up her quest for the aromatic condiment. It became too difficult to obtain.

After the incident with the cinnamon, her sleep pattern became more and more erratic. It was almost impossible to fall asleep, and the demons woke her every two hours. They kept her and the rest of the family in a state of exhaustion. It would take her hours to fall back asleep, only to be woken again. Sometimes they would poke her with their long fingers. Other times they screamed shrilly into her ears. When they weren't annoying her, they devoted their attention to her family.

It became extremely difficult for Nadia to concentrate on anything for any length of time. That's what the demons wanted ... for her to stay confused. They didn't want her to develop a strategy to fight against them. Her sleepless nights continued to the end of her summer vacation ... until she discovered something else they hated. Something they hated much more than cinnamon.

One Saturday while she was upstairs in the attic she accidentally bumped into a plant, scattering dirt everywhere. Nadia scooped up the dirt and held it for a few moments. Her eyes glazed over as she gently rubbed the dirt between her fingertips. A memory surfaced from the depths. She remembered demons despised fresh dirt. They hated plants as well, but it was the dirt that drove them away.

She ran into the shed and grabbed an empty pot, filling it with potting soil from a nearby bag. Eagar to test her theory, she placed the pot of dirt on her nightstand when it was time for bed. Her parents now went to bed before she did. They were suffering from the same ordeal and were exhausted all the time. It was the first night she actually slept soundly. She sensed they had entered her room, but they left before they could wake her. It was also the first night in months she had a good dream.

In her dream, she saw a tall figure in golden armor, standing in a grassy field. Nadia could tell it was a female by her figure. She had long red hair flowing from the helm. The helm's visor was down so Nadia couldn't see the woman's face. A red dragon was emblazoned on the breastplate. The rest of her armor looked like scales which covered her from neck to feet. There was also a red dragon etched in the metal of her helm.

She held a pulsing white sword in her right-hand which Nadia recognized immediately. It was the same sword she had seen from her previous dreams. Nadia guessed she was finally seeing the owner of the sword. There was something else unusual about the woman. A long set of red wings unfolded from her back. She looked fierce and powerful, but Nadia was not afraid of her.

The woman beckoned to Nadia. As Nadia slowly walked forward, the woman sheathed her sword. Nadia came to a halt, standing before the armored figure. The woman's left hand reached out and grasped Nadia's shoulder. Fire and ice coursed through Nadia's body. It didn't hurt, but it wasn't exactly pleasant either. After it was over, a great calm overtook Nadia and her fear of the intruding entities washed away. The woman began to open her helm, but Nadia awoke before she could see her face.

The dream had ended, but the calm within remained. She had a new sense of clarity and rejuvenation. Nadia glanced at her arm and was surprised to see the demon's mark had vanished. She rose from her bed and went into the kitchen to eat some cereal. It was Saturday but no one was home. Her father was answering an emergency plumbing call and her mother was shopping. Her brother had spent the night with a friend, so she was alone. They sensed she was out of her room and away from her precious dirt. They tried to frighten her by snarling and snapping, but she was no longer scared of them. She just looked at them and yawned. They immediately sensed something had changed … something within her. They were trembling in anger

"WHO TOLD YOU ABOUT THE DIRT!" Moe screamed.

"Wouldn't you like to know," she said, smirking.

The demon she called Larry grabbed her wrist and tried to wrench her off her feet. His hand passed through her like air. The other demons tried grabbing her as well, but they couldn't touch her either.

54

"Oh, stop it," she giggled. "you guys are tickling me."

Her laughter infuriated them further. They howled in frustration.

"So now," she smirked, as she poured herself some cereal, "I'm gonna put dirt all over the house. I don't care if I get in trouble for it either. It's time for you to leave my home!"

Moe stared at her for a long time before speaking. His eyes flashed evilly. He would have killed her at that moment if he had been allowed too.

"We shall leave for now, but I promise we will be back. You will regret this day my sweet little child. I swear to you. When we return, we will make you suffer like no soul has ever suffered on Earth," Moe promised, turning his back to her.

"Whatever," she said indifferently, "but before you go, can you answer a question? Who is the lady in golden dragon armor with long red hair and red wings?

Moe spun around as his eyes flew open. He gaped at her in shock. His mottled skin turned a deeper grey. The other two demons appeared equally stunned.

"Y … you saw Katrianna?" Moe stammered.

"Who?"

They disappeared in front of her before they could answer her question. The house felt bright and happy again. She breathed a sigh of relief. Nadia hoped she had seen the last of them … but she was wrong.

When they returned … they returned with a vengeance.

Nezatel was alarmed. Something had gone drastically wrong with his assignment. He needed to increase his activities, but he couldn't do so without the permission of his master. He wasn't looking forward to seeing Lucifer either. No doubt his master would be upset, especially once he learned about Katrianna. Nezatel couldn't believe he had lost his ability to touch her.

Humans had no idea how much energy it took for demons and spirits to manifest themselves. It took even more power to be able to touch the living. Lucifer had been gracious enough to supply him with ample amounts of power so he could do what he needed, but now something had changed. His two companions walked behind him, struggling to keep up. When they arrived in Hell, Nezatel quickened his pace to a run.

"Slow down, Nezatel!" Ieckisht complained. "I don't understand the rush."

Nezatel stopped and grabbed his companion by his shoulder, shaking him.

"Do you have any idea how upset he's going to be when I tell him about Katrianna? The longer I delay, the worse his anger. Now let's go!"

"I hate her!" Tyrient growled.

"You hate all warrior angels," Ieckisht mentioned.

"Well, shouldn't I? After all, they scarred my pretty face."

"I would have to say it's a vast improvement," Ieckisht laughed.

Nezatel ignored their banter and sprinted into the castle searching for Araphel. One didn't just waltz into Lucifer's chambers. Only his messenger was allowed that privilege. He found him lounging on a chair, reading a book. A flash of hatred filled him as he gazed upon Araphel. Nezatel despised Lucifer's messenger. His hatred stemmed from Araphel's past. As a fallen one, he still moved with grace. His mannerisms were delicate and precise as he carried himself with a sense of dignity. This wasn't the reason Nezatel hated him, however.

Demons hungered for knowledge and power. Araphel had knowledge most demons would never have … the knowledge of Heaven. Fallen angels were usually stripped of their knowledge of Heaven, but Lucifer allowed Araphel to keep his wisdom. It was his memories, and information Nezatel envied. Nezatel too had once been an angel, but Lucifer wiped his memories clean. He remembered nothing of his former life. Araphel was also arrogant and pompous, even more so than a typical demon.

"Yes? You desire something, Nezatel?" Araphel drawled, rolling his eyes.

"I have urgent news for the master. I must speak with him immediately," Nezatel urged, ignoring Araphel's haughtiness.

"Perhaps you should give me the message," Araphel suggested.

"Perhaps I should," Nezatel mocked, "that way it will be *your* head that rolls, not mine. Time is of the essence! I suggest you hurry."

Araphel stood up slowly and stretched.

"Very well," Araphel said, a soft smile playing around his

lips, "I shall inform Lucifer he has a … guest."

Araphel strolled into Lucifer's chambers and didn't return for a long time. Nezatel quickly grew impatient. Time on Earth was different than time in Hell. Hours in Hell were days on Earth. The longer he spent in Hell, the more time he was away from his job. There was a greater chance events could go wrong in his absence. Nadia was already growing stronger. Nezatel was worried she would figure out a way to dispel him, which would be disastrous.

Araphel finally opened the door and allowed him to enter.

"Lucifer will see you now," Araphel said, smirking.

Nezatel left his two companions and entered the room alone. It was easy to feel Lucifer. A cold seemed to envelop him, cold he felt in the depths of his soul. He bowed before Lucifer and waited to be acknowledged.

"Nezatel," Lucifer greeted coldly, "I must say I am surprised to see you. When we last spoke, I gave you strict instructions to never leave your post for any reason. And yet … here you are. Why?"

"Sire," Nezatel began quickly, "it was imperative I speak with you. I bring troubling news."

"I am waiting."

Lucifer glowered at Nezatel, making him very nervous.

"She has lost my mark on her arm and her fear. I need your permission to increase our influence."

"What do you mean she lost her fear? Explain yourself immediately," Lucifer ordered, anger dripping from his voice.

58

"My lord ...," Nezatel paused before continuing.

"SPEAK!" Lucifer barked.

"I believe Katrianna has visited her," the demon finished quickly.

"WHAT!"

"She described a woman she had seen. It fit the description of Katrianna exactly. And now, she has no fear of us."

Trembling with rage, Lucifer burst into blue flames. He grabbed a bookcase and heaved it into the wall, shattering it instantly. Papers rained down upon them.

"HOW COULD YOU ALLOW THIS TO HAPPEN!"

He picked up Nezatel by the neck and threw him across the room. He hit the wall with a thud. Nezatel scrambled to get away.

"My lord, I can rectify the situation," Nezatel gasped.

"YOU HAD BETTER RECTIFY THE SITUATION!" Lucifer screamed. "OR I WILL FEED YOU TO MY BEASTS!"

"I won't fail, I promise. I have a plan. I just need your permission to move forward," Nezatel gasped.

Lucifer stood shuddering for a few minutes before his anger subsided.

"What is your plan, Nezatel?" Lucifer asked, beckoning him forward.

Nezatel warily approached his master and whispered into his ears. Within moments Lucifer burst out laughing.

"You have my permission to implement your plan, and I

want frequent reports about your progress."

"Thank you, sire," Nezatel said, breathing a sigh of relief.

"It is a curious thing she was visited by Katrianna, is it not?" Lucifer asked more to himself than his demon. "This surely means Nadia *is* a warrior angel. I wonder if my enemy has finally decided to interfere. Katrianna *always* was his favorite," he said bitterly.

"I am not sure. It is curious, indeed."

"Well, no matter. If you succeed, you shall be heartily rewarded. I will make you a Captain in the Waru. You will have your own army to command. You have risen through the ranks faster than any of my fallen, and it's because you will do *anything* to accomplish your mission. That is a trait I greatly admire, and you are worthy of being my demon."

"Thank you, my lord," Nezatel said, bowing his head in gratitude.

"Tell me, do you remember anything about your life when you were an angel?"

"No, sire, nothing."

"You were a guardian angel of all things and quite inept at your job. At one time … you were my friend. You listened to me when no one did," Lucifer said softly, his eyes brimming with memories.

"I … I was?" Nezatel stammered.

"Yes. I promised you a grand position if you followed me. You fell like the rest. I rewarded you with the title of watcher and gave you powers most watchers don't have."

"Are you still my friend?" Nezatel asked.

60

"No. You are my servant and that is all. I have no friends in this place," Lucifer paused, settling his dark eyes upon his demon, "and should you fail … you shall suffer more than any demon in Hell. Your pain will be greater than any of the damned. All status will be removed, even a Kerbal will have a higher status than you. Do I make myself clear?"

Nezatel was shocked. To have no status in Hell was worse than being dead. Nezatel would rather have had his insides ripped apart a thousand times than have his status removed.

"I will not fail you!" Nezatel said, forcefully.

"I certainly hope not … for your sake. Many of my plans are dependent upon your success. You are dismissed."

Nezatel practically sprinted from the room. By now at least two days had passed. Two days gave Katrianna ample time to revisit Nadia. In two days, everything could change.

"Ah, I see you have made it back in one piece," Araphel goaded him.

Nezatel ignored him, motioning to his comrades before heading to the gate.

Lucifer emerged from the room and ordered Araphel to call an emergency council meeting. Lucifer stormed into the meeting room, eager to share his news. Unfortunately, Mortoc was fighting on the far end of the realm and couldn't return as quickly as Lucifer wanted. The delay did nothing for Lucifer's foul mood. When Mortoc finally arrived, everyone was already assembled. Elistax couldn't help but send a barb in his direction.

"Nice of you to join us, Mortoc," she sneered.

"Yes well, I actually have a job to do … unlike some," Mortoc returned.

"Enough!" Lucifer barked. "we have a far bigger problem on our hands then your petty squabbles."

When the room was silent, he continued.

"I have received disturbing word from one of my watchers. I believe Zavier may be directly managing the realm once more."

"Excellent! Finally, a real battle!" Elistax shouted, "send my army to scourge the Earth!"

"In time perhaps," Lucifer said smoothly, "but I need to see if it's true and for what purpose. I will not act rashly."

"What has happened to make you believe so, sire?" Mortoc asked.

"All of you know my plans to turn the human girl. I believe she is a reincarnated warrior angel. Nezatel told me she was visited by Katrianna. I'm sure you are all aware there is only one way Katrianna could have possibly visited her … through Zavier's direct interference."

The room exploded with shouting.

"How is that possible?" An advisor name Kered asked. "she was stripped of her powers and banished."

"That is what I intend to find out," Lucifer stated.

"What will you do if it's true? None of us want to see her return and reclaim her armies," Elistax asked.

"Aw, are you frightened little girl? Do you need a pillow to comfort you?" Mortoc mocked, taking the opportunity to needle her.

62

"Mortoc, ENOUGH!" Lucifer shouted, silencing the room.

Elistax was able to shoot Mortoc a sneer before Lucifer spoke again.

"If she has returned, I will resurrect the Crawlers."

The room fell silent once more. The Crawlers were an abomination, even the Varafe feared. They were huge, powerful lizards who wore heavy armor. They were vicious and hungry with no memory of their former selves. Humans were oblivious to the supernatural … but they could see the Crawlers. This was one of the reasons the Old Ones declared it a crime to summon them. They killed hundreds within moments and caused chaos by just their appearance.

"My lord! That comes with too great of cost to you," Nucaira, the historian shouted.

"I'm well aware of the price I have to pay, Nucaira, but I'll not see my plans destroyed by that woman!"

"So, what will ye do?" Yarish, the head demon asked.

"I think I shall pay a little visit to Zavier."

"But sire, you are not welcome there. I don't think that's a good idea," Kered sputtered.

"I am well aware I am not welcome in Heaven! I will go there as soon as this meeting is finished and demand an audience with him," Lucifer announced.

The council was so focused on Lucifer they didn't notice a Kerbal named Aurher enter the room, bringing flesh for them to eat. Aurher worked in the meat room and it was his job to deliver refreshments anytime the council was called. He wasn't the brightest demon, and never knew when to keep his mouth shut. He had heard most of what the council was discussing and thought it proper to give his input.

"Well, if you want my opinion," Aurher chimed.

For a third time, the council was completely silent as all necks snapped in his direction.

"What did you say?" Lucifer said softly.

"Maybe you can ask Xiere for help. I heard ...,"

Aurher wasn't able to finish his sentence because Lucifer quickly propelled himself over the table and ripped his soul from his body. Lucifer picked up the empty flesh sack and slammed it onto the table, splattering black blood all over the council. He repeatedly smashed the body until nothing, but bloody pulp remained. He hurled the carcass outside the door.

"Remind the underlings NO ONE is EVER to address me like that AGAIN! Do I make myself clear!" Lucifer bellowed. "I AM YOUR SUPREME LEADER, AND I DEMAND RESPECT. I NEVER WANT THAT NAME UTTERED IN MY PRESENCE AGAIN!"

They all quickly agreed in unison. They were used to seeing Lucifer angry, but he was beyond furious this time. He didn't like the Kerbal's speaking out of turn, much less addressing him without permission. The sheer audacity of such behavior was intolerable. Furthermore, Aurher mentioned the name of an individual so untrustworthy, Lucifer would rather cut off his wings before calling upon him. Aurher deserved to die for his lack of judgment.

"This meeting is over," Lucifer concluded. "I will call to reconvene after I speak with Zavier. Until that time Yarish is in charge."

In the Beginning...
Chapter Four

Zavier finished his daily tasks and sat down by a brook to contemplate. Soon he would have a special visitor to his realm. Lucifer didn't visit him often, but Zavier always knew when Lucifer wanted to speak with him. Zavier could have just as easily ignored him, but in his heart, he still loved his angel, even though he was a perverted version of his former self. Lucifer had so much potential and threw it all away. Compared to the rest, Lucifer had disappointed him the most.

Zavier, like many beings with great power, could switch appearances at will. He liked to appear as a vulnerable creature such as an animal or a small child. Zavier always believed he could judge another on how they treated a defenseless creature. As much as he enjoyed transforming, his true appearance was quite different. In reality, Zavier was well over seven-foot-tall with wavy brown hair. He had high cheekbones, a slightly hooked nose, and light green eyes. His skin was smooth with a bluish tint. He was more handsome than any of his angels. His looks were something he could have easily used to his advantage, but because of his integrity, he never did. There was an aura of kindness surrounding him and peacefulness in his heart, but it wasn't always this way.

Zavier had known great sadness in his long life but none as devastating as the loss of his wife. She was his everything, his soul mate. Her name was Stelline. She was tall with blazing red hair and crystal blue eyes. She was a Dragon Angel who lived on an entirely different realm and moved with the grace of a thousand angels. They had met years before he had been selected as a ruler. She gave him two beautiful children, a boy, and a girl. They were fraternal twins and couldn't have been more different. It was interesting his wife gave birth to twins. Twins ran in his family, he, himself having one.

Zavier remembered those early years with fondness. He had long given up on finding love. Never in a million years did he expect to find his soulmate on a peace mission. She came from a dying race. Zavier was ordered to form an alliance and offer safe passage to another realm. She didn't really need protection because she was a fierce warrior … one of the fiercest he had ever known.

The moment they locked eyes, their souls bonded. They became inseparable, and he courted her for many years. On a moonlight night, against the backdrop of a narrow waterfall, he asked for her hand in marriage. He thought his heart would burst with happiness when she said yes. It wasn't long after their marriage that Zavier became a ruler. He had everything a person could want.

Alas, their happiness was not meant to last. After many years of bliss, she fell into a state of hopelessness. He couldn't save her. Her soul was so devastated it could not be repaired. She disappeared never to be reborn again. When she died, she took his heart with her. He would never again find a love like hers. It was a dark time in his life. He was inconsolable and wept constantly.

It took him thousands of years to get over his crippling despair. He still missed her with every breath he took.

Furthermore, he had to raise two children and control a kingdom by himself. It wasn't easy but luckily, he had his angels to help him. It was challenging, but nothing is ever simple or easy, especially when it comes to raising children. And as he breathed life to his realm, many things changed over time.

Zavier's brother, Shivet, tried to help him, but he had his own calamities to contend with. Zavier and Shivet were fraternal twins, but their realms were identical … in the beginning. They once had the same land masses, same continents, and foliage. The Old Ones created twin realms eons before Shivet and Zavier were born. The purpose of having identical realms was so humans could be reborn from one realm into the next and have a sense of familiarity. The twins being who they were, altered their realms after a time.

Realms were collected into large groups called Chains. Zavier ruled the Meifilar realm in the Delaphina Chain. It was one small realm in an entire system of others. Human's called the realm Earth, but its actual name was Parium. Meifilar had many other planets besides Earth in the realm.

Shivet lived on a completely different set of realms called the Nanalder Chain. Shivet's Realm was called Pariseum, and war was brewing. His people were slowly uprising. Each brother had to deal with their trials alone. There was currently a small measure of peace on Shivet's realm, but Zavier was sure it wouldn't last long.

Zavier ruled from what humans called heaven, but its actual name was Eineitha. It was heaven to him. Humans always had a peculiar judgment about how his home should look. They always looked to the sky for heaven and thought it would look like a bunch of powdery clouds. They expected to arrive at a big gate manned by an angel. Once inside, they believed they would get wings and float around singing praises to him. He, of course, would be hidden by a veil of light, only to appear when he needed to bask in their praise, like some self-indulgent, pompous ass. It was utter nonsense. He would have been replaced a long time ago if he had been that useless. His people had such odd beliefs.

In fact, there were no human souls in Eineitha. Only his angels lived with him in this beautiful place. If someone had a kind soul when they died, they usually traveled on a different realm to reside until it was time for them to be reborn. Sometimes they were reborn immediately, especially if they didn't learn the lesson they were instructed to learn. If they had given their heart to darkness, they lived with Lucifer where they learned a far different lesson.

Zavier loved nature and felt most comfortable among living things. Most of Eineitha was an immense forest littered with all types of trees, many never seen on Earth. There were also vast areas of rolling hills and open fields. Brooks and rivers divided the land. They were teeming with fish and other water-breathing animals. Most of Eineitha was fixed in a never-ending season of spring, but there were areas specifically designed for winter, summer, and fall. Zavier loved all the seasons and wanted to incorporate their beauty. In the center of Eineitha, there was a humongous lake with a small island in the center. A large tree rose from the water, occupying most of the island. This island was where Zavier resided.

Zavier's home was created inside the tree and it was very comfortable. A winding staircase made of branches wound all the way to the top. There were several different rooms carved into the wood, but there was no bedroom. Zavier wasn't burdened with the need for sleep. A dome at the top opened so he could see the stars. Zavier treasured the stars. He loved them so much he made sure humans could see them as well. Something so beautiful had to be shared.

His smooth furniture was made of wood with intricate carvings etched into the surfaces. Huge tapestries made of different colors of grain hung on the walls. In the center was a waterfall which cascaded into a frothy fountain. The floor was a giant mosaic of different colored rocks. It was a beautiful and peaceful home. Zavier was very busy, but he came here when he needed to think. He would meditate for hours in a room near the top of the tree. It was how he kept himself grounded.

Zavier loved nature so much he made it a resilient species on all the planets under his watch. Parium/Earth had the greatest replenishing natural phenomenon, more so than the rest of his planets combined. He had to make it that way. After all, humans were the most destructive creatures he had ever made. Sadly, he hadn't meant for that to happen. Humans were the first creatures created and the most imperfect. Earth was far older than most humans could imagine. In fact, it was trillions and trillions of years old.

Zavier didn't like being a powerful ruler at times, and when he was younger, he wasn't always so kind. When his creations disappointed him, he destroyed them instead of giving them an opportunity for redemption. The first set of humans made war upon themselves almost immediately after he created them. His angels didn't even have a chance to guide them. Zavier couldn't understand what happened. They should have been perfect specimens, but they weren't. He wiped the slate clean and started over.

The second and third generations of humans were just as disappointing. They lived far longer than the first, but they still managed to disappoint him with their eventual turn towards barbarity. The second generation set fire to every living thing, choking the planet and themselves. The third destroyed all their females in a horrific act of violence. The males believed females to be a threat and sought to purge them. Their rash stupidity infuriated Zavier.

He destroyed the remaining male humans in his own barbaric manner. Zavier wanted them to suffer, so he killed off their food source. They died slowly and painfully, the strong preying on the weak. It wasn't his proudest moment. He had hoped they would learn, but they somehow refused to understand.

Zavier made changes every time he recreated them but still gave them free will. He had hoped they would freely turn toward the light so they could grow and learn. He didn't want them to blindly love him. He wanted them to love and help each other. His angels were used to guide them, but often, his people didn't listen. It was frustrating.

His fourth generation was seemingly perfect in every way. His people were a peaceful and loving species. They should have influenced others to live in peace and harmony. Something changed and somehow, they became corrupted.

72

Some of them became violent rulers. Hungry for power, they began enslaving their brethren and drinking their blood. They formed an army of lustful individuals whose only desire was absolute power. Filled with disappointment, Zavier began his cleansing process, but he couldn't finish it. He was stopped by the Old Ones. They were unhappy with his reign and ordered him to return to Galvadar. It wasn't a happy return.

The Old Ones ruled for as long as anyone could remember and desired balance above all things. There were thirteen of them all psychically linked. Most of their communication was done silently among themselves but when they spoke aloud, it was in unison. They always wore white robes, which concealed their bodies. Their frog-like faces peaked out from hooded cloaks. Zavier didn't realize it at the time, but he was being summoned for a hearing. His strive for perfection had upset the balance. In a central chamber made of stone, the council began their trial.

"Zavier!" The council began. "you stand before us, accused of upsetting the balance. How do you plea?"

Zavier was stunned.

"Accused? How have I upset the balance?" he asked, dumbfounded.

"Your PLEA!" they repeated louder.

"I'm innocent, of course. You placed me in charge ...," he tried explaining before they interrupted him.

"Very well. We will examine the evidence and make our decision."

"But ...,"

"SILENCE!"

Zavier sat quietly, shocked beyond words. They turned towards each other and communicated telepathically. After an hour of nodding heads and moving hands, they faced him, ready to continue.

"You have destroyed over 100 million living creatures. Do you deny this?" they asked him directly.

"No, but ...,"

"Then you are guilty," they concluded.

"Let me explain!" Zavier pleaded.

The council sat quietly, talking internally to each other. After a few moments, they spoke aloud.

"Very well, Zavier. Speak."

"You appointed me as protector of the realm. I am striving to create perfect inhabitants that live in harmony with each other. Every single one of them is flawed! I needed to cleanse the realm and begin anew after every disappointment. I am getting close to perfection. I shouldn't have to do this many more times."

The council frowned at him.

"*That* is your explanation for upsetting the balance?"

"I fail to understand how I have ...," Zavier blurted, trying to defend himself.

"We have heard enough! We will deliberate on your punishment."

"WHAT!" Zavier shouted.

The council ignored his outburst and quickly rose, filing

out of the room. They seemed to float rather than walk. He was left alone in the dimly lit chamber. He couldn't believe what was happening. His head was spinning. Fortunately, he didn't have to stew in his thoughts for too long. They returned shortly with his verdict.

"Zavier, as you know we find you guilty. We have come to believe however, you do not understand the ramifications of your actions. We wish to explain how you have tipped the balance before we begin punishment," they declared.

Zavier's mouth seemed dry and chalky. He had a hard time focusing on their words.

"When we placed you in charge of your realm, we told you explicitly you could run it any way you chose," they continued. "but instead of guiding your subjects on Parium you disposed of them like their lives meant nothing. That is only part of the problem. You have focused all your attention on one planet with the mad desire for perfection. The rest of your realm has been ignored. They have inhabitants on them who need your guidance, but because your attention is focused elsewhere, entire races are dying off. Your rule has been a disaster!"

"I ... I," Zavier couldn't finish.

"Zavier, these are living souls you are destroying. You are extinguishing them before they even have a chance to prove themselves. What you have done is an abomination! It takes time to match the correct soul with the body. Your actions have caused a massive influx of souls who cannot be reborn. They are left to wander the realms alone and many are turning evil in their uncertainty. Great unhappiness has filled them with despair. It is your pride and your lust

75

for perfection, which has done this."

Zavier fell to his knees, finally understanding. He hung his head in remorse.

"We find you guilty of tipping the balance and seek your immediate removal," they concluded.

"NO! Let me repair the damage!"

"There is nothing you can ever do to fix this, Zavier. As you are well aware, tipping the balance is a crime," they concluded.

"PLEASE! I beg you!"

The council fell quiet as they again communicated internally. After an extended period, they finally spoke."

"Very well, Zavier. We shall allow you to remain as ruler of your realm. However, as part of your sentence, we have removed your power to punish. You may only use your influence through others. If your inhabitants destroy themselves so be it, but you will never be allowed to kill them again. We will grant you permission to help them through your divine influence, but that is all."

"How can I protect them from evil influences if I cannot directly guide them?" Zavier asked, his head still reeling from their judgment.

"We shall allow you to create a special class of angel warriors to protect your people, but there is a catch ... they cannot know they are warriors until they have been deemed worthy by us."

"That makes no sense at all." Zavier protested. "how can I possibly use them as warriors if they don't know who they are?"

"You must continually test them, and they must always be born as humans. They can be guided, but they must figure out who they are on their own. Only when they are worthy will they have all their powers to fight against evil."

"My hands are tied," Zavier said, shaking his head. "what happens if they turned evil?"

"Then obviously they have failed their test and must be tested again or discarded," the council said, scowling.

"I thank the council for this chance to redeem myself," Zavier said, softly.

"And there is one more matter. You are hereby stripped of your powers and banished to Furuku Realm for a thousand years. No one will be allowed to speak to you. You shall be utterly alone. This should give you ample time to think about your actions and how they affected the rest of the realms. You may return long enough to place a leader in charge but choose wisely Zavier, for you will not be permitted to have contact while you are banished. If upon your return, should you use your warriors to hurt the innocent, you will be banished forever … in the Villands."

The Old Ones dismissed him, concluding their word was law. Zavier left the council in total confusion. He returned to Eineitha and called an emergency meeting. He didn't have time to explain what was happening. He informed them he would be gone for a while and left Lucifer in charge. It turned out to be the worst mistake he had ever made.

Lucifer, eager to prove he was a worthy ruler, slowly

turned the realm into a debased mockery of what Zavier had intended. Eineitha became divided and was in constant turmoil. Earth and the rest of the realm fared no better. At best, humans were ignored and left to fend for themselves. At worst, Lucifer used people as prey. He sent angels to hunt humans, and together, they slaughtered many innocent souls. Humans had little choice but to submit to Lucifer's wishes. It was a dark age ... the darkest in his realm's existence.

Zavier was grateful he didn't know what was happening during his banishment. It would have driven him insane knowing he couldn't do anything about it. During his long, lonely days, Zavier finally understood what he had done wrong and accepted responsibility. He swore he would never resort to such brutal methods again. He learned patience and humility, promising to create a better world filled with light.

When he returned from exile, he was appalled by Lucifer's rule. Truthfully, he was more disappointed than angry. He punished him by sending him away, but Lucifer wouldn't go quietly. A horrific war followed, resulting in a total upheaval of the entire realm. Per the Old One's punishment, Zavier had to watch as his angels fought each other. He decided to create a realm apart from his own, called Vox, or Hell as humans called it. He banished Lucifer and his followers.

Zavier decided all corrupt souls would live with Lucifer upon their death. He hoped during their punishment they might learn so when they were reborn, they would choose more wisely. He didn't expect them to be perfect. After all, he was far from perfect himself. Every soul was tested, and some of those tests were very difficult. What he was looking for were souls who endured and yet stayed honorable.

The idea of reincarnation was to allow souls to walk in someone else's shoes. It usually was the most effective way to learn. Zavier did create something rather unique on his realm to help people choose the right path. He created the system of Circle or Karma as many called it. Zavier wanted his creations to understand that although they had free will, there were consequences for their actions. Those consequences weren't always pleasant either. Humans usually caused their own misery as they looked for others to blame.

There were thousands of realms but none so insidious as the Villands. Eons ago, a powerful being created it although many have forgotten why. It is entirely cloaked in shadows and those who enter rarely return. The Villands twisted the strong and the weak. Once a soul was corrupted, it was very difficult for it to become pure again, but it wasn't impossible. To be banished to the Villands was to be banished from yourself.

It was often the last test for a ruler. Those chosen worthy to rule a realm had to spend an indiscernible amount of time in the Villands. Zavier himself spent over a year there. He saw horrors he wouldn't wish on his darkest enemy. He still shuddered at the memory of it. He never succumbed, even though there were times he desperately wanted to. It was the most malevolent realm ever created, but it did serve a purpose, as all realms did.

Since the Old Ones desired neutrality, there had to be evil to balance good. The Old Ones were forever moving realms around like chess pieces. To them, evil was simply a negative force to balance the positive force of good. If a realm became negative, the Old Ones would create a positive realm to balance it. Tipping the balance was considered a crime since it created chaos, which was the undoing of all.

Zavier's realm was unique in the sense it had both positive and negative forces occupying it. Most realms had some degree of one or the other but not in the same extent as his. It made things very challenging for Zavier. Lucifer was forever trying to tip the balance of Zavier's kingdom, but thus far had been unsuccessful. Zavier always hoped Lucifer might learn the error of his ways and return someday. After thousands of years, however, Zavier was beginning to lose hope. Lucifer was too arrogant, too selfish to change.

No one knew about the restrictions the Old Ones placed upon Zavier. He kept the secret to himself. Lucifer had spies everywhere. If Zavier told anyone, Lucifer would surely discover the truth. Some secrets had to be kept secret. It was better Lucifer believes Zavier still had the power to wipe him out with one swoop. Lucifer enjoyed playing games, but Zavier always had the upper hand

A fluttering behind him interrupted his contemplations. He knew it was his closest advisor Firthel, no doubt bringing him news.

"Yes, Firthel?"

"How is it I can never sneak up on you?" Firthel laughed.

"You couldn't sneak up on a deaf man, Firthel. You flutter like a drunken butterfly," Zavier quipped.

80

"Nice. Thanks. Remind me to spit in your drink next time."

"It wouldn't do you any good," Zavier chuckled. "I would know if you were going to do it."

"Ah, yes, Mr. Omnipotent," Firthel chuckled.

"I'm assuming you have interrupted my meditation for a good reason?"

"Of course," Firthel offered.

Zavier turned around and gave his angel an expecting look. Firthel was more than an advisor, he was a good friend. The two of them often bantered with each other for hours. Firthel belonged to a class of smaller angels. He had angler cheekbones and white hair, while his feathery wings were long and blue.

Angels were categorized according to their wing color. Advancement or a transfer took considerable effort since most angels were created for a specific job. They usually stayed in that job unless there was some reason for them to move to another profession. Every angel began with white wings and traded colors when they were picked for an occupation. Often angels weren't given a choice about their professions, which was a sore subject for many of them.

Guardian angels had yellow or green wings, and all advisors had blue. Black belonged to an elite group of assassins. They were vicious, taking care of business with a haunting glee. Lucifer had been part of that group. Looking back, Zavier knew it was a mistake to make Lucifer an assassin. He loved his job just a little too much.

There was a wide array of colors for different jobs, but

none was so recognizable than the red-winged. They were his warrior class and the ones who carried out Zavier's tasks as he was unable. They kept order in the realm. They were quick and deadly, striking the enemy with fatal blows. All of them were tall, elegant, and proud angels, sworn to protect the innocent and vanquish the wicked. It had taken him a long time to create the army of Red Wings since they were to be tested by the Old Ones first.

The most famous of the red-winged angels was Katrianna. She commanded, not only the army of Red Wings but a legion of dragons as well. Katrianna fought Lucifer during his uprising and destroyed over half of his army. Unfortunately, she rebelled when she wasn't allowed to kill Lucifer. She was young, impetus, and didn't understand why events happened as they did. She took her dragon army to other realms and began destroying any evil she could find. In the end, she slaughtered billions of good souls as well. Anything that stood in her path was obliterated. The Old Ones weren't pleased with her actions. They removed her powers and banished her from the realm until she was deemed worthy enough to return. No one, not even Zavier, could bring her back or even speak to her. It was a sad day for him.

Zavier never knew where she was most of the time. She had grown much during her punishment, but she still had a long way to go. He couldn't wait to have her back in his fold again. She was a great asset to his army, and he had a soft spot in his heart for her. He hoped she could learn from her actions and become the warrior she was meant to become. Her banishment was public knowledge, and everyone knew what happened to her. Lucifer rejoiced when his strongest enemy was removed from his path.

Zavier was waiting for Firthel to speak, but he just kept grinning at him like a Cheshire Cat.

"Well?" Zavier finally said, waving his hands.

"Yes, well, Lucifer is in the antechamber outside the main hall. He humbly … well, he requests your audience."

Zavier sighed.

All business was conducted in the main hall, which was built entirely of branches. Lucifer was allowed into Eineitha but had to be escorted into the antechamber and placed under close guard. Lucifer's powers were greatly diminished in Eineitha, but Zavier took no chances. Lucifer would seek any opportunity to create mischief.

"Well, I suppose I should see what he wants," Zavier yawned.

"Or not. I'm sure he would love it if you made him wait a millennium or two," Firthel suggested, smiling widely.

"I think not. His stench bleeds into the realm. I would rather have him leave as soon as possible."

Zavier teleported instantly to the main hall. He could hear Lucifer inside arguing furiously with the guards. He was screaming at the top of his lungs, demanding to be taken to Zavier. Zavier shook his head. It was always the same with Lucifer. He would never change. As Zavier entered the room, the guards fell silent, bowing their heads. Lucifer sneered and made a grand display of bowing formally.

"Hello father," Lucifer greeted, his voice dripping with

ice.

"Hello, son. It's been a long time."

Let the Games Begin!
Chapter Five

Nadia prepared for the worst. She gathered pots of dirt and hid them all over the house to drive them away. The demons returned after several days absence and immediately noticed her ploy. She thought they would be angry, but they didn't seem to care. The dirt still affected them, but they laughed at her instead of becoming angry. She was confused by their reaction.

"You will leave my house for good," she announced.

"Sweet child, you know we cannot do that. We have a job to do. I'm sure your parents will be quite displeased when they learn you are making their house dirty. Of course, I will make sure they find your little pots of dirt," the leader hissed evilly.

"I don't care. Dirt is everywhere. I will bring it in every night!" Nadia snarled.

"Suit yourself. I wish to inform you we won't be entering your room anymore. In fact, we will never," he paused, "directly wake you again. Enjoy your sleep … if you can."

"What does that mean?"

"You will find out soon enough my sweet child and remember … you can always end your suffering by simply joining my master."

They vanished before her eyes, but she knew they were still watching her every move. Nadia quickly found out what they meant. They decided to ignore her and concentrate all their efforts on her family. She soon grew weary of the constant arguing between her parents. Her mother looked haggard as she screamed like a banshee at her father. Her father in return bellowed at all three of them for the slightest infraction. They weren't themselves.

True to their word, her parents found her dirt and punished her severely for it. She was forced to stay in her room for a month, except when she had to go to school or the bathroom. They seemed to forget to feed her often, so she was always hungry. She wanted to hate her parents, but she couldn't. How could she, when she saw the demons whispering in their ears, controlling them like puppets? They had no strength to fight back.

The atmosphere at home became intolerable. Nadia escaped to Tasha's house every chance she could, but after a while, her parents wouldn't allow it anymore. Her father insisted Nadia stay home, but she just couldn't. There was no peace at home, only incessant arguing. After school, she would race into the woods, not caring what the weather was like. Nadia usually stayed there until her parents came home. Her father always yelled at her for leaving the house, but that didn't stop her. She needed the forest to help her stay sane.

The demons eventually put an end to her wooded haven. One night, she awoke to the acrid smell of smoke and the sound of fire trucks. She raced to the window, horrified at what she saw. The entire forest was aflame. She could feel the heat through her window. They were forced to evacuate until the fire was extinguished. Nadia's heart ached when she saw the scarred remains of her haven.

The authorities claimed it was arson, but they never

discovered who started it. Nadia knew, however. One day while her brother was at work, she went into his closet to look for a blanket. She found an empty gasoline jug and a box of matches. She knew it was the demons and their little tricks. Her brother would have never intentionally set fire to the woods. Nadia sobbed, feeling trapped. With no place to hide, she had to stay home … and home became a prison. Her brother tormented her constantly, calling her every name under the sun. She shut down to avoid escalating the situation, hiding in the attic as often as she could. Nadia wanted to disappear.

Her visions of the red-haired woman disappeared as Nadia became overwhelmed with negative energy. She didn't know what to do. She felt so helpless against the constant onslaught of misery. Her grades plummeted because she couldn't concentrate at home. As much as she tried, she couldn't claw out of the hole filling in on top of her. The demons badgered her, pleading with her to submit. They sounded so convincing, but she still found the strength to refuse them.

Nadia knew giving up wasn't an option. The demons offered her freedom from their torment, but she knew they were lying to her. Deep down, she knew they would give her a lifetime of misery. She often wondered why they were so intent on claiming her. She wasn't anything special, just an average girl in America. Nadia couldn't help but wonder if demons were doing the same to people all over the world. She wished she knew why her family couldn't see them … why she had been cursed with this gift.

"What if demons are influencing people everywhere?"

she pondered. "that would explain why there are so many wars."

The more Nadia thought about it, the more it made sense. She had read countless stories about ordinary people snapping and going on murderous rampages. People were always shocked when a good person suddenly became evil. Demons whispering from the shadows could do multitudes of damage to an unaware person.

Nadia began reading newspapers and watching the news. For every good story, there were ten horrible ones. She heard the old excuse 'the devil made me do it'. She always thought it was a lame justification for people not accepting responsibility for their actions. Nadia wondered if there was a war around everyone … and people weren't even aware of it. She promised herself to stay strong, but it wasn't easy, and it gradually became even harder.

After six months, the demon's decided to kick it up a notch. Screaming matches turned physical. Both parents launched themselves at each other and beat one another until they were bruised all over. On occasion, they hit her brother too, forcing him to fight back. The community knew what was happening. The angry screams resonated from the house like wailing sirens. Everyone shunned them, embarrassed by their behavior. No one called the police. Her parents never hit her, but they screamed at her constantly and told her to go away.

One particular hellish weekend, her mother sliced her father's bicep open with a paring knife. As blood poured from the wound, he managed to punch her face, splitting the delicate skin on her temple. They both needed stitches and headed to the car. Her mother turned on Nadia and grabbed her neck, screaming furiously.

"This is all your fault, Nadia!"

Nadia swallowed hard. She could see the demon Larry whispering in her mother's ear. He took his long-pointed finger and gently traced it down her mother's cheek as if to caress her face. Her mother seemed to feel nothing but grew angrier. Her eyes turned almost black as she spoke.

"If you would only give in, all this could stop. We could go back to being a normal family again," her mother pleaded.

"No," Nadia croaked, feeling the air tighten around her throat.

"You will give in!" her mother growled in a voice not entirely her own. "you will lose everything if you don't, and *you* will be to blame."

Nadia somehow found the strength within her. She shouted while pushing her energy outward.

"I WILL NEVER GIVE IN!" Nadia screamed shrilly.

The demon beside her mother was propelled outward and far away from them. He stood up slowly, glaring at her, hatred burning in his violent eyes.

"What happened?" her mother asked softly.

"You cut dad's arm open, and he punched your face," Nadia said flatly.

"Oh my god! What?" she blabbered, confused.

Her father appeared and dragged her mother to the car, whisking her away. They didn't return until after Nadia was asleep. That night was the first time in a long time she dreamed… of Katrianna. The fierce warrior stood on a grassy knoll, her dangerous weapon raised high in the air. Although Katrianna's face was shielded by a helm, Nadia could tell she was triumphant by her stance. Without warning, Katrianna let loose a battle cry that sent chills through Nadia's body.

When Nadia awoke, she felt rejuvenated … at least for a little while. It seemed after that event, the fighting between her parents intensified. Pieces of glass littered the floor as they used everything they could find as weapons against each other. Her brother, who still lived at home went to the hospital for a broken arm which he claimed was from sports. Their father broke Travis's arm using a tire iron. Travis managed to jam a screwdriver into their father's thigh to defend himself. It was now a war zone at home.

Her entire world came crashing down one windy night soon after her fifteenth birthday. Gunfire ripped through the house, waking her. Nadia sat up as fast as a bullet, hoping she had been dreaming, but she somehow knew it wasn't a dream. Another shot resounded throughout the house, revealing her worst fears. Terrified, Nadia quietly tiptoed downstairs. She could hear whimpering in the kitchen.

Nadia didn't want to go into the kitchen. Her entire being resisted because of what she might find. She wanted to go back into her room and hide, but she couldn't. Her body moved on its own accord. Nadia crept into the kitchen, unprepared for the horror facing her. Blood and bits of flesh painted the walls. Her father murdered her mother and sibling. He held them in his arms as he rocked back

90

and forth, mumbling to himself. A huge hole replaced her mother's heart. Her brother had his neck blown apart, his head held on by a few strands of flesh. A shotgun lay on the floor in a puddle of pooling blood.

"Dad?" Nadia asked softly.

Her father looked at her and grabbed his gun, pointing it at her. Sweat plastered his hair to his skull. His eyes were crazed and angry. The demons surrounded him and whispered softly into his ears. Slowly, he lowered the weapon and let it slip to the floor. Apparently, the demons didn't want her to die. The lead demon then did something strange. He released the hold he had on her father. Her dad finally saw the demons for the first time. They pointed and laughed hysterically at him. A look of terror was etched into his face.

The demon leader then turned towards her and spoke telepathically.

"Our work here is done. We will leave you now and return to our home."

Nadia couldn't say anything. She stood there, shaking with disbelief.

"Oh, and sweet child, there is one more thing I would like you to know before I leave. The loss of your family is entirely your own fault. If you had only submitted, we would have left them alone. You can take that tidbit of information to the grave with you. Have a good life, if you can, and when you are ready to join us … we will embrace you with open arms. My master is very forgiving," he snickered.

The demons disappeared, leaving her alone with her

father. With their disappearance, he returned to his normal temperament. He looked around in revulsion as he realized what he had done. He clutched his head and screamed. Nadia surveyed the scene with a detached sense of surrealness. Nadia had her father back … but to what end? He reached out and grabbed her arm, leaving a bloody imprint on her skin.

"Nadia," he blubbered uncontrollably, "please, promise me something. You have to promise me!"

"What?" Nadia asked, flatly.

Her voice sounded like it was a million miles away.

"Remember me … us before they came. Please remember what we were like … our family. Can you do that for me, honey?"

"Y … yes." Nadia stammered.

"I should have listened to you. I'm sorry. I'm so sorry for everything. Someday I hope you can forgive me for my weakness. I love you."

"Dad, I …," Nadia couldn't finish.

Unable to cope with his atrocities, her father reached down, grabbed the shotgun, and loaded a shell into it. Before Nadia could say another word, he plunged the barrel into his mouth and blew his head apart. Blood spewed everywhere, including over Nadia. His body fell to the floor with a thump. Within moments, everything had changed. Nadia slipped to the ground as her muscles finally gave way. She was unable to cry or even mourn. That night, the seeds of anger and hatred were planted within her. It wouldn't take long for them to bloom. She sat quietly in a loch of blood, listening to the sirens as they drew near and wishing for death.

"Why are you here, Lucifer?" Zavier asked directly.

"What? Can't a son visit his loving father?" Lucifer mocked.

"I do love you Lucifer, but sometimes a father knows what's best for his children. You would know that if you had any."

"You're right. I should have children. That way, I can throw them away when they don't perform up to my expectations," Lucifer countered, sarcastically.

Zavier groaned. It was always the same argument. He had heard it countless times. Nothing was ever Lucifer's fault. He could never accept responsibility for his actions.

"Once again … why have you graced me with your presence?" Zavier asked, growing weary of Lucifer's game.

"I think you know why I'm here."

"Son, we can play these games all day if you like, but I am rather busy. Humor me," Zavier sighed.

"I'm here because you have broken the agreement set forth by the Old Ones!" Lucifer shouted.

"I have?" Zavier chuckled. "hmmm, I think I would have remembered that. Seriously son, what are you going on about?"

"You know exactly what I'm talking about! Stop playing coy!" Lucifer screamed. "you violated the law, and I intend to make sure you're punished."

"Once again you have proven yourself to be rash and ill-informed, son. I have not broken any of the laws. Why do you even suggest this?" Zavier refuted.

Lucifer's voice became gruff. He wanted to remove his father's body parts.

"You've allowed Katrianna back into the realm without the Old One's approval!" Lucifer bellowed.

"I've done no such thing."

"Am I to assume you, who knows everything that happens in the realm, doesn't know Katrianna has been spotted?"

"As you well know, I am forbidden to contact her," Zavier said, rolling his eyes.

"Indeed," Lucifer mocked.

"Son, I have nothing to gain by lying to you," Zavier said, sighing.

Lucifer wanted to argue further, but he knew his father spoke the truth. It only intensified his anger.

"You disgust me! You claim to love your creations and yet you allow me to inflict torment upon them. You claim to love your angels and yet allow me to corrupt them. You claim to love me and yet tossed me aside. You preach forgiveness and yet know nothing about it. I think it's high time you know a little secret. I corrupted that fourth batch of vermin you created! I did it so you would see they are plague, but you will never see. You are blinded by your love for them."

Lucifer confirmed what Zavier had already suspected.

Zavier wanted to scream in return, but he couldn't bring himself to do it. His son was very shortsighted about a great many things. He felt sorry for Lucifer.

"I already knew that son. Once again, you fail to understand the big picture and learn any lessons. The universe is bigger than you … it's bigger than me."

"You knew? You knew, and yet did nothing! Once again you prove yourself a useless leader," Lucifer argued.

"Is there anything else you wish to discuss with me?" Zavier asked.

"No. However, I intend to inform the Old Ones of your meddling," Lucifer snarled.

"So be it. Good day, son. I trust you know the way out," Zavier said, dismissing him.

Lucifer disappeared with a flash of flame. He was furious. Anytime he returned to Eineitha, it made him angry. Repressed memories of betrayal always surfaced every time he stepped into that realm. It was the memory of Katrianna which burned him so bitterly. They had been such close friends, but his father's constant display of favoritism tore their relationship apart. He always wanted his father's approval, but he was never good enough. Jealousy turned to hatred.

When Zavier used Katrianna in the uprising, it tore Lucifer's soul apart. It wasn't that she went to battle against him, but rather that she enjoyed slaughtering his minions. She had a crazed blood lust look in her eyes as she tore through his army like tissue paper. When the two finally engaged on the battlefield, he was easily defeated. Katrianna lifted her weapon, a huge claymore named Rivaclore.

Singing through the air, her blade shattered his with one blow. As the splintered pieces sailed in the air, she cut inward, slicing his face temple to chin. A normal blade wouldn't have affected him, but Rivaclore was not a normal blade. Forged by the dragons and folded over ten thousand times, they sealed their fire, ice, and poison within the metal. It was a fierce and terrible weapon. The blade only answered to her. No entity escaped unscathed when touched by Rivaclore.

Screaming in agony, Lucifer fell to his knees as he felt the blade's magic take hold. He clawed at his face, but nothing could stop his torment. The skin around the laceration turned black as green pus poured from the wound. He wanted to die because the pain was so great. Through narrowed eyes, he saw Katrianna raise Rivaclore to decapitate him, but Zavier stopped her. Engrossed in his own suffering, he scarcely heard the argument around him.

Zavier forbade Katrianna from killing him and stopped his pain, but the damage had been done. His perfect face … his beautiful face, had been marred forever. That alone was enough for him to swear vengeance against his father. Lucifer could have forgiven Katrianna, but it was during his trial where she showed her true intentions. She pleaded to kill him. Her words were a dagger to his heart. After his banishment, he cursed them both and swore he would make them suffer.

From the depths of his new home, he made a deal with a powerful creature from the Nanalder Chain, who gave him the ability to create the Crawlers. He set them upon

Zavier's entire realm slaughtering millions. The accursed Old Ones then interfered. They informed him if he ever called upon them again, he'd be taken from Zavier's realm, stripped of all powers, and placed in a special prison. It would be a prison far worse than the one he was already in.

The Old Ones knew how to inflict the greatest amount of torture upon a prisoner. Each room was specially designed for an inmate. They promised him they would shred his wings and mutilate his body, scarring him beyond recognition. He would then be placed into a sealed room made entirely of mirrors. There he would stay for an eternity, unable to escape his image even with his eyes closed. Lucifer knew he would go insane. He would only raise the Crawlers again if he could use them against the Old Ones themselves.

Lucifer rejoiced when he heard of Katrianna's rebellion and banishment. He wasn't sure if she had reclaimed her powers or her army, but she was still a threat. Her return concerned him greatly. He didn't want her dead though, he wanted her on his side. Lucifer knew the grand puppeteer of Katrianna was his father. Corrupting Katrianna would hurt Zavier. If he had her army under his command, it would be the icing on the cake. He could finally take control of the realm and seize the Chain.

He stormed into his castle and demanded an emergency meeting. His demons expected their master to be angry and avoided him like the plague. He waited for the entire council to arrive before he spoke. At the end of the table, he impatiently drummed his long fingers, his eyes echoing hatred inside.

"I have spoken with my father. He claims to know nothing of Katrianna's return," Lucifer spoke angrily.

"He's lying, of course," his head demon offered.

"My father doesn't lie! He hates liars. You know this as well as I!" Lucifer shot back.

"Sire," Mortoc began diplomatically, "could it be possible that she is returning upon her own accord?"

"She isn't strong enough to do that," Elistax countered.

"You have no idea what that woman is capable of doing!" Mortoc snapped, "I was the one who fought her in battle. As I recall, you were sitting on your ass down here."

"IF," Lucifer interrupted loudly, "my *sister* … has found a way to return on her own, it changes our plans, drastically."

The room fell silent. Lucifer rarely acknowledged Katrianna was his sister. It hurt to know his sibling betrayed him.

"Sire … perhaps it would be best to wait and see how things play out," Mortoc suggested.

"For once, I agree with a plan of patience. I cannot rush things at this point. I think I will avoid speaking to the Old Ones about her appearance … for now," Lucifer said, stroking his chin.

A soft knock interrupted them as Araphel opened the door, bowing deeply.

"My lord, Nezatel has returned with news. He wishes to speak with you."

"Send him in Araphel. The council needs to hear what he has to say," Lucifer ordered.

Nezatel was eager to see Lucifer. He spent days celebrating with Tyrient and Ieckisht, but now it was time for him to be rewarded. He was ready to take command of his own army. While he wasn't keen on meeting Lucifer in front of the entire council, he wouldn't let his nerves affect him. He knew Elistax didn't like him, but she didn't respect any of the fallen. She would have sooner decapitated him than hear him speak. Mortoc didn't even look at him, as to gaze upon the fallen was beneath him. Nezatel heard Elistax snort as he passed her. He wasn't a coward, but he wasn't a fool either. There was no way he would confront her because he would undoubtedly lose.

"Ah, Nezatel, I trust you bring us good news?" Lucifer acknowledged him coolly.

"Yes, sire. We did as you required. We drove the family insane, and the father killed the other two."

"That is most excellent. Now, what of the girl?"

"I planted the seeds of guilt just as you instructed. She will not be able to escape them," Nezatel assured.

"Well, that is the first piece of good news I've heard today," Lucifer said, pleased. "now we must wait. If things go as planned, she will be easily corrupted, and I shall have another one of Zavier's warriors on my side … and the more, the merrier."

"It was my honor to be selected for this task," Nezatel said, expecting praise and compensation.

"Yes … I'm sure it was. You are dismissed, Nezatel."

Nezatel paused.

"Sire, I was wondering …," he began, before Lucifer

screamed at him.

"GET OUT!"

Nezatel felt embarrassed. He could hear the others laughing at him as he exited the room. He expected to be rewarded, not humiliated. Fuming, he stormed out of the castle. If he didn't get what was promised, Nezatel swore he would start making alliances of his own.

A Shrinking Light
Chapter Six

During the next year, Nadia slowly became the type of kid she hated. She was forced to live with foster parents since her grandparents were dead. She never stayed with any couple for a long period of time because she created chaos in their lives. She moved around always, switching school's numerous times. Everyone seemed to abandon her, and she hated them for it. She hated everything. Even Nadia's best friend wouldn't talk to her anymore ... not even a text. Her visions of Katrianna completely disappeared, leaving her in darkness.

She remembered that night vividly ... her father's blood all over her ... her mother lying in a bloody heap. She wanted to scream and cry when it happened, but she couldn't. The cops came along with their incessant questions. They wanted to know if her parents fought a lot, if they used drugs, if they were abusive and so on. She stayed at the police station for hours as they tried to comfort her, but they never managed to ease her mind. She felt dead inside.

When she was placed in her first foster home, she left everything behind except some clothes and her little red dragon. The first couple she lived with didn't like her dragon very much, so she kept it in her pocket. They were a devoutly religious couple, and Nadia immediately clashed with their beliefs. Every day she had to listen to them prattle on about God and the devil. She couldn't stand them. They wanted her to become their clone and read passages from the bible every night. Nadia refused and burned the family bible in the sink, earning her a fresh set of foster parents.

As hard as she tried, she couldn't stop herself from getting into trouble. Every time she did something bad, it felt good … just for a moment. Afterward, she felt terrible, as if her heart was stabbed repeatedly. She was shrouded with negativity and despair. Instead of helping people, she hurt them just so she could feel a brief moment of happiness. She was stuck in a never-ending vicious cycle.

The demons never bothered her again, much to her amazement. They made good on their promise … to take everything from her. She felt empty like a shell. They changed her forever, leaving her in a state of misery. Even though the demons no longer bothered her, Nadia knew someone … or something was watching her. She could feel eyes everywhere.

Sleep was virtually impossible. She woke up screaming almost every night. Nadia replayed that evening in her nightmares, often waking up covered in sweat. The dream always ended in flames. She could feel the heat on her face as the flames devoured her. The pain was exquisite. She learned to get by on a couple hours of interrupted sleep a night, but it was difficult to concentrate during the day, especially at school.

Her classmates knew her history. They shunned her at best. At worst they picked on her and accused her of having something to do with the death of her family. She was considered a goth kid, but she was rejected by that group as well. She felt utterly alone. Nadia refused to talk about the incident to anyone, assuming no one would believe her anyway. Consumed by hatred and pain, she gave in to the darkness in her heart, replacing sadness with anger.

She was called into the principal's office often for her constant bouts of fighting. One particular incident nine months after her parents' murder, she smashed a lunch tray into another girl's face, breaking her nose. The girl was taken to the hospital, and Nadia was arrested. After a brief stint in jail, she was released and ordered to attend therapy. She almost exploded in court but was whisked away before she could open her mouth.

The principal, Mr. Gunn, was displeased when he called her into his office, her first day back. Nadia entered his headquarters wearing the same thing she always wore to school, black pants, black shirt, and a black hoodie. Her hair was dyed black as well. Nadia would have worn black lipstick, but she thought it looked ugly on her. Instead, she painted her lips blood red, which was an odd contrast to her black attire. Earbuds hung around her neck, which normally played screaming metal into her ears. Her iPod was her only tool to block out the world. She had stolen it from a boy who left his backpack open. Nadia became good at thieving.

Mr. Gunn opened the door and motioned her to come inside. She rose slowly, glaring at him the entire time.

"Nadia, please sit down," he said, gesturing to the chair in front of his desk.

Nadia sat and scowled at him, through her razor cut hair.

"Now, I'm sure you are well aware of the school's policy about fighting," he scolded.

Nadia said nothing but continued to sneer at him. After a

few moments however, she began laughing.

"This is serious, Nadia. You were arrested. Technically, I should expel you."

"Go ahead!" she roared. "I don't give two shits about school."

"As is apparent by your grades. Look, I know you've had a difficult time as of late, but that does not excuse …,"

"What the HELL do you know about my life!" she yelled. "the kids in this school are always fuckin' with me cuz of what happened, and nobody does nuthin' about it. You turn away and let it happen. No one cares about me, so why should I care about them!"

"I didn't know that was happening," he said, trying to soften his tone.

"Of course, you didn't. You hide in your office all day doing what? I will defend myself from these assholes!"

"Enough! You will lower your tone immediately. Did you know you broke that girl's nose? The doctor said if you had hit upwards, you would have driven the bone into her brain. You could have killed her."

"Really? I will have to remember that technique for next time," Nadia laughed.

"Nadia! This is not funny," Mr. Gunn chided.

"Do you even care why I did it?" she asked, sarcastically.

"I assume she was picking on you."

"You assume wrong. She was telling people my dad killed everyone because he hated me."

"I'm sorry. I'll talk to her parents about the issue," he

offered.

"She's right, ya know," Nadia said softly.

"Come again?"

"She's right. My father hated me. I saw it in his eyes, but it wasn't his fault. It was mine," Nadia softly admitted.

A lone teardrop fell from her right eye before Nadia furiously scrubbed it away. She stood up abruptly and turned away from him. She refused to show anyone the turmoil she felt inside.

"Are we done yet!" Nadia snarled angrily over her shoulder.

"No, we are certainly not done. Please sit down."

Nadia spun and flopped into the chair, pulling her hair in front of her eyes so he couldn't see the redness.

"I want you to speak with the school counselor. I'll make an appointment for you after school."

"What! I don't want to see any damn head shrinker! Besides, how will I get home if I miss the bus? I know damn well, my stupid foster mom won't get off her lazy ass and pick me up."

"I'll take care of everything. You have been ordered by the court to see a therapist anyway. You *will* see the counselor today, and I want you to stop fighting."

"But …," she tried protesting.

"That is all," Mr. Gunn concluded, ignoring her objections.

Nadia stormed out of his office in a huff. She didn't want to see the counselor. The thought of just leaving at the end of the day crept into her mind, but she knew the principal would just take her from the bus, embarrassing her further. All she wanted was to be left alone. She didn't want to talk about it. Everyone was always asking her about it. It seemed every time she started a new school, someone would catch wind about her past and spread it like wildfire. She really wanted to drop out of school. Living on the streets alone would be better than having to deal with so many nosy people. Every time someone asked her about it, she was brought back to that night … that horrible night she lost everything, because she wouldn't surrender. Sometimes she wished she had.

After school, she stormed over to the counselor, prepared to unleash her fury. She paced outside the room, waiting to be called into the office. Nadia glanced around the room while she waited. The décor was hideous and pointless. The walls were painted peach and were plagued with motivational posters. Her least favorite was one, 'Destiny is not a matter of chance, it is a matter of choice'. Bile rose within her.

"Admiring the poster?" a feminine voice spoke behind her.

"No," Nadia said, spinning around, "some people don't have a choice."

"Everyone has a choice."

"Yea, whatever."

"Hello, you must be Nadia. I'm Adriana," she said, extending her hand.

Nadia looked at the woman's hand like it was a viper, refusing to shake her hand. She examined the woman in

106

front of her. She was a tall Hispanic lady with jet black hair. Her brown eyes reminded Nadia of marbles. Her face was slender like her build, and she moved gracefully. Nadia didn't trust her as far as she could throw her.

"Please come into my office and find a seat."

Adriana's office was packed with more motivational posters smothered in upbeat sayings. Nadia flopped onto one of the overstuffed leather seats and scowled.

"I hope you don't mind, but I took the liberty of researching your life. You've had quite a traumatic year."

"Ya think?" Nadia asked sarcastically.

"You have lived with six foster families. It must be hard being shuffled around like that, from school to school."

Nadia shrugged her shoulders.

"It's been nine months since … the event …," Adriana began.

"You mean, since my dad blew my mom and brother apart?" Nadia growled. "you don't have to tiptoe around it."

"I want to know how you are dealing with it?"

"Dealing with it? Dealing with it!" Nadia's voice rose. "if those fuckin' assholes at this school would leave me alone, I'd be doin' a lot better."

"Yes, I've heard what happened. I've made a few phone calls. Those girls won't be bothering you again."

"Great. Can I go now?" Nadia sneered.

"No. How you would feel if you knew you had a family member who was desperately trying to acquire custody of you?"

Nadia was shocked. She thought all her family members were dead. She wasn't sure how it made her feel. Part of her was elated that someone actually cared, while another part was fearful of the future.

"Who?"

"You have an aunt, your mother's sister. She has been fighting the court system ever since that night."

Nadia vaguely remembered her mother had a sister she didn't often mention, except to say she was weird. She wondered why on earth, this lady was fighting for her. Nadia was nothing ... a nobody with a worthless life. She would have killed herself if she hadn't been afraid of dying. She knew where she would go if she died, and that thought terrified her.

"She has been in court several times, and as your only living relative, there is a good chance she will get custody of you," Adriana explained.

"Where does she live?" Nadia asked, her curiosity briefly overshadowing her despair.

"South Dakota."

"SOUTH DAKOTA!" Nadia snarled. "I'm not moving to South Dakota! Is that even a fuckin' state!"

"It certainly is. You will have to move there if she gets custody. You won't have a choice on that matter."

"I should be used to that by now! I never have a choice with anything. I will run away, I swear!" Nadia screamed.

"And where will you run to Nadia?" Adriana asked quietly. "you don't have a source of income."

108

"I could live on the streets. I could …," her voice faltered.

Nadia knew in her heart that choice wasn't desirable. Her chest swelled with hatred. She loathed everything about her life. Most of all, she despised those demons and what they took from her.

"I know you are in pain." Adriana said, softly. "your body is consumed with it, but there is a light at the end of the tunnel."

Nadia felt cold all over. She hated talking about herself to anyone. She rubbed her arms for warmth. In her quest to warm herself, she pushed her long sleeves up her forearms, exposing the horizontal scars. She caught Adriana looking at her arms. Nadia quickly pulled down her sleeves and crossed her arms over her chest.

"How long have you been cutting?" Adriana asked, tilting her head.

Nadia knew it was pointless to lie. She had been cutting herself for several months. She discovered the only thing that made her feel alive by accident. She was peeling an apple when the knife slipped and plunged into her flesh. After the initial shock of pain, Nadia discovered it felt good to bleed. She began cutting herself with a razor blade regularly. It made her feel better … more in control.

That wasn't the only dangerous thing she tried. One time she drank so much liquor, she put herself into a coma. Her foster parents had left their alcohol cabinet open, and after one particularly bad day at school, she decided to drink her worries away. She finished two large bottles of whiskey before puking all over the floor. Nadia ended up passing out in a puddle of her own vomit. Her foster parents found her unconscious and whisked her to the hospital where they pumped her stomach, another very unpleasant experience.

When she was discharged from the hospital, she was forced to live with another set of foster parents since her previous ones refused to foster her again. Nadia didn't really care. She wouldn't allow herself to become close to anyone again. If she didn't love anyone, it wouldn't hurt when she lost them. She moved in with the next set and was equally miserable.

After that experience, she refused to drink again. At first, alcohol made her feel free, but reality swiftly came crashing down as soon as the effects wore off. She didn't like feeling out of control. It was easy for her to avoid drugs for the same reason. Cutting was different, however. Cutting gave her a rush without feeling woozy and sick. Cutting heightened her sense of awareness. It made her feel alive.

"A couple of months," Nadia answered.

"I see."

There was a long pregnant pause before the counselor continued.

"Why do you cut yourself?"

"I dunno. I feel better when I do, so I do it," Nadia said, becoming irritated.

"Does anyone else know you cut yourself?"

Nadia shrugged her shoulders. She hoped not. She was secretive about it, wearing long sleeves, even in the heat of summer.

"Do you cut yourself because it gives you a high?"

110

"No."

"I think it does. It makes you feel good because your body sends endorphins into action, and they make you feel better. It's like the high, runners get when they are running."

"I cut myself because that's the only time I feel anything. It's better to feel pain than nothing at all. It's the only time I know I'm real," Nadia admitted.

"I see," Adriana said. "well, I have to report this. You are deeply troubled, and this is beyond my skills as a counselor. I'm going to recommend you stay at a facility in town so you can get the help you need."

"What! That's just fuckin' great! I knew seeing you was a bad idea. Now I have to go to some nut house!"

"It's not a nut house. It's a place where people can help you deal with your feelings."

"Well, fuck that! I'm not going!" Nadia shouted, jumping to her feet.

"Yes, you are. Now, wait in the next room while I make a few calls. And don't try to run away. The principal will be watching you."

Nadia left the room in a daze. Every time she turned around, she was uprooted and sent away. Now she was being sent to a mental hospital. She wanted to run and hide from embarrassment. The kids at school would really have something to talk about now.

The principal was guarding the door just as Adriana told her. She scowled at him and threw herself into a chair. She could hear Adriana talking to someone on the other side of the door. It wasn't long before two men came and escorted her out of the building. They were both wearing blue shirts. She was glad the school was empty. They put her in a van and drove her away. She heard them telling her everything would be OK, and her things would be picked up from her foster parents. She didn't pay much attention to them.

The van stopped after a while, and they guided her into a large building. Serenity Springs was written above the door in large blue letters. A woman in her late forty's stood outside to greet her.

"WELCOME NADIA!" she shouted enthusiastically. "WELCOME to the first day of the rest of your life!"

Nadia wanted to puke.

Zavier listened inattentively to his angels, arguing amongst themselves. He hated meetings. He thought they were a complete waste of time. On occasion however, he had to attend because they needed his input or authorization. This particular meeting was about altering the duties within the angel ranks. After a few moments, he realized they had fallen silent. They were waiting for his response.

"Zavier? Do you want me to repeat the question?" an angel named Treceler asked.

"No," Zavier said, rising from his seat. "let me think upon the matter. In the meantime, I must dismiss myself from this meeting."

He left the room, certain they were surprised by his behavior. Normally, he sat through all meetings, regardless of how boring they were. Zavier traveled to his house and opened the door to a special cabinet which held his arcane orb. The orb was immense and heavy. Strange colors swirled inside. Once activated, it became crystal clear and allowed him to see everything in his realm.

"Ararya," he said softly.

The murkiness inside the orb shifted and swirled until the orb became a window. He gazed into his orb, diverting his attention from one region to another. He wasn't sure what he was searching for exactly. He heard the millions calling out to him for help. His creations expected him to fulfill all their requests. Zavier couldn't do that, however. People had to learn to help themselves. The more positive energy they sent out to the universe, the more it was returned to them. The same applied to negative energy. Those who were mired in negativity created their own difficulties, and those who hurt others ultimately hurt themselves.

In the beginning of his reign, he learned a lesson about only helping those who truly deserved it. Zavier remembered a young man who desperately wanted a large fortune so he could marry a girl above his stature. Zavier granted his wish and suddenly he won a windfall of money. The man married his beloved and had several children. Unfortunately, his lust for money corrupted him. He quickly became arrogant, bragging to everyone about his wealth. He eventually boasted to the wrong people. During the night, a band of thieves broke into the home and slaughtered everyone.

Zavier now searched far into an individual's future to determine if granting aid was acceptable. He could see every possible choice a person could make as well as the results of that choice. Their free will gave them opportunities to live rich and meaningful lives if they chose it. Sadly, most of them decided to live in despair.

The same theory applied to rulers and their offspring. Zavier missed his children. He closed his eyes and remembered long ago they would run into his arms and giggle. Even with his vast infinite amounts of wisdom, he was shocked they ended up warring against each other. It was a sad day when he asked his daughter to fight against her brother. It was even sadder she had been so excited to destroy him.

His beautiful daughter was so stubborn, and now she was paying the price for it. She wouldn't listen to him. She believed Lucifer betrayed her, and perhaps he did. The two once close siblings were forever bitter enemies. Katrianna believing she served the light was so blinded by hatred she actually served the darkness, including those who sought to use her. Now he was alone, his soulmate gone and both children were banished to different areas. He shook his head and sighed. He couldn't change the past. He could only learn from his mistakes.

Most of all, he missed his beloved wife. Nothing could ever fill the emptiness of her death. He pushed her memory to the side so he could focus on his task. He explored the orb. Suddenly, he found the object of his search. He closed his eyes and hummed a strange tune. Slowly, the orb resumed its colorful appearance, returning to its slumber. As his hand reached to shut the door, he greeted Firthel. The angel had been standing behind him for quite some time.

"Can I help you with something, Firthel?" Zavier asked, spinning around.

"Just wondering what's happening. The committee was quite shocked when you left like that. Is anything the matter?"

"Oh Firthel, you know I detest meetings. I was simply looking for a reason to leave," Zavier said lightly.

"I know you better than that. What's going on?" Firthel asked, concerned.

"I'm not sure. I just felt more hopelessness than usual in the realm," Zavier replied, rubbing his face.

"Is something troubling you?" his friend asked.

"I am always troubled Firthel, you should know that." Zavier laughed. "I am the ruler of one of the most chaotic realms in existence."

"Well, that is certainly true," Firthel joined Zavier in laughter. "I often wonder why you don't simply start over."

"They need more time. It's not their fault Lucifer sullied the realm."

"Zavier, you have given them ample time to turn towards the light, and still, they turn towards darkness. I never understood why you decided to stop disciplining your people," Firthel sighed.

"I thought it best to let my warriors handle the disciplining, you know this Firthel. Why even bring this up?" Zavier asked.

"Because the realm is in pandemonium and yet you do nothing!" the angel shouted.

Zavier was shocked. He wasn't accustomed to his angels raising their voices to him and never his best friend.

"I'm sorry, sire," Firthel apologized, falling to his knees.

"Get up already Firthel. I'm not angry," Zavier sighed. "I hold a great many secrets you are not aware of. I kept them secret because if such information ever fell into the wrong hands … it would be catastrophic."

"I'm sorry. It's not my place to question you," Firthel apologized.

"Don't worry about it. You are my greatest friend, and I trust you," Zavier began, "but you must promise never to utter a word of what I'm going to tell you."

"You don't have to tell me," Firthel breathed.

"Promise me!" Zavier insisted.

"I swear I will never reveal your secrets."

Zavier motioned Firthel to sit. For the next hour, Zavier revealed his most inner secrets. Firthel was astonished and agreed no one could know, especially Lucifer. Firthel once again swore his silence after Zavier finished.

"Thank you for trusting me," Firthel said.

"Thank you for being trustworthy," replied Zavier.

"I meant to ask you. Why were you using the orb?"

"Oh, there was someone who needed just a bit of luck," Zavier chuckled, winking. "and now if you excuse me, I do believe my brother wants a word with me."

"Of course," Firthel said exiting the room.

Zavier was always happy to see his twin. They were both

116

so busy, they didn't have time to see each other as often as he would have preferred. Shivet's realm was just as chaotic as his own, but his brother handled things differently. They were similar in so many ways, even down to their personal tragedies. As similar as they were, they looked nothing alike. Shivet had short spiky blond hair … so pale, it was almost white. He was shorter than Zavier but more muscular. His eyes were clearly his most striking feature. They were ice blue and seemed to swirl when he was thinking

"Shivet!" Zavier greeted warmly. "how are you, my brother?"

"I am good!" Shivet responded as he knocked Zavier in the head.

The two spilled to the floor and became tangled in a heated wrestling match. It was a common trend for them. They enjoyed beating each other senseless, but it was all in good fun. Exhausted, they disengaged and flopped into the chairs.

"So, what news of your daughter? Is she free?" Shivet asked.

"She is unavailable," Zavier sighed.

"That is most unfortunate. I could use her to clean up a mess building on my realm."

"Have faith, brother. I think she will be out sooner than later. And when she is with me once more, I will ask her to help you if it is allowed."

"Thank you, Zavier. I just hope it's not too late."

Hope

Chapter Seven

Nezatel was furious. A great time had passed, and he still hadn't received word from Lucifer. He knew he was being ignored. Rewards meant everything in Hell. It was different than in heaven where angels believed helping someone was reward enough. Angels were stunned when they received praise or incentives. Demons were quite the opposite. They wanted compensation for every task they did, especially those out of the ordinary. Demons were liars, but they didn't like being lied to.

As much as he hated seeing Araphel, Nezatel knew he needed to speak with Lucifer. He traveled into the castle via the dungeon where the souls of the damned were being tortured by his fellow demons. It was always the same thing … flesh being ripped apart, eyes being gouged out, fire being laid on the victim and so on. No one in Hell had any kind of imagination. He shook his head. Nezatel was glad he was given the job as a watcher. He would have been bored to death working in the dungeon.

Watchers didn't have regular work hours. They only worked when they were called upon, so he had ample time to himself. Watchers also could leave Hell anytime they chose … if they returned when they were summoned. In fact, when they weren't on a mission, they were expected to spend a certain amount of time spying on humans. Lucifer used their information to help make decisions. One of the greatest perks of being a watcher was having his own quarters far away from the rest of the rabble.

As Nezatel walked towards the stairs, he spied a door down a lonely corridor. He had been down this path countless times, but never noticed it before. Watchers had keen powers of observation. He wondered why he had never seen it. Curiosity got the better of him, and he opened it. It was a simple storage room filled with tools and different torture implements. It was apparent the room wasn't used much because everything was covered in a thick layer of dirt. As he was about to leave the room however, he heard voices coming from the far corner. Slowly he pulled the door closed, killing any light in the room. He crept to the far corner and knelt. There was a sizeable crack in the stone, just big enough for Nezatel to see into the other room. He was not prepared for what he saw.

The room opposite him was Lucifer's meeting room. Lucifer was in a lengthy discussion with Mortoc. Nezatel listened until the meeting was over. He sat back against the stone and shook his head in disbelief. He couldn't believe his luck. Now, he could spy on Lucifer and learn his innermost secrets. He had to be careful. If he were ever caught, the results would be disastrous. There was no doubt in his mind Lucifer would rend him limb from limb. He pulled a cabinet to the corner, giving himself just enough room to squeeze behind it. He would be hidden if anyone happened to walk into the room while he was there. It also concealed his peephole quite nicely. He moved the tools around in the room and swept his footprints away.

Nezatel couldn't wait until Lucifer was in a meeting again. He skulked from the room as quietly as possible, waiting in the shadows. As a watcher, he could easily move around the castle undetected. He planned on using the room to gain whatever upper hand he could on Lucifer. It was a dangerous game he played, but luckily, he was good at playing games.

The room wasn't the only interesting thing Nezatel had found in the castle. Lucifer's home had many secrets, some which his master didn't know. For instance, Nezatel was sure Lucifer didn't know there was a third gate. It was concealed in the lower dungeons, nestled between two walls far in the back. It appeared as if it was made by someone who wanted to escape rather hastily. It didn't look like it had been used for a long time. It was half the size of the other gates and emitted a different type of energy than the other two. One could simply walk towards the back and disappear without anyone even noticing … especially a watcher.

He chose to keep the information about the gate to himself. If Lucifer knew he would surely close it. Nezatel knew the demons in the dungeons would never find it. They were a dimwitted bunch of festering imbeciles. Instead, he 'encouraged' the shadows to grow ever darker between the walls. No one would ever even suspect it was there and he could use it anytime he desired.

He continued on his path until he reached Araphel's chambers. Nezatel burst through the door without knocking. A split-second look of annoyance crossed Araphel's face before his irritating calm demeanor returned.

"Yes, Nezatel? Is there a reason you have disturbed my break?" Araphel asked smugly.

"I must speak with Lucifer. I need you to arrange a meeting."

"Why? Your current task is done. There should be nothing troubling you at the moment. Are you bored? Do you want another assignment?"

"I am not here to discuss my affairs with the likes of you! Now waddle off and arrange a meeting," Nezatel growled.

"Waddle? I can assure you I don't waddle," Araphel chuckled. "I will speak with Lucifer when my break is over. Now go away so I can enjoy some intelligent conversation with myself."

Nezatel spun around and departed without another word. He knew Araphel was purposely forcing him to wait. He wanted to stick a blade into Araphel's withered soul. He returned to his chambers but was too agitated to relax. As he paced around the room a memory surfaced, one he thought was long gone … one that *should* have been long gone.

He remembered his favorite place in Eineitha. It was of a tree which never stopped blooming and grew near a small sparkling brook. There were little pink flowers all over it which smelled ever so sweet. The grass was incredibly thick that it was almost like a carpet. He would often sit under the tree with his back to the trunk, inhaling the fragrant perfume of the blooms. That was his special place, and it always filled him with joy.

Nezatel shook his head violently to clear his thoughts. He wasn't supposed to have memories of Eineitha. Lucifer stripped all of them away. A trickle of fear rushed down his spine. He didn't know what it meant, but it couldn't be good.

"What's going on?" he muttered to himself.

122

A sudden knock brought him from his thoughts. Nezatel hoped Araphel was bringing him some good news.

"When is the meeting?" Nezatel asked as he opened the door.

"Once again Nezatel, you presume too much. Lucifer has no desire to meet with you," Araphel gloated.

"What do you mean? This is important!" the demon huffed.

"Important to you perhaps, but not to him," Araphel sneered. "he told me to inform you not to bother him again. He will call upon you when he has another task for you."

"WHAT! He told me I would be rewarded! He told me I would be a Captain in the Waru!" Nezatel ranted.

"Yes well, perhaps you misunderstood," Araphel retorted.

"You filthy Kerbal excrement! I should tear your head off!"

"Now, now, don't be upset with me. After all, I am simply … the messenger. Why would you want that job anyway? After all, as a Captain, you would actually have to work," Araphel laughed.

Araphel turned and slithered away, leaving Nezatel seething in anger.

After staying a month in Serenity Springs, Nadia was sick to death of listening to people talk about their problems. She was surprised to learn some people were actually worse off than she was, but that didn't mean she felt sorry for them. Most of these people created their own problems, spoiled little rich kids with nothing to do with their time. None of them had a demon problem like hers. She hated everyone in the place.

When she first arrived, she immediately isolated herself from them. She couldn't be entirely alone since she had a roommate. Her 'cellmate' as Nadia preferred to call her, was a lanky girl with long blonde hair named Megan. She always talked about killing herself if her daddy didn't buy her a Ferrari. Her parents put her in the Springs because they were worried about her. Nadia thought if they didn't spoil their daughter so much, she wouldn't be in the Springs, to begin with. Megan continuously prattled on about material things, especially the Ferrari. Nadia did her best to ignore her, putting in her earbuds as soon as Megan opened her mouth.

Nadia only got into two fights … quite a remarkable feat for her. A boy named Jack pushed her into a closet, attempting to grope her. She quickly rammed her knee into his crotch. As he bent over screaming, she lifted her other knee and struck his nose. Blood spurted from his broken beak as he reeled backward into a pile of mops. She got into a little trouble for that incident, but it was worth it.

Her other fight was with a girl who took her dragon. Nadia was sitting in a group session listening to everyone blather on about themselves. She became quickly bored and pulled the dragon from her pocket. Nadia turned it over and over in her hands like she always did, trying her best to ignore the group. A girl sitting next to her grabbed it from her hands. Nadia reacted without thinking, punching the girl in the stomach. She briefly heard everyone erupt

124

with shouting, but she didn't pay attention. She scooped her dragon from the floor, put it in her pocket, and left the room. That fight earned her a lot of trouble. She had to listen to even more lectures about being a good person.

Nadia was mostly bored with everyone and everything in the place. She was thrilled to be called to the main office one particularly drab day. It meant she could skip the group meeting, which Nadia dubbed the hug-a-long. A woman was sitting in the office with the lead head shrinker. Nadia didn't recognize her and suspected she was just another person sent to question the hell out of her about her past. She barged into the room without knocking and stood defiantly.

"Ah, here she is now," the psychologist chirped. "please Nadia, have a seat. I have some exciting news."

"Yea?" Nadia asked sarcastically. "have I been given permission to burn this place to the ground?"

The two women looked at each other briefly before the psychologist continued.

"This is your Aunt Lillya. She has won custody of you. You are going to live with her in South Dakota. Isn't that wonderful!"

Nadia examined the woman seated across from her. She was tall and thin, almost frail looking. Her gray hair was wound around in a tight bun on the back of her head. She had a hooked nose, thin lips, and glaring grey eyes. Her veiny hands were folded tightly in her lap. Nadia guessed she had to be somewhere around sixty. She looked old, boring, and strict. Nadia decided she would not be happy living with this woman, but she wasn't happy living anywhere.

At least this woman was family … the only family she had left. She didn't want to leave with her, but she didn't want to stay at the Springs either. It seemed like once again, she had no choice.

"Greaaat," Nadia mocked, "jus' where I've always wanted to go. Somewhere where there are more cows than people."

"Actually, South Dakota is quite nice," her aunt spoke up. "it's a very pretty state."

Aunt Lillya had a sharp tone which reminded Nadia of a schoolteacher.

"Now, pack your belongings. We have a flight to catch," she instructed.

Nadia was suddenly eager to leave the Springs. Her aunt seemed strict but anywhere had to be better than this nut house. She gathered her meager items. She only had a few things that were important to her. Besides her dragon, she had one picture of her family. These few items were the only things that reminded her of when her life was normal. She carefully placed her cherished possessions into a small bag.

The rest of her stuff wasn't important. Nadia ripped her clothes from their hangers and stuffed them into an old suitcase. She didn't even look at anyone when she followed her aunt to a cab. They went to the airport where Nadia found something else that annoyed her. She didn't understand why she had to stand in line for so long and remove her shoes. She felt like a cow being pushed to the slaughterhouse. Luckily, the plane ride seemed almost a blur. Her aunt made small talk with her but mostly did crossword puzzles. Nadia had so many questions, but she

126

wasn't sure if she should ask them. In the end, she decided to wait until they were off the plane. Part of her hated moving somewhere completely different, but she couldn't help feeling a little excited as well.

Nadia had never been on an airplane before. She should have felt exhilarated when the plane launched into the air, but she wasn't. She peered out the window, unimpressed as the earth grew smaller and smaller. She slammed her window shade down and put in her earbuds. After a while, she dozed and dreamed about something she hadn't seen in a long time. She dreamed about the sword with the glowing blade.

The planes rough landing jolted her from her slumber. She noticed she didn't feel quite as bad as usual. Nadia didn't want to believe it, but in her heart, she knew change was in the air. She glanced over to her aunt, who gave her a thin smile. Nadia wasn't sure if she should trust this woman she just met. She wondered why her aunt fought to gain custody of her and if there was some hidden agenda. It didn't matter though. In a little more than a year, she would be 18, and she could do what she wanted.

It was late evening when they arrived in Rapid City. Nadia's nostrils were assaulted by a wave of cow manure. She crinkled her nose and made a face. Nadia peered into the darkness. There was enough light for her to see the rolling hills of nothingness for miles. She saw lights from the town glittering in the distance. The town didn't look very big. It was February and cold. The wind howled like a wraith, kicking up the snow covering the ground. Nadia pulled her coat tightly around her and followed her aunt to her rusty Jeep Wrangler.

"You live here?" Nadia asked, yanking the car door tightly shut.

"Oh goodness gracious no." Her aunt replied.

Nadia felt relieved. She didn't like being in such a desolate place.

"I live about an hour east of here in the middle of nowhere."

Nadia's face fell. She slumped back into her seat, wanting to disappear. Things as usual, were going bad to worse.

"You will like it, I promise."

"Yea, right. Whatever."

"My, such an attitude," her aunt clucked disapprovingly. "we shall have to work on that."

"Whatever," Nadia repeated, feeling irritable.

The ride seemed to last forever. Darkness covered everything. As far as Nadia could tell, there were only a few houses in the area. Her aunt slowed to a halt a few times to avoid herds of deer crossing the road. It felt like she was in the Twilight Zone. Finally, they pulled into a driveway which led to an old looking farmhouse with a wrap-around porch.

Lillya parked the Jeep to the left of the garage and turned it off. The engine growled with a hiss.

"You don't park in the garage?" Nadia asked.

"No. I use the garage for other things."

"What's the point of having a garage, then?"

"For … other things," Lillya responded.

128

Her aunt led her inside. Five cats came running into the room mewing and rubbing themselves all over her legs like snakes.

"Holy crap! How many cats do you have?" Nadia asked.

"Just the five, but I have many more animals outside. In the morning, I will give you a tour of the barn."

"Aunt Lillya, why am I here? Why did you want custody of me?" Nadia finally asked.

"Please, just call me Lillya or Lil. I answer to both. I will explain everything to you in the morning after you have had a good night's sleep."

"That's something I almost never have," Nadia said, sighing.

"What's that?"

"A good night's sleep. I can't remember the last time I slept all night without having a nightmare."

"I promise you will sleep well here," Lillya assured.

Nadia wanted to deliver an angry retort, but she just didn't have the energy. Lillya showed Nadia to her room and told her to feel free to investigate while she made dinner. Nadia's room was bigger than any she had ever had and far finer. A massive canopy bed was located on the far wall. There were two immense wooden dressers on the opposite side. She had her own bathroom, which was a happy surprise. A small ornate nightstand stood by the left of the bed where a beautiful Tiffany lamp was placed. She turned it on, sending shards of colored light across the room. Nadia took her little dragon out of the bag and put it next to the light. She tossed her clothes into the dresser drawers.

Nadia plopped onto the bed, feeling almost like royalty. She glanced around the room. There was a large painting of a red dragon on the wall, opposite her bed. It looked elegant laying peacefully on the edge of a cliff. Snowcapped mountain peaks were in the distance. A puff of white smoke trailed from the dragon's nostrils. It was so realistic Nadia half expected it to move. A familiar name was in the corner of the painting.

"So, she's an artist as well," Nadia said softly to herself.

Nadia began exploring the other parts of the house. There were five bedrooms, three bathrooms, and a large living room with a built-in slate fireplace. A huge plate glass window took up most of one wall. The kitchen could have fed an army. The whole house seemed like an illusion. It certainly looked smaller on the outside. Nadia briefly explored the upper rooms. They were mostly bedrooms and one small room which held her unfinished paintings. Thankfully, there was no cellar in the house. It felt peaceful and quiet … quiet except for the cats which followed her everywhere, mewing as they went.

Nadia heard her aunt putting food onto some plates. Her stomach rumbled, reminding her she hadn't eaten in hours. As she walked downstairs, she finally took a good look around. Her aunt had dragons everywhere. There were paintings, figurines, drawings, and even plastic dragons which came in a set. Every nook and cranny had a dragon. Once again, it reminded Nadia of how surreal her life had suddenly become. There was a statue of a great blue dragon on the floor just inside the kitchen. Its green eyes were so clear it was almost as if it was looking at her. She tentatively reached out and felt its back. It felt warm to her touch.

"That's Brutus," Lillya explained. "he guards the kitchen."

"Oh," Nadia said, feeling like she was in a movie, rather than real life.

"I hope you don't mind, but I reheated some roast chicken I made this afternoon. Please sit."

"You have lots of dragons," Nadia said between mouthfuls of food.

"Yes … dragons are protectors," Lillya responded.

"Maybe I should have had a few more growing up," Nadia sneered, "then maybe my family wouldn't have been ripped apart."

"Now listen to me Nadia," Lillya said sternly. "that wasn't your fault. There is nothing you could have done to prevent what happened."

"Oh yea! What the fuck do you know about it! You know nothing about loss!" Nadia screamed, slamming her fork down onto the table.

"I know quite a bit about loss young lady. Never forget as you lost a mother, I lost my only sister. It's true we weren't close, but that was her choice, not mine!"

Nadia stood up, ready to walk away. She didn't want to hear about how much they had in common because they both lost loved ones. She didn't think losing a sister was the same as losing a mother. Her whole body trembled with rage.

"You and I have nothing in common!" Nadia shouted.

"Oh, no? I think we have quite a bit in common. Now SIT!" Lillya ordered, pointing to the chair.

Nadia slowly sat down, seething inside.

"Now as I was saying … none of this is your fault. You mustn't blame yourself."

"Yes, it is," Nadia said softly. "it's my fault they are dead."

"Nadia, look at me," Lillya clucked.

Lillya paused for a few moments until Nadia locked eyes with her.

"Trust me, if you had given in to them, it would have been far worse. They would have taken more than your family."

Nadia jumped as if electricity shot through her.

"W …who, are you talking about?" Nadia stammered.

"The demons, Nadia."

"But …,"

"Come, come, my child," Lillya whispered. "you didn't think you were the only one who could see them? Why do you think I fought so hard to get custody of you? Yes, I am your only living relative, but I am also one of the few people who know exactly what you are going through. So, you see my dear, we really do have quite a bit in common."

The iron-clad dam Nadia had built to keep her emotions imprisoned, finally shattered and she was swept away with the surge. Nadia burst into tears. Lillya quickly slipped over to Nadia and hugged her. Wave after wave of sorrow wracked her body. She wailed until she couldn't cry anymore.

"I … thought … I … was … the only one," she said

through the tears. "I thought I was going … crazy."

"I know. I felt the same way when I was your age. I had no one to talk to about it. I had to learn everything on my own. That's when I swore if anyone ever had the same problem, I would help them. No one should ever have to deal with something so horrific alone."

"What did they do to you?" Nadia asked when her tears subsided.

"That my dear is a story for another day, but I can assure you, it wasn't pleasant. You have the sight. It runs in our family and is passed down from mother to daughter, but you … you have gifts well beyond the sight. You are far stronger than you could ever imagine."

"Wait!" Nadia interrupted, "my mother could see them too?"

"She could when she was a child, but she chose to deny her gifts and closed her sight."

Nadia ran into the bathroom to vomit. Too many feelings rushed through her, and she couldn't handle it. After she finished purging what little food was in her stomach, she washed her face and spilled water into her mouth. She felt relieved, anxious, and stunned. Mostly, she was exhausted. She had forgotten how crying drained her. She dried her face on an embroidered towel and returned to the kitchen.

"Feeling better?" Lillya asked.

"A little. Mostly I'm tired. I'm not hungry anymore."

"Well, maybe it's best if you go to bed. In the morning, we'll talk more."

"Yea I'm ready for sleep now," Nadia admitted.

Nadia stumbled into her bedroom and threw on her pajama's. She really wanted a shower but was too tired. She managed to brush her teeth as her aunt opened the door.

"Goodnight Nadia. I know you will sleep well tonight," Lillya said softly.

"Thanks," Nadia mumbled.

Before Lillya could leave the room, Nadia stopped her.

"Lillya, what other gifts do I have besides seeing demons?"

"Ah, you will find out soon enough, but for now, just sleep. My dragons and my cats will watch over you."

Nadia flopped into bed and picked up her little dragon. Her eyes glanced at the painting on the far wall. She realized after a few moments her dragon looked exactly like the painting. It should have struck her as odd, but at that moment she was too tired. She fell into a deep slumber without any nightmares. The morning light caressed her face waking her. She glanced at the old-fashioned clock on her nightstand. It was well after nine, the longest she had slept in a while. She stretched and tried to move her feet, but there was a lump lying next to her. As she sat up, she spied all five cats in bed with her. They all looked up at her at the same time.

"What the hell?" she said aloud.

The cat by her shoulder seemed to wink at her. She reached out and stroked its silky fur, making it purr instantly. Without hesitation, the rest of the cats bounded over demanding to be petted as well. Nadia sniffed the air and caught wind of something delectable cooking in the kitchen. She gently pushed the cats to the side and jumped out of bed. She was overcome with a strange feeling. It was something she hadn't felt in a long time … something she thought she would never feel again. It was the feeling of hope.

Criss-Cross, Double-Cross

Chapter Eight

Nezatel spent many hours spying on Lucifer and the council. He became obsessed with knowing what was happening with the inner ring. His anger grew towards Lucifer and his refusal to see him. It seemed like Lucifer had forgotten him altogether and his promise. Usually, he would have had a new mission by now or something to occupy his time, but nothing was passed down to him. Most demons would have enjoyed the break, but not him. Boredom was his greatest enemy. Boredom left him alone with his thoughts … and subtle memories long forgotten. Lately, he had been feeling strange. Every memory brought forth emotions … emotions he didn't want to have.

When he wasn't spying on Lucifer, he wandered without purpose, which didn't give him much satisfaction. He wasn't allowed to act on anything without permission. He spent his days in the woods avoiding humans, but the animals always knew he was there. He could never get close to any of them. Demons cloaked themselves and usually were only seen when they wanted to be seen. Most animals and some of the more gifted humans could sense a demon's presence. Cats were a different sort, however. They were one of the few animals which saw demons even when they were cloaked.

Cats had always been revered as protectors throughout human cultures. Most households had at least one cat, or they did until Lucifer convinced people cats were evil. He sent many watchers to manipulate people into believing cats sucked the air out of babies, that they were always accompanied by witches, that they brought bad luck, or they were the spawns of Hell itself. People of many cultures began killing cats by the thousands, but the mindset was starting to change. Cats were becoming popular again. Nezatel guessed Lucifer would eventually try something different.

He hated it when a human had a cat. The watcher had difficulty getting close to his subjects and had to find different methods to manipulate. There was another animal which could see demons, but they generally weren't as popular. A horse's psychic abilities were far superior, using their eyes to peer into a human's soul. Fortunately, horses weren't house pets, so he didn't have to contend with them very often.

A violent shove interrupted his thoughts.

"Nezatel! Thar ye be ye worm. Where have ye been lately?" Yarish demanded.

"Doing my job," Nezatel countered. "unlike … others I know."

"YE disgust me!" Yarish growled.

"And I should care … why?" Nezatel laughed. "what do you want?"

"Lucifer wants to see ye."

"My, my, my, Lucifer sends his head demon to summon the likes of a watcher. Things must be quite busy in the castle, I think. I thank thee," Nezatel mocked, bowing deeply.

"Filthy maggot! Go see him 'fore I rip yar head from ye

neck."

Nezatel chuckled as he strolled away from Yarish. He could hear the head demon growling curses behind him. He never did like Yarish, and the feeling was mutual. Yarish didn't like any watchers, believing them to be lazy. Nezatel knew Lucifer would replace Yarish fairly soon. The day Nezatel fell, Yarish took him under his wing to 'help' him. He snorted at the memory.

The only thing Yarish helped him do was look like an idiot. He followed Yarish's set of erroneous protocols and was immediately reprimanded by Lucifer and Mortoc. Yarish told him to run up to Lucifer, fall to his knees and loudly proclaim he was ready for service. It didn't go over well. His first day in Hell was a complete disaster. Later, he saw Yarish outside the castle telling some of the Waru about it. He was laughing and having a grand time. Nezatel swore to get revenge someday.

He hurried along the corridor leading to Lucifer's chambers. He wondered why he had been summoned. He was ready for another task, but he still hoped to be rewarded for the last one. Ignoring Araphel's smug expression, he entered the room and bowed before his master.

"Ah, Nezatel. You may rise," Lucifer ordered.

Lucifer waited a moment before continuing.

"I wish to know how Nadia is coming along. It has been quite some time since you left her. Do not interact with her. Just watch for a while and report back to me. Is that clear?"

"Yes, my lord," Nezatel answered.

Nezatel stood quietly for a few moments waiting for

Lucifer to speak further. Lucifer simply stared at him, finally waving his hands.

"What? Do I need to explain myself further?" Lucifer growled.

"No, sire … it's just, you promised me a high position after I was successful with my last task."

"I don't throw rewards out to just anyone Nezatel. I think perhaps you misunderstood me."

"No, I …," Nezatel began.

"ENOUGH!" Lucifer roared. "you are DISMISSED!"

Startled and confused, Nezatel scooted from the room as fast as his legs could carry him. Araphel laughed at him as he departed the room.

"So, tell me Nezatel, did you receive good news?" Araphel chimed.

Nezatel wouldn't give him any satisfaction.

"Yes, I did."

"Oh?" Araphel asked, cocking his head to the side.

"Now if you will excuse me, I have a job to do," Nezatel said, flatly.

"Yes, you had better run along now. It wouldn't look good if our master saw us chatting when he comes out. He has a crucial meeting soon."

Nezatel sprinted away from Lucifer's messenger. Araphel's words kept replaying in his head … crucial meeting. He wondered what made the meeting so vital. Instead of heading to the gate, he decided to take a little detour … to his spying room. He took the long way around, avoiding any guards or punishers. When he felt no one was watching him, he slipped silently into the room. Pulling the door tightly closed, he heard muffled voices coming from the chasm. Nezatel slipped behind the cabinet and peered into the meeting room. His head reeled when he spied Lucifer's guest. Lucifer was in a very private meeting with … an angel.

"Firthel, how very nice of you to visit me," Lucifer chuckled. "I was beginning to think you switched sides."

"Never, my lord," Firthel laughed.

Nezatel's head was spinning.

"Why is an angel calling Lucifer his lord?" Nezatel wondered.

He put his face closer, so he wouldn't miss any details.

"I bring you news … news which will make you very happy," Firthel beamed.

"I'm listening," Lucifer replied.

"This news will change everything."

Lucifer sat waiting.

"It is something you have been wondering about for thousands of years," Firthel continued without revealing anything.

"TELL ME instead of babbling on about it!" Lucifer bellowed.

"Oh, I don't think so, fallen one," Firthel chuckled. "I must be guaranteed suitable compensation first."

"Confound you!" Lucifer laughed and embraced Firthel

141

like an old friend. "you haven't changed at all during your stint in Eineitha, have you?"

"Of course not," Firthel chortled. "I deserve compensation for having to befriend that moron in the first place. He thinks I'm his best friend, which is revolting."

"I agree. I have put you through a lot. Now my friend, tell me what I need to know, and you shall be rewarded beyond your richest dreams. I shall make you my head demon, and all my subjects will answer to you. Here, take my hand, and I shall give my vow."

Firthel grasped his hand as Lucifer began speaking in an ancient tongue. A strange red glow encompassed their hands. The light faded as soon as the ritual was over.

"Excellent! My promise is bound to you."

"Is that the only way you keep your word?" Firthel asked, curious.

"Yes. I make many promises to my demons, and I usually break my word. It keeps them guessing. In fact, I recently broke a promise to one of my watchers. He actually had the nerve to confront me about it," Lucifer laughed.

"He must be either quite stupid or quite brave," Firthel offered.

"I am betting on the first. Now my friend … tell me."

"Zavier cannot directly punish anyone in the realm. The Old Ones stripped his power from him as punishment for upsetting the balance. Now, he can only reward his creations but never punish … and he can never directly engage you in battle." Firthel blurted.

142

Lucifer's eyes widened. He slowly lowered onto a chair as he processed the information.

"So that's why he uses his warriors," Lucifer concluded.

"Yes."

"Do you know what this means Firthel?"

"It means my lord, you can empty Hell onto the upper realm. You can destroy the masses, and Zavier cannot interfere. He can only send his angels and warriors to combat them on Earth. You can obliterate Earth and the entire realm!"

Lucifer tilted his head back and laughed.

"Oh, glorious day!" Lucifer shouted. "and so, it shall be done! Thank you, Firthel. You have proved your worth to me time and time again. I will call my council together to formulate an attack on Zavier's darlings. What grand news this is!"

"Indeed," Firthel agreed.

"But before I reward you, I have another task. You must stay a bit longer with Zavier. Push him for information about Katrianna. See what he knows."

"As you wish, master."

Firthel mumbled something else, but Nezatel wasn't paying attention. He was stunned by the stolen information, and furious Lucifer never intended to reward him. He felt like a fool. The horrible things he had done left him with little satisfaction. He wondered why he bothered to follow Lucifer in the first place. There was no doubt in his mind Zavier was clueless about his angel's betrayal.

Slipping silently from the room, he used the secret gate and teleported to the upper surface. He knew what had to be done.

Nadia followed Lillya to a huge red barn carrying two buckets of feed in each hand. Her aunt carried four more by herself. Nadia could hear the animals inside clamoring for breakfast. Lillya opened the door and sent a large gaggle of goats pouring from the barn. They jumped and flipped into the air, circling her like a shark. A little black goat found her pants tasty and began chewing on them.

"Um, Lillya?" Nadia stammered, unsure if they were dangerous.

"Just pour the feed into that trough over there," she replied, pointing towards the corner of the fence.

As she poured the feed, the goats swarmed her, pushing her in all directions. Nadia tripped over them, falling backward onto her ass. Several baby goats pranced over to her, bleating and cocking their heads. Nadia reached out and gently stroked their soft little backs. She had never seen anything so cute in her life. A brown one with a long-curved face and floppy ears began chewing on her hair. Instantly, they were away in a flash, bouncing and twisting in the air. Nadia couldn't help but giggle. The sound of her laughter sounded strange to her. She hadn't heard it in a long time.

"Oh wow, they're cute!" she exclaimed.

"Yes, they are. There is nothing cuter in the whole world than a baby goat," Lillya agreed.

144

"Look how they twist in the air. It's like they don't have a spine," Nadia laughed.

"This is my small herd of goats. There are fifteen nannies and seventeen kids. I don't keep a male around because they tend to make the females' milk stink. Billy goats are terribly smelly because they pee all over themselves."

"Gross!" Nadia said, making a face.

Lillya rattled off their names but Nadia only remembered a few. She led Nadia inside where she kept the rest of her animals. Chickens were roosting in wooden boxes on the right side of the barn. They clucked and scattered, happy to be outside. On the opposite wall, rabbits with black ears were housed in several pens. The largest occupant in the barn was a humongous white horse with a long flowing mane. He had a single black star in the middle of his forehead. His eyes were the most unusual attribute about him since they were light blue. The entire rear half of the barn was his stable. He whinnied loudly when he saw them. The sheer volume of his call made the entire barn reverberate.

"Easy boy," Lillya cooed. "we'll get you some breakfast and let you out."

"What a beautiful horse. Do you ride him?"

"All the time. You can ride him too if you like. He's quite gentle," Lillya offered.

"Me? The only thing I've ridden was a pony at the fair when I was a kid, and that wasn't thrilling."

"Well, it's always nice to learn how to do new things," Lillya said, smiling.

Her aunt grabbed a halter and gently placed it over the horse's massive skull. He shook his head in protest while stomping his left front foot repeatedly. She took one of her buckets and dumped it into his trough. He didn't dive right into his food, however. He brought his head over the railing and stared at Nadia. His eyes gazed at her with such intensity, it made her feel uncomfortable. Nadia felt like she was being scrutinized. After he felt satisfied with his inspection, he returned his head into the stable and began munching with great enthusiasm. Lillya stroked his neck and hummed while he ate. When he finished, Lillya took him outside, releasing him into an immense corral.

Nadia thought it strange such a big animal was completely docile in her aunt's hands. Once released, he reared and charged, racing around the pen at top speed. Nadia knew he was showing off. After a while, he became bored with them and turned his attention to the grass beneath his feet. It was dry and brown, but the horse decided it was worth eating.

"Where did you get him?"

"I bought him as a foal. I was actually looking for a mare for riding. Instead, I came across him. He looked at me with his beautiful eyes, and I knew I had to have him. I spent way more than I should have, but he's worth it," Lillya explained, smiling at the memory.

"What's his name?" Nadia asked, awestruck by his beauty.

"Gabriel," Lillya replied.

That name churned up a feeling within her … as if she should know it.

146

"Interesting name. Sounds familiar," Nadia said softly.

"Does it?" Lillya asked. "It's the name of an angel on another realm. He is a powerful warrior. It was a bedtime story my grandmother used to tell me. She loved telling me stories about different angels and gods. I believe this horse has an ancient spirit within him. He's … different. Come, we have one more inhabitant I must feed."

They walked past the barn to an enclosure in the back of the property. A vile stench greeted Nadia's nostrils. A lone pig occupied a muddy pen, it squealed loudly, demanding food. Lillya picked up a bucket of foul-smelling muck and poured it into his trough. She patted its back as the pig grunted through mouthfuls of food.

"And what's this one's name?" Nadia asked.

"Bacon," Lillya laughed.

"Wow, that is just so wrong!"

"He won't be around for long. I'm taking him to the butcher soon. I never get attached to my pigs. They are simply food for me." Lillya said. "even though … I must admit they are adorable when they are young."

Nadia wandered away to investigate the animals by herself. She enjoyed watching them. It made her feel like she was at a zoo. They seemed to like Nadia, especially the goats. Her aunt had sixty acres in the middle of nowhere. A small stream ran through the property with many huge cottonwood trees on either side. There were a few other trees on the property, but it wasn't like the northeast. Mostly it was rolling hills of dead grass and nothingness in all directions.

There was a stark beauty about the land. Even the rocks were different, colored with wild patterns. Nadia wasn't keen on the weather, however. It was bitterly cold, but since it was winter, she assumed it would warm up eventually. This strange land oddly gave her peace. She knew she could start over here … a place where no one knew her past. Finally, she had someone who understood her.

As Nadia walked to the creek, she spied patches of thick ice along the sides. It gurgled noisily as it cut through the land. A huge willow tree dominated the shore. Devoid of leaves, the branches swayed around noisily. Something wet touched her cheek. It was beginning to snow, sending a chill through her. She ran to the warm house to thaw. She hadn't realized how cold she was. It felt good to slip into a nice warm kitchen. Nadia kicked off her sneakers and left them by the door.

"There you are," Lillya greeted, placing a cup of hot cocoa before her.

"Thanks. This place is something else. How long have you lived here?" Nadia probed.

"I moved to South Dakota in 1977, and it's been my home ever since. I bought this place in 92," she said, before changing the subject, "now, I'm sure you are wondering about school."

Nadia groaned, "yea don't remind me. Which armpit will I be going to?"

"None."

"What? You're gonna let me drop out of school? Awesome!"

"Not hardly, dear," Lillya laughed. "I'm going to home school you. I used to be a teacher after all. It's good to put my skills to work again."

"Huh?" Nadia asked, confused, "you mean, you're gonna teach me? I don't have to go to an actual school?"

"No. I figured it will be better for you. You won't have to deal with nosy kids and their questions."

"That's freaking AWESOME!" Nadia shouted happily. "I can stay home all day. Yay!"

"Before you start celebrating, I must warn you. Your days will be far harder than if you went to public school. I will begin lessons at seven AM promptly … after we take care of the animals. You will learn a wide selection of subjects, including those not taught in school. I will instruct you until four thirty PM. You will have a fifteen-minute break every hour and thirty minutes for lunch. After schooling, we will put the animals to bed because it will be dark by then. You will be allowed some free time until dinner, which will be at six PM. You will only have Sunday off to rest. You won't have homework because you will do everything as I am teaching. As the days become longer, we will adjust your schedule."

Nadia stared at Lillya like she was speaking gibberish.

"After dinner, around seven thirty," Lillya continued, "you will learn Tai Chi, Arnis or sword fighting depending on the day. We will conclude all lessons by nine PM and the rest of the day is yours. I suggest you turn in early."

Nadia thought her aunt had lost her mind.

"What the heck is Arnis?" Nadia demanded.

"Arnis is the Filipino art of stick fighting."

"Who's gonna teach me Tai Chi and sword fighting?"

"I am."

Nadia looked at the frail woman sitting across from her and almost laughed aloud. Her aunt's arms looked spindly and weak. She didn't look like she could even pick up a sword, much less use one.

"What about summer vacation?" Nadia asked.

"Ah, summer. You won't learn school subjects during the summer. Summer is when I will teach you magic."

"Wha … what!" Nadia exclaimed.

"Magic. You know … the thing that ties the fabric of the cosmos together."

"Ooooo," Nadia mocked, "will I be getting my very own wand too?"

"This isn't Hollywood rubbish I'm going to teach you. Magic is part of you. It's in your blood, and you will learn to wield it."

"I've heard enough!" Nadia barked, heading for the door. "I'm going outside. The animals make more sense than you do!"

"Tell me, Nadia," Lillya spoke softly. "have you ever dreamed of a sword with a glowing blade?"

Nadia spun around so fast she almost fell over, her mouth hanging open.

"Hmmmm, thought so," Lillya chuckled, walking away.

150

"You have a visitor," a female angel named Hurebala, informed Zavier.

Zavier was surprised. He wasn't expecting anyone for a visit. He was aware of most things on the realm, but on occasion, he could still be surprised. He didn't like surprises either. Surprises usually meant a bad situation.

"Who is it?"

"Well … actually, it is a demon. He insisted on speaking with you and you alone. He says he has important information for you."

"What's his name?"

"He wouldn't tell me. In fact, I couldn't even see his face. He wore a shielding cloak," Hurebala said nervously.

"Most interesting. Send him to me."

"Zavier, it could be a trap."

"It could be indeed, but I am not worried about it. Send him … and make sure no one knows he's here. Bring him to me via my private entrance," Zavier instructed.

"Yes, of course."

Zavier thought it remarkable this demon wore a shielding cloak. Clearly, he didn't want anyone, including Lucifer, to know where he was. Demons generally weren't allowed into this realm. They could only visit the area outside of Eineitha called the Scerabala and enter if they were escorted inside. He wondered what could have possibly driven a demon from Lucifer's realm.

He heard a sharp rapping on the door. After dismissing Hurebala, he invited his guest to sit. Zavier knew who it was immediately, even before he removed the cloak. It was one of his fallen.

When Nezatel left Hell, he decided to visit Zavier. Time was of the essence because Firthel wouldn't be with Lucifer for much longer. It was important he speak with Zavier before Firthel returned or it would be a disaster. Lucifer would … be upset at his betrayal. His soul would be unmade, and he would cease to exist. He had seen it done to demons before, and it looked to be a harrowing, unpleasant experience.

Nezatel felt he lost his mind coming back to Zavier's realm. He had no idea why he was so compelled to speak with Zavier, but something called him home. Zavier had to know what was happening. When he entered the Scerabala, he was lucky to find it mostly empty. There was only one angel inside. He had startled her, and she almost fled, but his incessant begging paid off. She agreed to inform Zavier.

He felt utterly vulnerable here, and he didn't like it at all. He constantly looked over his shoulder as the angel led him to her lord. Zavier must have sensed his need for discretion because she took him a secret way, where they wouldn't be seen. Bits of memories flashed through his mind as he looked around. He shook his head to clear his thoughts. More than anything, he wanted to stop and visit the tree, but he knew now was not the time. He wondered how long he had been away … how long he had been a demon. Time seemed to disappear in Hell.

When the angel left the room, he removed his cloak. Zavier seemed the same and yet different. He looked more world-weary. He locked eyes with his former leader and let the memories flood his soul. An uncomfortable sense of pain overcame him. He willingly gave up a beautiful existence for what … a chance to fill people's souls with hatred. So many emotions ran through him. He felt things he hadn't felt in a long time. Shame coursed through him. He hung his head, unsure how to even begin.

"Welcome, Renuphen," Zavier greeted, "it certainly has been a long time."

Nezatel's head rose, and he stared at Zavier. 'Renuphen' was a name he hadn't been called in ages. It was his name before he fell.

"So, what brings you to my realm, Renuphen and why the secrecy?"

"My …," Nezatel stopped himself from calling Zavier his lord. It was so easy to say, it almost fell from his tongue. "I bring you grave news."

Zavier leaned forward in his chair.

"Tell me," he said, softly.

Fire Wind

Chapter Nine

Nadia soon fell into a routine of school, work, and more schooling. It was difficult in the beginning. She didn't like waking up so early, but she did enjoy taking care of the animals. They ran to her every time she came close. Nadia even grew to like the pig. He grunted whenever he saw her. As he ate, she scratched his back. He squealed, enjoying the attention and the food. She convinced her aunt to keep him. Lillya wasn't happy about it but agreed to move his pen further out to give him more room.

Lillya's cats were always around her. They followed behind her like a little army, everywhere she went. At first, it was annoying, but after a while, she grew to enjoy their company. Even Lillya's aloof horse seemed to warm up to her. He would nicker a greeting when she approached him. She still felt unnerved by the way he peered into her. He almost seemed to read her mind.

Gabriel loved being brushed. It was during one of his brushing sessions, she discovered he had a ticklish spot. He was sensitive right under his left forelimb. When she tickled him, he snorted and bucked. He glared at her as if to say it wasn't dignified for him to act that way. She continued to tickle him until he gave her a nip on her ass. Even though he was gentle, he still gave her a large bruise. Nadia learned her lesson and avoided tickling him after that.

The horse's favorite spot for a good scratch was on his forehead. His eyes would almost roll back into his head.

Eventually, Nadia lost her fear of him. He was always careful not to step on her just as he was with Lillya. Lillya usually rode him on Sundays, though she never used a saddle or even a bridle. Her aunt just hopped up on him and held on tight, directing him with her knees. It was a strange sight.

Before she knew it, it was her birthday, and she turned seventeen. Lillya bought her a camera for her birthday and several lenses. Nadia never thought she would have enjoyed a camera as much as she did. She always took it with her when she was outside, snapping pictures of random objects. It felt good to capture beautiful things. Nadia would have preferred more time with her camera but Lillya kept her constantly busy with school.

The subjects Lillya taught were vastly harder than what she learned in a regular school and infinitely more interesting. Her aunt taught her Latin, which she never dreamed she could learn. She didn't have any trouble paying attention. The evenings were especially fascinating since Lillya taught her all types of martial arts. Nadia now understood why her aunt didn't park in the garage. It was set up as a training area. She even had a punching bag where Nadia practiced her hits. Nadia preferred Arnis and sword fighting to Tai Chi because they were more action oriented.

After a while, Nadia was bruised all over. Her hands ached from holding tightly on to the sticks. More than once her aunt 'accidentally' rapped Nadia's knuckles with a stick when she wasn't quick enough. Nadia promptly learned to move like water, especially when she was defending herself. Sword fighting was even more painful. Even though she wore protective equipment, it still hurt when her aunt poked her with the blade. It was a painful process, but within months she wielded the sticks and swords like she always knew how to use them.

Her aunt was an exceptional teacher, and Nadia was continually surprised by her strength. Lillya never seemed to tire and could train for hours. Nadia, on the other hand, was exhausted and sweaty after each lesson. By the time they were finished for the night, Nadia was so tired she practically fell into bed. She lost the urge to cut herself, although she knew she would carry the scars with her forever. It felt strange to experience emotions other than anger.

Nadia felt her hatred and agony disappearing, although on occasion her anger returned when she thought about her family. She missed them dearly, but she was finally able to mourn. Some nights she fell asleep crying. In the morning, her eyes were often red and bloodshot. Lillya never said anything to her, but Nadia knew her aunt was aware. Lillya let her work through her sorrow. There were times she raged against God. She felt he abandoned her in her time of need. Eventually, she even made peace with her anger, but it was a hard process. Nadia didn't have all the answers, but in time she hoped they would come. As winter passed into spring, she changed much like the seasons. Smiling and laughing became easier for her. Everything was intriguing. The magic of life had returned, and she felt happy.

She no longer dyed her hair, opting for her natural color. Lillya took her to get her hair styled at the local salon. Lillya's favorite stylist Heidi, gave Nadia a modern haircut. Nadia beamed, loving it … and herself. She also gave up wearing makeup. It was too much work to apply, and there was no one at home to impress or shock. Lillya wasn't surprised by anything Nadia did, and the animals didn't care what she looked like. She forwent her usual attire and dressed in jeans and t-shirts. One day on a whim, she took all her old clothes and threw them in the trash. After showing up for 'class' in her pajamas for five days in a row, Lillya told her to put on some clothes. Her aunt was less than pleased when she learned Nadia disposed of her attire. They drove to Wal-Mart on her day off to buy new clothes.

Nadia was horrified to be seen out in public in her PJ's, but after entering the store, she realized she would blend in nicely. Lillya wasn't very upset with her because she understood why Nadia purged her wardrobe. A fresh start meant new clothes as well. Lillya let her pick out a few pieces so she could change before they went to Kohls. Nadia felt guilty for forcing her aunt to spend money on her, but Lillya dismissed her worries.

Nadia really enjoyed Rapid City. It had an 'old west' mentality, which was far different than the primeval towns northeast. The town's center was her favorite area. It was bustling with people, traveling from one local shop to another. There were bronze statues of the presidents on every corner. She noticed people smiled everywhere they went and seemed happy.

Lillya took Nadia to her favorite store on Main Street, Worldwide Market. The store exuded a heady aroma of incense. Books, dragons, crystals, and other metaphysical items were crammed in every corner of the place. Lillya

158

only bought two things, a dragon of course, and some white sage. Nadia picked up the sage and sniffed it. It had an offensive and pungent odor to it. She crinkled her nose and dropped it as fast as she could.

The rest of the town was almost as charming as the center. Lillya took her to a mountain with immense concrete dinosaurs on top of it. She could see the brontosaurus from far away. There were a few areas which were dull and ugly, but not many. One boring street had rows and rows of car lots and fast-food joints lining the sides like soldiers. Electric wires crisscrossed the streets haphazardly. It was Nadia's least favorite place to visit.

She couldn't wait for summer … and warmer days. Lillya told her about all the hiking places in the Black Hills, which seemed exciting. There was another reason she was looking forward to summer. She wanted to know what her aunt meant by 'magic.' She asked her about it many times, but her aunt simply said she would tell her when it was time.

South Dakota grew on her. Even the cold wasn't so bad. The only thing she could have done without was the crazy windstorms. Every month there were a few days where the wind howled furiously. The whole house would shake and rattle, waking her in the middle of the night. It was annoying, and Nadia quickly grew to despise windy days, specifically when she had to feed the animals.

She awoke on a Friday morning to hear the winds wailing for the third day in a row. She marched outside carrying the feed bucket when a particularly strong gust of wind caught her. Nadia tumbled to the ground, spilling feed all over herself. The goats, now much bigger, began climbing on top of her to eat the grain. She shook them off angrily and screamed up at the sky.

"ENOUGH WITH THE WIND ALREADY! MAKE IT STOP!" she bellowed.

Annoyed, Nadia went to get more grain so she could finish feeding them. It was after she let the chickens out that she realized the winds had ceased. Nadia slowly walked around gazing at the sky. Her mouth fell open. She couldn't help but wonder if she was responsible for stopping the wind. It could have been a coincidence, but somehow Nadia knew it wasn't. A thrill shot through her. She ran excitedly to the house to tell her aunt.

"Lillya! Guess what? I told the wind to stop!"

Lillya cocked her head to the side listening.

"Sounds like the wind has stopped," Lillya admitted.

"Did … did I do that?"

Lillya sighed, unsure of what to tell her.

"Those with gifts can often change the weather for short periods," Lillya revealed.

"REALLY? AWESOME!" Nadia shouted. "I'm gonna make it ninety degrees and balmy every day."

"You have to be careful with that, young lady," Lillya cautioned.

"Uh, why?" Nadia asked, shaking her head.

"It is best to let the weather do its own thing," Lillya said, softly.

"But why? If I can change the weather, then why not

160

change it?"

"Having the power to do something doesn't mean you should rush out and do it."

"Then why even bother having powers?" Nadia retorted. "I mean, what's the frickin' point!"

"The point is to help people. Using your gifts to benefit only yourself creates a negative karma balance on your soul."

"That doesn't even make sense," Nadia argued.

"This is a discussion for another day, young lady," Lillya said sternly, "it is time for school and today is a test day."

"Greaaat," Nadia said sarcastically.

Nadia didn't want to learn about school stuff, she wanted to learn about changing the weather. She did her best to put it aside and concentrate on her tests. By lunchtime, everything was completed, including her tests. She felt drained and chose to eat quickly so she could go to her room. She didn't like watching her aunt grade her tests. It was torture. Her thoughts turned towards the discussion earlier. If she could change the weather, she wondered what else she could do. The possibilities were endless and thrilling.

She wondered if she could influence people as well. It would be easier to try if she hadn't been so isolated. If she could control people, then she could have everything she ever wanted. As she glanced in the mirror, she caught a glimpse of someone else on the other side ... someone vile. It was her, but it wasn't. This version of her had blood red hair and cruel eyes. An evil smile was on her blood-covered lips. Nadia had never seen anyone so heinous.

Nadia shook her head to clear it. The image in the mirror was gone when she looked again. A feeling of shame filled her. She felt repulsed by her earlier thoughts. There were so many strange things happening to her and she wanted to know what was going on. Nadia needed information from her aunt. Somehow, she had to pry it from her. A soft knock on the door was startling.

"May I come in?" her aunt asked.

"Yea, of course. It's your house," Nadia said, feeling puzzled.

"So, I graded your tests, and I am quite pleased. You scored high on all of them. In fact, you scored an A on math, which is quite a feat."

"I guess I'm pretty smart. My parents always said I was gifted," Nadia said, smiling.

"True … but Nadia this is college-level material I'm teaching you. This material is advanced … far advanced. People going for their master's degree learn this. You are far beyond gifted, dear."

"Really?" Nadia said, suddenly happy.

"Yes, and such an effort deserves a reward."

"REALLY?" Nadia repeated, louder this time.

"Yes. All classes, academic and otherwise, are dismissed until Monday."

"For real!" Nadia shouted.

"Yes, and I couldn't be prouder of you. You deserve a break," Lillya praised.

162

"Holy crap! Thank you!"

"You earned it dearie. Besides … I sense you want to talk, and we certainly cannot do that between your lessons, can we?"

Nadia was speechless.

"How is it she always knows what's goin' on with me?" Nadia wondered silently.

"Thank you," Nadia repeated after a few moments.

"Rest for a bit. We'll talk after dinner."

Her aunt smiled and left the room. Nadia sat down on the bed and thought about her reward. A million dollars wouldn't have felt better. She had been going at it almost nonstop since arriving in South Dakota. Nadia had no idea how tired she was until that moment. She laid down on her bed and examined the dragon painting on the wall. It was amazing how real the dragon looked. It was almost as if she could reach out her hand and feel its scaly skin.

The smoke from its nostrils seemed to swirl. She wanted to rise and go closer to the painting, but her body wouldn't move. It was as if she had turned to stone. The dragon in the painting began to move its head. That should have alarmed her, but nothing was what it seemed in her aunt's house. The dragon turned towards her, nodding as if to greet her.

Suddenly, the room around her wavered and disappeared as she was transported to a clearing in a forest. For a few moments, she was unable to move. The grass under her body felt soft and comfortable. The forest around her was alive with noises. She could hear the animals scurrying in the trees. She looked up and caught the sunlight gleaming through the pine needles. It was a peaceful place. Eventually, Nadia was able to move, and she slowly rose. She inhaled deeply, allowing the rich, earthy smells to fill her.

A sudden movement in the distance caught her eye. The dragon from the painting stepped into the clearing. It wasn't as large as some of the dragons she read about in stories, scarcely bigger than a truck. She felt no fear when she saw it. It was almost as if he was an old friend. Nadia surprised herself as she rushed to the dragon and tightly hugged its neck. Tears of happiness streamed down her face.

"It has been a long time, FireWind. I'm most pleased to see you," she said in a voice not entirely her own.

She stepped backward and kissed the dragon on the nose. He snorted in surprise.

"Yes, it has," the dragon replied smoothly.

"Is it almost time?" she asked eagerly.

"Who is that talking?" Nadia wondered.

"Not quite," he replied, shaking his head.

"When? When will it be time!" the voice demanded.

"Time for what?" Nadia asked herself.

"Soon, I suspect. Remember to have patience youngling. You have brought me here, and that is a good omen. Events are moving forward."

Nadia's head was reeling. She had no idea what the dragon was talking about. She wanted to ask him how she knew him or what she was waiting for. Instead, she continued talking with him about things that didn't make sense.

"Ah yes ... patience. The hardest lesson to learn as of yet," she laughed. "come, let us fly."

She climbed onto FireWind's back and held onto his scaly mane. He surged into the air, saturating her soul with ecstasy. The steady beating of his wings drowned out all other noise. The ground beneath them fell away as they rose into the clouds. Moist droplets caressed her cheeks. She gave into the joy of riding a dragon … of becoming one with him. It was exhilarating.

Nadia realized after a time, she was falling. FireWind disappeared into the mist. Terror gripped her as she fell to the earth, but before she could scream, she landed onto a soft surface. She sat up, unsure of her whereabouts. Looking around wildly, Nadia realized she was in her bedroom. The room was bathed in the soft glow of moonlight. She fell asleep and had a dream.

"But it felt so real," Nadia said aloud.

She picked up her little dragon and held it tightly in her hand. It was uncanny how the little dragon looked like the painting. She rose from the bed and went to the painting on the wall. The moon's glimmer made his skin shine.

"FireWind," she said, placing her hand on the canvas.

Nadia felt the dragon tremble beneath her touch. She quickly removed her hand and glanced at the clock. She had been asleep for almost six hours. The smell of food wafting under the door made her mouth water. She raced out to the kitchen to see what her aunt was cooking.

"Hello, sleepy head. Have a good nap?" Lillya asked, winking.

"Wow! I was out forever. I can't believe I slept so long."

"You obviously needed rest," her aunt said, placing a heaping plate of food onto the table for her.

"Boy, did I have a weird dream. It felt like … it was real," Nadia blurted.

"Really?" Lillya asked, cocking her head to the side. "tell me about it."

"What's the name of the dragon in the painting in my room?" Nadia asked.

"His name is FireWind."

Nadia dropped her fork onto her plate. She gaped at her aunt.

"What?" Lillya asked. "that's his name."

"I dr… dreamed about him and I knew his name. How is that possible? I mean, I rode on him for Christ's sake!"

"Interesting," Lillya said, smiling.

"It was really weird. I was laying on the bed one minute and then the next I was in a forest. Then FireWind came into the clearing, and I was chattin' with him like he was my buddy about stuff I don't know anything about, and then I got on his back, and we were riding around, and THEN he disappeared, and I woke up in the room," Nadia blurted in one breath.

"Well, that was an exciting dream. A visit from FireWind is certainly lucky."

"Why is that?"

"Because he's a very important dragon. That's why I painted a picture of him."

166

"Wait, wait, wait," Nadia protested, holding up her hands. "are you telling me … you know him too?"

"I do."

Nadia handed her aunt the little dragon.

Lillya smiled and gently plucked it from Nadia's hand.

"How long have you had him?" Lillya asked.

"My mom gave him to me when I was a little girl."

"Hmmm, interesting," Lillya repeated, handing the dragon back to Nadia. "Nadia dear, just because you don't see dragons, doesn't mean they aren't real. If you study history, all cultures have some form of dragon in them. They are considered lucky in most civilizations. It's only the Christian based religions that associate dragons with Lucifer, which is utter poppycock. They have been around since the dawn of time watching us."

"But … how do you know this dragon?"

"He has visited me before in my dreams," Lillya said.

"This felt so real."

"You were probably doing something called lucid dreaming. One explanation could be your true self took over, and that's why you knew FireWind," Lillya explained.

"My true self?"

"Yes … who you are when you aren't in this form."

"Geesh, the more you tell me, the more confused I get," Nadia breathed.

"You will understand in time, I'm sure. Perhaps a better explanation is, what you dreamed wasn't actually happening to you. You could have simply watched a conversation happening."

"But it sure felt like it was happening to me."

"A vivid dream will certainly feel that way," Lillya offered.

"I don't know, but it was sure strange."

Nadia finished eating and offered to help her aunt with the dishes. Lillya asked her if she would like some tea. Nadia however, opted for hot chocolate, stating her tea was 'gross.' She followed her aunt to the living room. Nadia knew she finally had the opportunity to talk with her.

"So why can't I change the weather?" Nadia probed.

"Somehow I knew you would bring that up," Lillya laughed. "it's alright to make little changes in the weather. For instance, I usually ask for snow on Christmas Eve. I like it when it snows for Christmas. However, if I ask for snow every day, think about what that might do for everyone else. I am not the sole inhabitant in this world, so it is not OK for me to act that way. The weather will basically do its own thing, however someone powerful … wishing hard enough could actually change the weather patterns. Think about what a ninety-degree winter would do for the area, Nadia."

"Well people would pay less for heating," Nadia suggested.

"True. And more for cooling. Crops would be devastated since many types depend on colder weather. There would be an astronomical influx of parasite bugs since there would be no cold weather to kill them off. The entire ecosystem would be altered, causing the death of hundreds of animals. There would be more tornados, more fires, and an increase in human population … something I would entirely despise. More people would move here, which would disrupt everyone's way of life. Traffic would increase, creating more pollution. A warmer climate would be disastrous for this area.

"Wow, I didn't think about that," Nadia admitted.

"I know. That's why I'm here to teach you. It's important to think of others when performing magic … or rather how your actions may affect others," Lillya explained.

"Wait … I did magic?"

"Yes. It's what others call magic. I call it simply using your energy."

"Cool! I did magic!" Nadia said, beaming.

"Are you even listening to me?" Lillya asked, waving her hands in the air.

"Yea, I'm sorry. I'm just excited. So, no changing the weather … got it. Tell me about demons."

"Demons are vile creatures which make people's lives miserable."

"Yea I know that," Nadia said bitterly.

"Ah, but what you don't know is they are really weak creatures, pimples actually, Lillya revealed."

"But the ones who tormented me were strong. They tore my family apart."

"Here's the thing, Nadia. For centuries people have been told they are weak, helpless creatures. They are told about demons, and yet they are too afraid to really believe they exist … and that the only way they can fight against them is to turn to one god or another. It's complete rubbish. The truth is humans are strong. They just don't know how to fight against them."

"For real?"

"Yes. Demons work mostly through manipulation. They manipulate people to do horrible things. They are scary, especially when they manifest themselves. Fear and anger make demons stronger. They feed from it as if it were a succulent steak," Lillya explained.

A memory sparked in Nadia's consciousness, something the one demon said to her. Something about feeding it anger.

"If you had known how to fight them you could have easily gotten rid of them," Lillya said.

"I knew they hated cinnamon and … dirt!" Nadia exclaimed.

"Well, that depends on the demon. Some of them actually like the smell. Most demons really hate dirt, especially with a plant in it. They hate anything natural. They are not big admirers of sage either. There is a misconception that sage drives them away, but it won't. Sage merely cleanses negative energy and makes them very uncomfortable. However, enough plants in the house will force them out. It's best to go with your instinct."

"Sage? You mean the stinky stuff you bought in that store? That stench would drive *me* away for sure," Nadia laughed

"I think it has a very pleasant odor," Lillya chuckled. "you will get used to it. I promise."

"Blech! If you say so," Nadia said, grimacing.

170

"Always remember … they must leave if you order them out."

"But … my demons wouldn't leave," Nadia said confused. "I told them to leave many times."

"Oh, they won't leave right away. They will cling to you until the very last second. In the end however, they have no choice," Lillya replied. "they fool people into thinking they're weak. They work through people's feelings. It's easy to manipulate those who can't control their emotions. Eventually, people lose hope and when that happens, they become puppets. So, they run to doctors to get put on pills … which only masks the problem or makes it worse. I have lost so many friends over the years whose lives have spiraled out of control. I didn't know how to fight demons until the day they came after me. I was thirteen when five of them moved into my house. I couldn't tell my parents and my sister refused to believe me. They made my life a living hell. My parents thought I was going through some kind of depression and forced me to see a doctor. That's where I made my biggest mistake. I admitted to him what I was seeing."

"What happened?" Nadia asked breathlessly.

"They forced me into a mental ward and that's where I learned to lie really well. The demon's followed me, so there was no escaping them. Mental wards are filled with them. You see, demons are drawn to negativity. When they find a place that has it, they make a nest and invite their friends. That place I was in was filled to the hilt with negativity. They were everywhere whispering in the ears of patients, waking them up at all hours. The people who were really lost were always hurting themselves."

"How long were you in there?"

"A week. I lied like crazy and told them I made everything up because I was mad at my parents. They let me go home, and I swore to find a way to rid myself of them. It took a lot of meditating to finally find peace, but it was within that peace where I found the answers. You see, demons love hurting people in general, but they truly desire those with powers. If they can corrupt us, then they can use us to hurt others by proxy … by large numbers. For instance, like putting thoughts into your head about changing the weather or convincing you to start an unstoppable chain reaction."

"So that's why they were so interested in me!" Nadia exclaimed.

"Exactly. You have gifts far beyond mere mortals. The damage you could cause is profound."

Everything finally made sense. That's why they came after her when she was so young. They wanted to groom her. Nadia then admitted her thoughts about influencing people and the strange vision in the mirror.

"Demons may no longer be influencing you Nadia, but sometimes you will still feel the effects of them, having been in your life for so long. The vision was of yourself if you would have followed an evil path. You were miserable after that horrible night, but you have never been evil … at least not in this life. Now that you are living with me, I can guide you on your path. Your conscience will tell you when you are straying, just as it did by making you feel ashamed," Lillya clarified.

172

"I am so glad you got custody of me," Nadia admitted. "um … what did you mean by 'in this life'?"

"That is a story for another time. I'm happy to have you living under my roof. It was so strange. I fought for months, but the judge wouldn't help me. Then my lawyer called one day and told me the judge had a change of heart. I was so happy I cried. I knew it would be difficult for you, but I suspected you would come around. You still have quite a way to go, but I am very proud of your progress."

Nadia smiled at her praise. It had been a long time since anyone praised her. She suddenly felt tired, even though she slept most of the day. She slugged her hot chocolate and got ready for bed. It had been a wild and interesting day. Nadia hugged Lillya good night.

"Lillya … what makes FireWind so important?" Nadia asked suddenly.

Lillya paused a few moments before answering.

"It is said that FireWind is Katrianna's dragon."

"Katrianna! I've heard that name before!" Nadia exclaimed. "the demons mentioned her. They seemed freaked out."

"And for a good reason," Lillya chuckled.

"Why? Who is Katrianna anyway?"

A New Endeavor
Chapter Ten

Zavier was reeling from the information the demon gave him. His best friend, his confidante, had betrayed him. Initially, he wanted to accuse Renuphen of lying, but he could sense the demon was telling the truth. Zavier wondered why he didn't see it sooner. Had his love blinded him? There were so many questions running through his head. The biggest question was … why? Why had Firthel deceived him?

Looking back, he should have known. Lucifer seemed to know things Zavier kept most private. Firthel was always around him, asking questions, and offering suggestions. When Lucifer lived in Eineitha, Firthel was the angel's friend. Apparently, he never stopped being his friend either. Zavier was hurt beyond belief, but mostly he felt foolish for revealing his secret to him.

"How could I have been so irresponsible!" he shouted.

"I am sorry to bring you this news, but I thought you should know," Nezatel said softly.

"Why did you? What do you want as payment?" Zavier demanded.

Nezatel paused for a long moment, looking at the floor. After a few moments, he spoke.

"I want to come home."

"I beg your pardon?" Zavier asked, bemused.

"Home! Please let me come back!" Nezatel begged.

Even though Zavier had powers beyond anything imaginable, he managed to be stunned twice in a short period of time.

"You wish to be an angel again?"

"Yes! More than anything! I've done vile things to people for no reason. I hate what I have become." Nezatel said, furiously.

"Come with me," Zavier ordered, holding out his hand.

The moment Nezatel grasped Zavier's hand, they were instantly teleported to a different area of Eineitha. Nezatel released his grip, immediately recognizing the place Zavier brought them. It was the place from his returning memories … the flowering tree.

"Do you remember this place, Renuphen? You used to come here to seek solace after your missions," Zavier said.

"I … I remember," Nezatel admitted, reaching out to caress the soft petals.

When his fingers touched the tree, the petals turned black and fell to the ground. Nezatel looked back at Zavier in horror.

"You see? I CANNOT CREATE ANYTHING! I CAN ONLY DESTROY!" Nezatel wailed, falling to the ground.

The demon covered his face with his hands and wept. Great black tears fell from his eyes onto the grass. It withered and died, increasing his anguish. He crawled into a fetal position, lost to his misery. He wished for death at that moment because nothingness would be better than the life he was living. He had given up everything … everything he once held dear.

As he lay on the dead grass, more memories came to him. He had been in love, and she was to be his wife. When Nezatel told her he was following Lucifer, she told him she couldn't be with him. She never screamed at him, however. No, she did something far worse. She looked at him with disappointment as her eyes overflowed with tears. She walked away and he never saw her again. Nezatel had also given up good friends who shared many laughs with him. He had known happiness, and he tossed it away … for despair. He didn't know how long he was on the ground crying, but it was Zavier's voice that brought him from his misery.

"Of course, I will let you return, Renuphen."

Nezatel slowly rose to his feet, his body still wracked with sobs.

"I … I am sorry I destroyed this place. It was special," he apologized.

"Ha!" Zavier snorted. "I can repair this in a second."

Zavier waved his hand, and the tree came back to life. The grass sprang up, returning to its lustrous green.

"You see," Zavier said, "no harm done."

Nezatel couldn't believe his eyes. He felt a trickle of bliss for the first time in ages. He smiled and wiped his face.

"I need you to do something for me before I allow you to come back," Zavier said.

"Anything!"

"I need you to go back to Hell. I want you to use your special room and spy for me. Keep me informed about

Lucifer's plans."

"I will be happy to do that for you," Nezatel chirped, "but if I may be so bold as to ask …, why is it you don't know what's going on in Hell?"

Zavier sighed.

"When I was punished for my arrogance, I was purposely blinded from seeing into my son's domain. The Old Ones told me it was so I could learn patience and humility. I have my spies Renuphen, but I cannot directly see what he is up too."

"I found a hidden gate in the bowels of the castle. I can easily shift between realms without anyone's knowledge," Nezatel offered.

"Ah yes … that gate."

"You know of it?"

"Of course. I had one of my agents make it a long time ago. That is how they travel into Hell."

"Interesting. I placed a shadow around it to conceal it further."

"Return to me only when Firthel is in Hell. I don't want him discovering our ruse. I will grant you special access to my home so you can directly teleport here. When you are in Hell, attend to your business as you normally would, following Lucifer's orders. When you have gathered enough information, I will end your employment with him. Don't get caught because I cannot intercede. You must be very careful," Zavier cautioned.

"I will be. He just sent me on a mission to spy on someone

178

I hurt. I'm afraid of what I will find. I don't know if she will recover from what I did to her," Nezatel sobbed, hanging his head.

He was ashamed for his actions.

"She is doing better, much, much better," Zavier said, cheerfully.

"She is? Really?" Nezatel asked, perking up.

"Yes. I gave her a bit of luck. I knew what was happening to her Renuphen, but everyone must find their path. Everyone is tested. No one is given a free pass. That is the only way anyone ever learns. Even I was tested, and I failed miserably, but luckily I have learned from my mistakes. Those mistakes have made me a better leader."

"I'll lie to Lucifer. Whatever I see, I won't reveal the truth," Nezatel proclaimed.

"Just be careful when you're spying on her. There is one there who could hurt you if you step an inch across the line."

"I will. I'm a watcher after all," Nezatel laughed.

"Well, you best be off. I'm sure Firthel will be returning soon, and it wouldn't be good if he saw you here."

"True. One more thing before I forget. Lucifer asked Firthel to probe you about Katrianna. I think Lucifer believes you are planning an invasion with her in the lead."

"Most interesting indeed. I think I shall have a bit of fun with that news," Zavier laughed.

Zavier waved his hand and sent Renuphen away. He felt exhausted. More than anything, he wished he could actually sleep. His best friend had been betraying him for who knows how long. Their entire friendship was a fraud. On the other hand, an angel he thought was lost forever wanted to come home. Zavier shook his head at the strange turn of events.

He closed his eyes and composed himself. He didn't want to give any indication something was wrong when the traitor returned. Firthel would undoubtedly cleanse himself from the stench of Hell before he visited him. The angel often disappeared for days, claiming he was 'looking for evil on Earth'. Zavier didn't think anything of it at the time. He never even thought to question him. Firthel was supposed to be his best friend … someone he could depend on through all his trials. Zavier guessed Firthel used some form of special energy to conceal himself when he disappeared. He would now pay attention to Firthel and his travels.

"Deep thoughts?" a familiar voice behind him spoke.

Zavier sent Renuphen away just in time, for Firthel had returned. He took a deep breath and spun around with a huge smile on his face.

"Firthel! Good to see you … my friend. You've been gone far too long. Where were you off to this time?" Zavier asked, smiling.

"Oh, you know, ridding the earth of evil doers and what not," Firthel lied.

"Yes … I know how much you abhor evil. Care to have a drink with me?"

Firthel smiled widely and leisurely sat down. Zavier

examined the traitor carefully. There were so many signs he shouldn't have missed. Firthel's appearance was changing. He carried himself with arrogance, which Zavier mistook for confidence. He had been blinded but now he saw his 'friend' for who he really was.

"So, I am here for a reason, Zavier," Firthel began slowly.

"Yes? I can hardly wait for the news you bring me," Zavier said, thinly masking his sarcasm.

"I've heard whispers ... well more like gossip amongst the angels."

"Gossip? Well clearly, I am not giving them enough work if they have time to sit around gossiping. I shall have to remedy the situation," Zavier countered, immensely enjoying the game.

"No Zavier, it's not that they are gossiping. It's what they are saying."

"And what pray tell is that?"

"They are saying Katrianna is coming back. They say *you* are bringing her back," Firthel revealed.

Zavier then did something he hadn't done in a long time. Something he hated doing. Something he swore he would never do. Zavier lied.

"My friend," Zavier began, his voice dropping to a whisper, "speak not a word of this to any of the angels. It is true. I trust you with this vital piece of information because I know you would never betray me."

"Of course not," Firthel whispered, a little too eagerly.

"You know I cannot directly battle Lucifer. I made a deal

with the Old Ones. They have allowed her to return to my home. The day after next, she will march her army of dragons and angels into Hell and destroy Lucifer forever."

"Where will she be entering Hell?" Firthel asked, excitedly.

"Directly in front of the castle. You know as well as I do, Katrianna isn't one to skulk in the shadows. She plans on entering Hell with a magnificent display. It should be a quick and effortless battle, especially since she was given her sword back."

"Her sword? They gave her ... the sword!" Firthel asked, his mouth fell open.

"Oh, yes! It will be wonderful to finally put an end to my son and his shenanigans. At long last, our enemies will be purged from the land!" Zavier proclaimed, clapping Firthel on the back.

"But won't that tip the balance?" the angel asked.

"Yes! But the Old Ones have already given me permission to do so. They grow weary of the chaos on this realm."

For the next hour, Zavier filled Firthel's head with images of the bloody battle, which would never happen. He went into great details of his fictitious plan so Firthel would have plenty of information to give Lucifer. After they had concluded their meeting, Firthel raced away, claiming he had urgent work on earth. Zavier put a trace on him to find out which gate he was using. Firthel, in all his arrogance, had been using a gate next to Zavier's house. Once again, he felt foolish putting so much trust into his friendship. He couldn't wait to see what happened next.

Zavier started laughing at the top of his lungs.

182

"Let him run and tell *that* to Lucifer. I can't wait to see what he does when my son discovers it isn't true," Zavier chortled, tears squeezing from his eyes.

Things were going to get much more exciting.

"What on earth is Gabriel carrying on about?" Lillya asked, peering out the window.

The giant horse was racing around in his pasture. Every few moments he would rear and kick, whinnying loudly. Lillya rarely saw her horse act so upset. After kicking at a tree, he stopped and stared into the distance. Lillya moved the curtain so she could see further and found the source of her horse's fury. There was a demon hidden in the shadows just beyond the protection circle around her property.

"Ah, well there's the problem," Lillya said, heading for the door.

"What is it?" Nadia asked.

"A demon is spying on us."

"What! A demon!" Nadia shouted.

Stay inside. Don't come out unless I tell you too. Is that clear?"

"Yea sure, but aren't you afraid the demon might hurt you?" Nadia asked, worried.

"HA! Not likely. There isn't a demon alive that's stronger than me," Lillya snorted.

Lillya marched straight to the demon. He didn't realize he had been spotted until she was right in front of him.

Suddenly, he found himself unable to move. He felt a trickle of fear race down his spine. He wasn't supposed to be seen. Nezatel thought he was a better watcher than that. The woman in front of him ferociously glared at him.

"Why are you here, demon!" Lillya spat.

"I … I," Nezatel stammered, attempting desperately to free himself from the binding spell she used.

"I will rip you to pieces! Now talk!" Lillya growled.

"Please! I am here only to observe."

"Yes, I am quite aware you are a watcher, but you are something else as well. You are far more powerful than a typical watcher. If you don't start talking, I will make you wish you had never been a demon."

"I already wish that," Nezatel said quietly.

"Lies! All of you are liars, incapable of telling the truth!"

"I was sent here by Lucifer to find out how she is doing. I was the demon who destroyed her family. I was able to trace her energy here," Nezatel admitted.

"Ah, an honest answer. That must be a new thing for you … honesty," Lillya mocked.

"I will never tell him what I see. I'm going to tell him she's miserable and lost. That should buy her enough time."

"Now, why would you do that? Why do you care if she has more time?"

"Because I'm done serving Lucifer!" Nezatel declared.

"Liar!"

"I'm not lying!" Nezatel snorted.

184

"Look at me, demon," Lillya said, softly. "Do you know who I am?"

She grabbed his face and forced him to look into her eyes. Her touch sent shards of exquisite pain through his body. He opened his mouth in a silent scream as wave after wave of piercing agony wracked his flesh. She released him after what seemed like an eternity. Nezatel knew precisely who she was, and that he was in deep trouble.

"I know who you are," he gasped.

"So, tell me … why should I let you live?"

"It doesn't matter. Kill me if you want. I'm already dead inside," he breathed.

"Fascinating," Lillya said, "you aren't begging for your life like the rest of your pathetic rabble. Perhaps it is a trap of a different sort."

"It is no trap. I simply hate who I have become," Nezatel admitted.

"Who are you?"

"I was once called Renuphen before I fell. Now I am known as Nezatel, but I hope to return to my former name."

"A demon who has repented his evil ways?" Lillya laughed. "How amusing."

"I would like to live so I can correct my wrongs, but if you choose to kill me then so be it," Nezatel sighed, resigned to his fate.

Lillya truly wanted to end his life, but something stayed her hand. She couldn't bring herself to kill him. She released him from her spell.

"Go. I'm done with this conversation. If I find out you lied to me … well let's just say I will make you suffer immensely," Lillya said, heatedly.

"Thank you. Please … please tell her I'm sorry," Nezatel began crying. "if I could do anything to take it back, I would."

"I'm not sure she will appreciate your apology, but I will tell her. It's time for you to leave now demon," Lillya said, pointing.

Nezatel got up slowly and bowed. He could feel her eyes burrowing into his back as he walked away. He should have been more careful. He didn't know how close he was to death until she touched him. He never felt such power … ever. He was lucky she decided to let him live. He wanted more than anything to repair some of the damage he had caused. He teleported to a gate and passed through it.

Nezatel wanted to relax in his room before he even attempted to see Lucifer. He was a mess. Along the way, he passed scores of damned souls being tortured. They screamed in agony as the whips cracked. He knew their crimes were heinous, but he couldn't help but feel sorry for them. They were led astray by demons just like himself. They paid the ultimate price for their weakness.

Nezatel laid down on the floor and shut his eyes, enjoying the heat of the air swirling around him. After a short rest, he felt composed enough to see his boss. He would have to give his best acting performance or Lucifer would see right through him. When he arrived at Lucifer's room, Araphel told him he was in a meeting with someone important. Curiosity got the better of him, so he stole away to the

186

secret room. He heard loud voices on the other side.

"Yes! Yes! Yes! A thousand times, yes!" Firthel argued. "as I *said* before that's all he told me."

"What time will she arrive?" Lucifer demanded.

"The day after next."

"What time, you imbecile!"

"I don't know! I can't ask him for every piece of information. It might tip him off," Firthel complained.

"Go back and find out!" Lucifer snarled.

"But the information I gave you should be enough," Firthel countered.

"I swear if I didn't need you I would tear you to shreds!" Lucifer shouted. "I need a precise time. What don't you understand about that! Now go and ask him!"

"Yes, my lord."

"How can this be? What deal could my father have possibly struck to allow her, *and* the sword back into the realm?" Lucifer asked. "and to be allowed to tip the balance?"

"I don't know. He wouldn't tell me."

"It doesn't matter. I will find out in time. In the meantime, I must develop a trap for her."

"You … you have the ability to trap her?" Firthel asked, stunned.

"Yes. While she was in banishment I made a bargain with a wraith. I gave him some of my souls for a powerful spell. I've been waiting eons to use it. This spell will trap her and then I can cleave her head from her body. I shall claim the sword as my own! With its power, I can conquer my father. Why are you still here? Didn't I give you an order!" Lucifer berated.

Firthel scrambled as fast as he could to get away from Lucifer and ran out the door.

Nezatel smiled at what he just learned. He suspected Zavier implanted this news into Firthel's head. There was no way Zavier could have brought Katrianna back from banishment by himself. Surely Lucifer knew that. Nezatel often wondered why none of the other demons staged a coup. Lucifer's anger blinded him to act rashly. He waited until the room on the other side was empty before he crept back upstairs. Lucifer was in a foul mood but agreed to see him.

"What news do you bring me, Nezatel?" Lucifer growled.

"Sire," Nezatel began, bowing, "she has strayed far from the path and is very lost. Her anger causes her to hurt anyone she is around."

"Excellent! That's the first bit of good news I've heard all day. Where is she living?" Lucifer cheered, clapping his hands together.

"She moves around constantly. When I was there, she was living on the streets."

"Hmmmm, no one is taking care of her?"

"No, my lord. She looks after herself," Nezatel lied easily.

Lucifer scrutinized Nezatel with his piercing eyes. The demon thought he might have been discovered, until his master smiled.

188

"Most wonderful. Let us hope she continues down this path for quite some time. I will have a new task for you shortly. You may return to your watcher duties until I call for you."

"Thank you," Nezatel said, bowing.

A wave of relief washed over him. He glided out of the room, putting as much distance between him and his master as possible. If Lucifer thought something was off, he would have grilled him for hours. Lucifer often believed those closest to him were lying. He killed many demons just on suspicion alone. There was an excitement in the air, Nezatel could feel it in his bones. Something was happening … something big. He wondered if he should return to Zavier and tell him what he heard. In the end, he chose to wait until he collected more intel.

Eventually, he wandered back into his special room and waited. He lay waiting in the shadows for a long time before he heard a noise inside the opposite room. It wasn't just a noise, it was more like a bellowing. Lucifer was screaming at the top of his lungs.

"WHAT DO YOU MEAN!"

"My l … lord, she is coming with her army the day after tomorrow at dawn," Firthel stammered.

"That leaves us even LESS time to prepare than I thought! If you had only done your job and learned this earlier than I would have had more time!"

"I'm sorry Lucifer. Spying is tricky business. I can't ask for too much information at once. I might give myself away."

"You are useless, Firthel!"

Nezatel smiled. Firthel was learning the hard way, being friends with Lucifer was a double-edged sword. He slipped from the room and entered the hidden gate. Within moments he was in Zavier's house. Zavier must have known he was needed because he appeared moments later.

"That was a speedy return, Renuphen. Firthel is spilling some news I suspect."

"Yes … my lord," Nezatel greeted, smiling. "I was going to wait, but I decided against it. Firthel told Lucifer …," he paused.

"Yes, please continue," Zavier encouraged him.

"That Katrianna is invading Hell under your instruction."

"HA!" Zavier laughed. "I bet that got Lucifer's knickers in a twist."

"That would be putting it mildly. He's panicking and plans to trap her. He wants her sword."

"Of course he does, but he shall never have it. Katrianna is still in exile of sorts and her sword is safely locked away. I don't have the power to go against the wishes of the Old Ones. I simply lied to Firthel."

Nezatel shook his head and laughed. It was a brilliant scheme. When Katrianna didn't show, Lucifer would lose all faith in his angelic spy. Firthel would be lucky to get out of Hell with his wings intact.

"That … is a magnificent plan," the demon laughed.

"I thought it was rather amusing myself," Zavier chuckled. "I need to know what Lucifer is planning after his great battle doesn't happen. After I gain this knowledge, I will deal with Firthel, and you shall become an angel once more."

"Thank you!" Nezatel exclaimed, falling to his knees.

"Enough of that, Renuphen. I should be thanking you. You are helping me more than you know."

Nezatel bowed and returned to Hell, eager to see the events unfolding.

The Price of Betrayal
Chapter Eleven

Lucifer called a meeting so he could discuss his battle plans and trap for Katrianna. Every warrior was to fight in this battle with the Varafe leading the charge. This news angered Mortoc, and he argued that his army should be in the lead and not a bunch of pathetic females. The argument escalated almost to the point of violence between Mortoc and Elistax. Elistax demanded Mortoc apologize or she would march her army out of Hell permanently. Lucifer knew there was no way he could win any battles without them, so he forced Mortoc to apologize.

Mortoc, of course, refused until he was threatened to lose his position. He finally gave a half-hearted apology, triggering delighted smirks from Elistax. She sneered at Mortoc every time he spoke, which only angered him further. His neck was bulging with purple streaks, and he shook with fury each time he spoke. Elistax used every opportunity to discuss her importance to the plan.

It didn't help matters Lucifer brought Firthel to the meeting. They protested, claiming an angel couldn't be trusted, especially one who betrayed his 'master' so easily. Lucifer explained numerous times Firthel had been working for him since his fall. His reassurances didn't seem to appease his generals as they eyed Firthel warily. Elistax crinkled her nose, claiming Firthel stunk and should wait outside. Mortoc seized the opportunity and insulted her, creating more pandemonium. The meeting was utter chaos for some time until Lucifer was finally able to quiet them long enough to discuss everything.

Lucifer's acquired spell would turn the ground into an inescapable mire. The soil would appear solid, but once Katrianna stepped onto it, she would be unable to move. The more magic she used to free herself, the more she would become entombed. The spell would only work on his enemies. His demons could wander around as if the ground were solid. The trap wouldn't hold her for long, but it didn't matter. It only needed to hold her long enough for Lucifer to remove her head. Once he had her sword, it would have to obey him. It was the only way the blade would switch alliances.

In the meantime, his soldier demons would slaughter the rest of her army. Worker demons would not be part of the battle since they offered little support with their skills. Instead, he would have them seal the exits in case anyone tried escaping. They were instructed to alert the Waru if enemies were lurking in hidden areas. The armies would be strategically placed to annihilate their enemies.

The damned would be moved to the far reaches of his dungeons, in case Katrianna had plans of rescuing any of them. His watchers would be sent to patrol the upper surfaces and report any movement back to his generals. They were the eyes of Hell. Lucifer depended on them to make accurate assessments

His council wanted alternative plans in case everything went sideways. Lucifer fought his sister in battle before and knew her strengths. If it appeared the battle might turn against him, Lucifer would raise the Crawlers. Should the Old Ones discover his plans, it would cost him dearly, but he needed her sword to finish their father and seize control of the Delaphina Chain. Nothing ventured ... nothing gained. It was a chance he was willing to take. It would be glorious. He dismissed everyone except his historian, Nucaira. He wanted to speak with her in private.

"Nucaira, what are our chances of winning this battle?" he demanded.

"Sire, there is nothing in our history about such a battle," she replied cautiously.

"I have fought her before! Are you telling me there is nothing in our past which can predict the outcome?"

"Sire, as you know, I can only predict the future from past events. This is an entirely new event. I'm sorry, but I cannot help you," she said slowly.

"Damn you, Nucaira! I must be sure!" he shouted.

"Then I suggest you see the dark priests. They should be able to give you the answers you so dearly seek."

Scowling, he stormed into their chambers. Unfortunately, they couldn't give him the answers he wanted either, electing to speak in vague riddles. Lucifer killed them all, leaving their bodies in puddles of blood. He had grown tired of their listless behavior and elusive answers. He decided at that moment he wouldn't use priests for predicting events. Since nothing was set in stone, he would make his own future.

At the opportune time, he released his spell for the trap. His demons rushed around, getting everything in place. Hell was churning with excitement and nervousness. Nezatel, of course, knew every detail of the plan. He pretended to be excited and promised to constantly make reports. He couldn't wait to see how Lucifer reacted when nothing happened. The demon would then slink to his spying room shortly after. The thought of his upcoming wrath after nothing happened made him snicker with glee.

When the hour approached, everyone was tense and ready. Lucifer led the army, flanked on either side by Elistax and Firthel. Lucifer wielded a huge, black halberd, with a long, curved blade at the end. His hands gripped tightly upon the staff. A hushed silence fell over the area as they waited and waited. Every little sound brought more tension.

The hour came and went. They stood waiting for hours, yet nothing happened. The watchers reported everything was quiet on the upper surface. There wasn't a sign of any army. Firthel grew more and more nervous, shifting from one foot to another. Elistax scowled at him every time he caught her eye. After a long wait it became clear Katrianna wasn't coming … at least not at the time, Firthel claimed. Lucifer grabbed the angel and took him aside.

"WHERE is she!" Lucifer barked.

"I don't know! Zavier said she would be here at that time," Firthel blurted, wanting to be anywhere else at the moment.

"BUT SHE'S NOT HERE, IS SHE!"

"That's what he told me," Firthel whined. "maybe he lied."

"MY FATHER DOESN'T LIE!" Lucifer screamed.

"But …," Firthel stammered.

"You know what *I* think?" Lucifer snarled, his brown hair flowing wildly. "I THINK YOU'RE THE ONE WHO'S

LYING. I THINK YOU INTENTIONALLY PLAYED ME.

From a distance, Nezatel could see the events unfolding. He covered his face so others couldn't see him laugh. He then shrouded himself with a shadow and slowly crept closer to Lucifer.

"NO!" Firthel protested. "I wouldn't stay by your side if I was playing you. That's what he told me!"

"YOU'VE BEEN WORKING FOR HIM ALL ALONG, HAVEN'T YOU!" Lucifer screamed loudly.

Before Firthel could utter another protest, Lucifer grabbed him by the neck and shook him like a rag doll. Lucifer shoved his fingernails into Firthel's face, permanently marring him. Mortoc and Elistax spied Lucifer assault the angel and rushed over, hoping to take part in the destruction. Lucifer momentarily glanced away from him, which gave Firthel an opportunity to escape. Using all his energy, he pushed outward and slipped from Lucifer's grip. The moment his feet touched the ground, he ran … he ran for his life with a hoard of demons on his tail. He managed to slide into one of the gates milliseconds before it shut.

Lucifer burst into flames, shrieking loudly at his failure to capture the angel. He raised his fists to the heavens and yelled every curse imaginable. Nezatel departed hastily so he could listen to the private discussion. Everyone was distracted by Lucifer's fury, and it was easy to slip away to spy on him. Nezatel couldn't wait to hear what Lucifer was going to tell his council. He waited in darkness for only a short time. The boom of the crashing door on the other side startled him. Lucifer was in a foul mood.

"I CAN'T BELIEVE THIS!" he screeched.

The rest of the council filed in behind him and quietly sat down. They did their best to avoid eye contact with their master. When he was this angry, it was always best not to look at him.

"ALL MY FUCKING PLANS ARE RUINED!"

"My lord," Yarish spoke quietly. "we can have part of ye army ready in case she does come."

"SHE'S NOT COMING!" Lucifer shouted, spittle flying from his lips. "AND EVEN IF SHE DOES, MY SPELL WON'T WORK. IT WASN'T A PERMANENT CURSE. BY NOW IT HAS DISSIPATED."

Lucifer struck the table with a mighty blow sending shards of material everywhere. He wanted nothing more than to kill everyone in the room. He put his head into his hands and tried to calm himself. He knew he would not have his revenge against his sister today. He couldn't even go forward with his other plans. If Firthel lied about Katrianna coming, surely he lied about his father's inability to defend the realm. Everything Firthel said was either a ploy from his father or some scheme the angel was playing. Lucifer didn't know who to believe. He slowly sat down in his chair.

"We cannot go forward with our other plans at the moment," Lucifer confessed, finally calm.

"What is our next step?" Mortoc asked quietly.

"I have to find out if anything Firthel told me was true. For all I know, he could have been lying about everything. I was wrong to put so much trust into him," Lucifer admitted.

"What will ye do?" Yarish asked.

"I will visit the Old Ones and demand an answer. If my father is bringing my sister back, they should be advised. This way, they will be in my debt and grant me some information. In the meantime, send all my watchers and spies to the surface. I must rely on their sight."

"As you command!" the council said in unison.

"Go now and let me rest. My fury has weakened me. Yarish, bring me Nezatel when I am rested. I have a special task for him."

Nezatel didn't like hearing his name mentioned. Whatever the task was, he wanted no part of it. He was out of the room and into the gate before any of them left the room. When he arrived in Eineitha however, Zavier was nowhere to be found.

"Firthel! You look terrible! What happened to you?" Zavier asked when he spied his former friend leaning against a tree.

Firthel did indeed look awful. His face was scarred with large gaping wounds across his cheek. His left wing was broken and hung limply by his side. He left a trail of blood everywhere he walked. When the other angels saw him, they rushed to get Zavier.

"I got into a bit of trouble with some demons," Firthel wheezed.

"Well, it certainly looks that way. Is your wing broken?"

"Yes. Can you heal me?" Firthel asked.

"Heal you? Of course, I can heal you. I am ... a god after

all," Zavier laughed.

Firthel didn't understand why Zavier was acting so jovial. He was growing annoyed.

"Well hurry and do so. I'm in a lot of pain."

"Yes," Zavier said, dropping his voice an octave, "betrayal often is painful, isn't it Firthel?"

Firthel's eyes widened. He knew he had been discovered.

"And you used a gate closest to my house to carry out your plans. I was an idiot to trust you," Zavier groaned, shaking his head.

"I … I," Firthel stammered.

"ANGELS TO ME!" Zavier shouted.

Within a few moments, every angel from every corner of the realm stood before Zavier wondering what was happening. Their eyes darted from Firthel to Zavier.

"FIRTHEL HAS BETRAYED US!" Zavier shouted, his voice echoed.

The angels turned their attention towards Firthel and scowled.

"HE HAS MADE AN ALLEGIANCE WITH LUCIFER AND HAS REVEALED MY SECRETS TO HIM."

Angry chatter erupted all around them.

"Sire," Firthel begged, "I'm sorry! I wasn't thinking clearly."

"Firthel," Zavier began, "you not only betrayed me, someone you called a friend, but you also betrayed them," he pointed at the hoard of angels surrounding them.

200

"But I ...,"

"YOU ARE UNWORTHY OF BEING AN ANGEL!"

"NO! Let me fix things! Please, I beg you!" Firthel pleaded.

"There is no fixing this, Firthel," Zavier said, shaking his head with disappointment.

Zavier spun Firthel around and ripped his wings from his body. Firthel screamed and fell to the ground, fresh blood pumping from his wounds. It was disgraceful and painful to have your wings removed. Everyone who saw a wingless angel knew what it meant.

"YOU ARE HEREBY BANISHED FROM THE REALM. YOU WILL BE A SHADOW WALKING AMONG THE MORTALS. YOU WILL BE HUNTED BY DEMONS AND SHUNNED BY ANGELS. NO ONE WILL HELP YOU. You ... are alone," Zavier concluded.

"N... noooooooooo," Firthel blubbered.

"Goodbye, Firthel. When I have deemed you worthy, you may return, but not a second sooner."

Zavier waved his hand blasting Firthel from Eineitha. It was always a sad day when one of his angels did something regrettable. Those who fell needed to learn a lesson.

"Zavier," an angel near him, spoke quickly, "I am sorry for your loss. Is there anything we can do?"

"No Bealustat but thank you. I have some business to attend to at my home."

Zavier knew Renuphen was waiting for him. It was time to reward him with the one thing he wanted more than anything. It was strange how easily Firthel gave away what a demon desperately wanted.

"Ah, I'm sorry I had to keep you waiting Renuphen. I had some business with Firthel."

"It's fine," Nezatel said, smiling, "your little lie created quite the chaos in Hell. After Katrianna didn't come, Lucifer accused Firthel of lying and roughed him up a bit. I think he would have killed him if he hadn't escaped."

"No doubt," Zavier agreed. "what are Lucifer's plans now?"

"Well now he thinks Firthel lied to him about everything, so he has halted his campaign."

"Funny how nicely that worked out," Zavier laughed.

"Yes. He's going to see the Old Ones and demand answers."

"Ha!" Zavier snorted. "that will go over like a lead balloon! Thank you, Renuphen. I am truly in your debt. You have fulfilled your end of the bargain. Are you ready to return as an angel?"

"Not quite. There is something else I must do first. It won't take long."

"Oh? And what might that be?"

"Something which will create a little more chaos in Hell," Nezatel laughed, winking.

"Well then, I shall await your return," Zavier said, smiling.

When Lillya told her niece about the demon's apology, Nadia flew into a rage. She wanted to run out and stick a knife into him. There was no amount of apologizing which could change the past. She took her sticks out to the garage and attacked the bag until she was drained. Lillya, sensing this was something Nadia needed, allowed her to get it out of her system. Afterward, she fell into an exhausted sleep and once more dreamed of FireWind.

"When? When will it be time, FireWind?" she asked in that strange, familiar voice.

"It will be time when you are ready," he replied.

"I *am* ready. It has been far too long."

"Who are you?" Nadia asked the person speaking.

The person didn't answer her.

"If you were ready, then the time would already be here." FireWind countered.

"I suppose your right," she agreed.

"Patience, youngling. It won't be long now."

The dream changed, and she was standing in front of an enormous stone door. There was something powerful on the other side. She could hear its heartbeat calling out to her. She beat her fists against the door, but it wouldn't budge. Tears sprang from her eyes as she cried in frustration. She ran from the door and entered yet another place. She was in a forest. There was a small pond in the center. Nadia bent over to gaze at her reflection, but the water wavered, and she awoke. Instead of anger, she felt refreshed and peaceful. She thought about the demon's apology, but it no longer filled her with rage.

"If a demon could learn remorse than there was hope for the world, I suppose," she said to herself.

She still hated all of them, but her anger was spent. Something was changing within her ... something mysterious.

As spring turned to summer, Nadia was able to truly appreciate the beauty of her surroundings. The grass was so green it reminded her of pictures in Ireland. Wildflowers bloomed everywhere, covering the prairie like a quilt. Every morning her eyes were greeted with a different collection of colors and scents. She loved being outside, even when it was windy. Her favorite place was by the willow tree. She liked to hear the water bubbling as it travelled down the stream.

Nadia learned a new skill after the goats had their babies. She became an expert at milking them. At first, they kicked her as she squeezed their utters in a vain attempt to produce milk. After some coaching from Lillya however, she was finally able to milk them effectively. The only goat that continued to give her problems was a black and white one named Sally. Sally would do everything in her power to avoid being milked. She only allowed Lillya to touch her. Nadia did her best to befriend Sally, but the goat had nothing to do with her. She ran away the moment Nadia came into the barn. It was infuriating.

As summer vacation approached, Nadia grew antsy, eager to learn about magic. Lillya wanted Nadia to split her vacation. She was off for a few weeks in June, July, and August. At first, Nadia didn't want any breaks. The thirst for knowledge was so great she was willing to skip time off. She soon discovered kindling magic was far more difficult than she had anticipated. It came naturally to her, but it was difficult for her to control it. She never dreamed it would be so exhausting to learn magic. The first lessons were about controlling the energy she took.

"Everything is made of energy. The rawest form comes from the Earth. The purest form comes from the heavens. In time you will learn to use both," Lillya explained.

"So, when you are talking about the heavens, are you talking about god?" Nadia asked.

"No, I am talking about the universe …. that universal energy that binds us all together. We are all connected because of it."

"Um, where do god and the devil fit into all of this?"

"Do you want a lesson on theology or a lesson on magic?" Lillya asked, sounding cross.

"Magic of course."

"Well then pay attention. Most people think there are two kinds of energy in the universe, positive and negative. All energy is basically neutral. It's what you do with it that changes it. Positive yields positive results, whereas negative yields negative. In other words, when you play with negative energy, part of itself attaches to you, making it increasingly difficult to do positive things. Positive energy is free. It travels through the universe, and the universe returns more of it to you. There have been countless books written on this, *but* they fail to mention how demons come into the story. Demons roam the Earth looking for those playing with negative energy. They are drawn to them like moths to a flame.

"Ugh! Demons suck!" Nadia proclaimed.

"They feed on it and become stronger as the person puts out even greater negativity. Unless people change, they will be sucked into a miserable life of their own making. Heaven forbid, someone dies in a home filled with demons. They will never let a soul pass on. It will be tortured for eternity unless someone intervenes."

"Why aren't demons attracted to those with positive energy?" Nadia asked.

"They are *extremely* attracted to them … but it's difficult to get close. Positive energy is almost like a protective shield."

"So that's why I could never feel happy when they were around," Nadia breathed.

"Yes. Demons suck happiness away. Once you were aware of their presence, you could have changed your thought patterns and drove them away."

"So, which is better, the energy from the Earth or the universe?"

"That depends on what you are using it for," Lillya answered, "and every kind of magic has a price to pay. In other words, if you go around pulling energy, you can expect changes … mostly positive, to your body. I will teach you how to pull the natural positive energy from your surroundings".

"Can a person work with just neutral energy?"

"Only those who are experts at energy manipulation can wield neutral energy. It has the components of both positive and negative, and it's highly volatile. I heard stories of entire cities wiped from existence because someone tried to play around with neutral energy."

"Holy crap!" Nadia exclaimed.

"Exactly. Now stand up and close your eyes. Imagine your feet growing roots. These roots go down to the center of the Earth. At the center it's brilliant green. Now begin pulling up the energy until it reaches your body and hold it there."

Nadia opened one eye and peeked at her aunt.

"Are you serious? This is magic?" Nadia joked.

"Yes, the beginnings of it. Now close your eyes and try it."

Nadia wondered how her aunt knew her eye was open. She tried to do what her aunt instructed, but she couldn't visualize anything. Try as she might, she couldn't even envision the center of the earth. After a few moments, she gave up and opened her eyes. Nadia was startled by the sight of her aunt … bathed in green light. She blinked a few times as it disappeared.

"Uhhhhh, you were glowing like a traffic light," Nadia hooted.

"Shhhhh, I know. Giving up already?" Lillya asked.

"Nah, I'll try it again."

Nadia struggled for hours, but she couldn't seem to grasp the art of visualization. Lillya made her sit quietly and meditate. Nadia liked meditation because it seemed to calm her inner storm. After weeks of meditating and visualizing, Nadia had a breakthrough. She was standing in the living room, as always during this exercise. She felt a surge of energy encompass her. Lillya's voice broke her concentration.

"You did it! I'm proud of you."

"I did?" Nadia gasped, looking at the greenish glow around her. "holy crap! I did it."

After a few moments, the glow disappeared, and Nadia felt the rush of energy leave her. She stumbled almost falling to the floor. Lillya caught her before she hit the ground.

"Wow, I'm dizzy."

"This is the price of magic I was telling you about. It affects everyone differently," Lillya described.

"What's your price?" Nadia mumbled.

"Me? I don't have one."

"But I thought you said …," Nadia protested.

"Yes, yes, yes, I know what I said. I am different. Rest a few moments, and when you feel up to it, you can try again."

Nadia relaxed until she could rise to her feet. This time when she reached for the Earth's energy, it came to her easily. When she brought it up however, she couldn't stop it. It kept coming and coming until her hair was standing on its end. The air popped and crackled with energy.

"Lillya!" Nadia screamed.

"Stop the flow!"

"I can't! It hurts!"

Pain overwhelmed Nadia. Her head felt like it was going to explode. She felt her aunt's arms around her. Lillya took the energy she was producing and sent it back to the Earth. For a long time, they stayed locked in a loop, unable to break free. After what felt like forever, Nadia was able to break contact with the Earth. The remaining energy flashed into the air destroying several of Lillya's glass dragons.

"I'm sorry," Nadia mumbled.

"It's alright. Let's get you to bed. After a good night's sleep, we will try again, but this time in the garage."

Nadia briefly chuckled before she fell asleep. She awoke in the forest once again climbing onto FireWind's back. The thrill of flying on a dragon overwhelmed her. It felt so real. Everything about this dream was vivid beyond anything she had ever experienced. She didn't want it to end, but it always had to. She touched the covers and knew she was in her bed. The house was silent. It was still early morning.

She was too excited about learning magic and couldn't fall back asleep. Instead, she chose to meditate and calm her center. She did this for an hour until she heard her aunt in the kitchen.

"I dreamed of that dragon again," she told her aunt.

"FireWind?"

"Yea, this is like the third time. The second dream there was a bunch of talking about something with time and other random stuff. I didn't understand any of it."

"Seems to me that you are either tapping into someone's memories or their conversations, but who, I wonder," Lillya suggested.

"Maybe this Katrianna person?" Nadia offered.

"Perhaps. It is her dragon, after all."

"Tell me about her please," Nadia pleaded.

"It's a long story."

"I got nothing but time," Nadia said, smiling.

Lillya cleared her throat and began.

Katrianna

Chapter Twelve

When Katrianna and Lucifer were born, they were loved by the entire kingdom. Katrianna was the first to arrive, bald and screaming like a banshee. The whole room shook and wavered as she wailed. Her mother Stelline clasped her hands to her ears to block the sheer volume of noise. Zavier gently put his hand on her head and whispered, calming her immediately. Her brother Lucifer arrived only a few minutes later. He screamed just as much as Katrianna, but the effect wasn't the same.

Both children were beautiful beyond reproach. Katrianna had flaming red hair with hazel eyes while Lucifer had brown hair and eyes so dark, they looked like tiny marbles. Katrianna had little red wings while her brother had white. Both children had a curiosity for everything, but Katrianna was drawn towards the natural world while her brother was interested in how things worked.

Children of higher beings age differently than mortals. They age slower and are considered adults when they reach the age of five hundred. It takes thousands and thousands of years to gain the wisdom to rule a kingdom. Many realms were destroyed in the past because a young, impetuous ruler was placed at the helm. The Old Ones only interceded when the balance was tipped beyond a simple repair … and when they interfered, it was never a blessing. They were often unforgiving with their judgment. Usually, they stayed out of a ruler's business and only interceded as a last effort.

The Old Ones always watched the heirs of rulers warily. Higher beings produced offspring which were quicker, stronger, and vastly more knowledgeable than any mortal. Often, they looked down upon mortals, deeming them weak and useless creatures. It took time for higher beings to understand mortals, but some of them never did. Katrianna and Lucifer had difficulty appreciating mortals and the other creatures which roamed the realm. Katrianna never hated them like her brother, however.

Katrianna was very interested in dragons. She even acted like she was a dragon, roaring at her brother whenever he annoyed her. Dragons were everywhere on Zavier's realm, but they couldn't be seen by humans. When she was three, her mother gave her a tiny blue dragon name Rort. He became her constant companion, much like a mortal's dog. Rort liked to wake her in the morning by blowing smoke at her face. She would giggle, cuddling him close to her.

Both children loved to hear stories and would pester their parents until they gave in. One day, Zavier told them an extraordinary story ... a story of how they were named.

"Did I ever tell you how you two were given your names?" Zavier asked them.

"No!" They shouted, "tell us, tell us!"

"Katrianna, you were named after your grandmother."

"Your mom?" Katrianna asked.

"No. Your mom's, mom. She died before you were born, but she was a fierce warrior and protector. She led her people to victory in the ancient Rurka wars. She was such a remarkable woman, and I see many of her traits in you.

Just like your mom and you, she too was a Dragon Angel."

"Really?"

"Yes …," Zavier said before he was interrupted.

"Who was I named after father?" Lucifer asked eagerly.

"Son, you were named after my brother's finest angel. You probably don't remember this, but he came to visit you when you were just a baby."

"He did? What does he look like?"

"Beautiful beyond words … long blonde hair, chiseled face, and light blue eyes."

"Do you think I'll get to see him again someday?" Lucifer asked.

"I'm not sure, son. Shivet's angel has recently fallen and now resides in a dark place. He has given in to hatred. I'm not sure any of us will ever see him again."

"Oh," Lucifer said, sounding disappointed.

Katrianna and Lucifer usually asked to hear stories repeated again and again, but Lucifer never wanted to listen to the story of his name after that. It was almost as if he felt tainted by the tale. Instead, he chose a new activity, which was to annoy his sister.

Although Katrianna and Lucifer were very close at a young age, cracks between them eventually occurred. Stelline would become upset every time the two of them arguing, which was quite often. Lucifer knew precisely how to push his sister's buttons, and he would tease her for hours. She only took it for so long and ended the fight by punching him in the face. He tried fighting back, but she was far stronger.

"When I'm older I'm going to take over the kingdom," Lucifer teased.

"Nuh, uh I AM! I'm older, and I will be the leader," she returned.

"No way. I'm a boy, and a stupid girl can't possibly be left in charge."

They would argue for hours about who would be a better ruler and why. Any argument usually ended badly for Lucifer, since his sister would bash him in the head. He would run screaming to his parents, who rarely took his side.

To make matters worse, Katrianna was given a chance to pick out a dragon to ride. Nothing like this was ever offered to Lucifer. He was extremely envious of her steed, and while he would never admit it, he desired one for himself. Even though her dragon was small by dragon standards ... it was still a dragon ... something he would never have.

As Katrianna grew older, she began showing signs of the power she would someday hold. She was strong, willful, and very stubborn, but she also had the capacity for great kindness. Her brother, on the other hand, was just as willful but lacked humility and compassion. Lucifer became more and more jealous of her as she blossomed. She could do things he couldn't, and it drove him mad. There was no way he could ever beat her in a physical fight, so Lucifer learned how to manipulate, and he did it quite well. Quite a few times Katrianna was a victim of Lucifer's ploys until she learned what he was actually doing.

Katrianna loved both her parents and had a special bond with her mother, but it was the bond with her father that eventually tore the twins apart. Lucifer hated seeing so much attention doted on his sister. Even though he knew deep down, it wasn't true, he felt like he wasn't loved enough. Every time Katrianna was showered with attention, he would start whining about how no one loved him. Zavier and Stelline grew weary of continually reassuring him and eventually quit trying to prove they loved him. No one could ever love Lucifer enough.

In time she noticed her brother was spending more time with their mother than by himself. At first, she didn't think anything of it. After a while, however, she noticed her mother became more and more depressed every time Lucifer finished chatting with her. Katrianna always tried to cheer her mother up, but Stelline was spiraling out of control. Nothing could be done to fix the situation. Lucifer didn't seem upset that his mother was having difficulties. In fact, he seemed rather happy about it. Katrianna couldn't prove it at the time, but she knew Lucifer was the reason her mother lost the will to live.

After Stelline's death, Katrianna became filled with anger. She hated her brother and took her rage out on him. He would take her punishments so he could whine to their father about how he was abused, and no one loved him. Zavier had a difficult time dealing with the loss of his wife and the workings of his realm, much less two children who hated each other. He was frustrated and exhausted.

When Katrianna became older, an opportunity arose, and she took it. The leader of a dragon realm in the Gerimel

Chain asked Zavier if he could train her. He recognized Katrianna's potential as well as her shortcomings and hoped to mold her. The leader of the dragon realm, Rivaclore wanted an alliance with Zavier. In time, Zavier hoped they could unite the realms with Katrianna leading an army of dragons and angels. It was a sad day for the kingdom when she left. Zavier missed her terribly, but he knew it was an opportunity he couldn't give her … a chance to learn from the dragons. Katrianna was more than happy to leave. Everything reminded her of her mother, and she couldn't stand being around Lucifer.

This wasn't the first time she had been to their realm. She went there with her father when she was young to select a steed. Katrianna didn't pick the biggest or strongest. She picked the dragon with the most heart. The two bonded on a spiritual level. In time, FireWind earned quite the name for himself.

The dragon realm, Meinashar had various natural environments much like Earth. Many different types of dragons lived on Meinashar. Dragons could be found on every realm in the universe, although they much preferred to live in their home realm. It was the only place they could truly feel at peace.

The fire dragons predominantly stayed in the fire lakes at the base of Mount Kerkel. Water dragons played in the ocean in the center of the realm. Ice dragons lived on the icy plains of Esacal. Poison dragons were the least liked by their kin and were 'asked' to stay far away because of their horrid stench. They made their home in a noxious swamp on the outskirts of the great desert where the sand dragons lived. A special breed of shadow dragon lived only on Mount Kerkel. There were small dragons which lived in the great forest and were often used as nursemaids.

Each type had their own unique abilities and could speak telepathically to each other as well as verbally. Human stories often spoke of fire-breathing dragons, whooshing through the air, slaughtering everyone with their fire. Dragons, particularly the fire breathers, had a bad reputation because they looked frightening. The fact was, dragons rarely bothered with people, placing them in a category of 'short-life' creatures. They mostly lived in peace with other realms and only went to war as a last resort. When they did however, they never stopped fighting until all their enemies were defeated.

Many dragons could breathe fire but needed to rest between burst of flames to restore their spark. Fire dragons were different, however. Their flame never died, which gave them the ability to breathe fire forever without resting. Their scales were shades of red and orange and they were relatively large. They used the fire lakes to restore their health by bathing in flames. All dragons believed in honor, but fire dragons were the proudest of all.

The sand dragons were the second largest type and weighed close to eight thousand pounds. They produced sandstorms to hinder a foe's activity and expelled a lethal mixture of fire and sand. They were chameleons and blended so well with their environment they became invisible … even to other dragons. They used this ability not only for surprise attacks in battle but also to startle their fellow dragons. They were known as pranksters with the uncanny ability to hide within seconds.

Poison dragons used fire to drive the poison from their mouths, killing anything instantly caught near the noxious cloud. Their height and weight were about average for a dragon with their skin color often green, red, or black. Their entire bodies leached poison and, although it didn't hurt the others, their stench was nauseating. They had nasty tempers and were mostly shunned by everyone else.

The ice, water, and shadow dragons didn't breathe fire at all. Ice dragons were the largest of all dragons. An adult could weigh up to twenty tons and easily have a wingspan of five hundred feet. They were usually blue, but some were black as well. They blew shards of ice which punctured their enemies and turned them into ice.

On the top of Mount Kerkel, time stood still. The shadow dragons wielded time as their weapon but were only called upon in battle as a last resort, because tampering with time was dangerous. They could increase or decrease time to their advantage. They were the oldest and wisest of the dragons. They only appeared as shadows flitting from place to place.

Water Dragons were smaller and the most agile of the dragon breeds. They had snake-like bodies and preferred to swim rather than walk. They were greenish blue in color with small legs and a flat tail for movement. Their wings were held tightly to their bodies as they swam. While they could fly, it took considerable effort. They shot streams of water at high speeds which stunned their adversaries. These dragons could breathe both water and air.

Dragons didn't have cities like humans, preferring to

live in their natural environment. There were only two buildings in the whole realm, the great hall of Delentar and Zavier's armory. Delentar was large enough to hold every dragon in the realm. It was where Rivaclore resided, the most magnificent dragon in existence. Rivaclore had all the abilities of each type of dragon and could flit between them when needed. He chose to teach Katrianna because she possessed abilities, he couldn't find in anyone else.

Under their tutelage, she unlocked the magic within her and became far stronger than anyone anticipated. She made peace with her mother's death and concentrated her efforts on reaching her potential. Katrianna also learned to sword fight, practicing constantly. The dragons enlisted the best trainer for her ... a man by the name of Alastar. He was short, athletic, and fast as the wind. His skin was the color of night, and his eyes were brilliant white. Many speculated about where he came from, surmising he was a dark elf who left his clan to find a better life. Everyone knew he was the best sword fighter in all the realms and an ideal teacher.

Alastar spent many hours every day instructing Katrianna on the fine arts of sword fighting. She picked up the skill easily but had difficulty learning the proper timing for striking. Patience was never her strong suit, and often lost matches because she rushed into a situation. He fooled her a few times by feinting attacks, but she learned to watch his movements and switched her strikes.

Her weapon of choice in the beginning was a rapier, but as her strength grew, she fell in love with the broad sword. In time, she became so advanced she easily bested him every time they fought. Alastar departed when there was nothing more to teach her, which saddened her greatly. He became her best friend, and she loved him like the brother she never had.

It was during the latter part of her training when she learned things were not going well back home. She was not happy when she discovered her father was away from the realm and placed Lucifer in charge. She heard whispers of what he was doing to their home, which upset her further. She felt she would have been a better choice. She didn't understand why her father hadn't even asked her to rule in his stead.

She lost herself in her training to push away the feelings of betrayal. The dragons taught her every kind of magic, including wielding time. She grew very powerful, and the dragons loved her. In time, she found peace living among them and learned to trust her heart. When she reached her potential, Rivaclore took her aside and told her she was to be given a special gift … a sword only the dragons could forge.

They crafted it in secret, forging their fire, ice, and poison into the blade. Rivaclore summoned her to the main hall, where he presented it to her. It was light as a feather and easy to wield despite its great size. There were symbols etched into the metal that only the dragons understood. She held it high above her and screamed, her voice echoing. Every dragon in the hall returned her cry with their own. The sound was deafening. After the ceremony, Rivaclore took her aside to speak with her in private.

"Youngling, do you know why I have chosen you?" he

asked her telepathically.

"No, but I am overwhelmed with gratitude," she returned, bowing.

The dragon chuckled before continuing.

"I don't think you will be so grateful in the future. I am giving you a great responsibility."

"I am to command the army then?" she asked.

"Yes youngling, you are."

"But … I'm not even a dragon. Why would they follow me?" Katrianna probed.

"Ah, but you are part dragon," he laughed. "as you know, your mother came from a long line of shape-shifting dragons."

"Are there any others… like me?"

"I am not sure, young one. I think you may be the last of your kind. Your soul is both angel and dragon."

"That explains my connection with dragons," she said softly, finally putting everything together.

"Yes. They will follow you to the end of all the realms," Rivaclore declared. "I am growing too old for war. It must be you who leads."

"But if I do this, I can never return home," she assumed.

"Nonsense," he chortled, "you may live wherever you choose. War is brewing on your realm. I can feel it in my bones. Your brother has committed many deplorable acts. He is selfish and greedy."

"My brother! I will have his head on this sword!" she swore.

"Remember youngling, death to save another can be justified. We only go to war if it's needed. Revenge is never a reason to go to war. It will leave you hollow and empty. If you follow that path, you will corrupt yourself."

Katrianna sighed, "I shall do my best to stay on the right path."

"Good. And remember for as long as you hold this sword, you will command my army."

Then Rivaclore did something she didn't expect. He grasped the sword with his long talon and plunged it into his chest. Katrianna gasped in horror as she thought he meant to kill himself. He smiled and gently pushed her aside. When he withdrew the sword a part of his soul attached to it making it glow brilliantly. As she grasped the hilt, a surge of energy poured through her. She couldn't let go of it. Katrianna screamed as the energy overcame her. When it was over, she lay panting on the ground.

"What happened?" she asked.

"I infused part of my soul with the sword. It is bound to you and will only answer to you. You will know where the sword is always, even if it isn't by your side. It is a part of you as you are of it. You can only be separated by death."

"Then I shall name it after you ... Rivaclore!" she shouted, thrusting the sword into the air.

It was shortly after she claimed her sword, she received word to come home. Her father returned only to find his realm in chaos. Everything was aflame both in heaven and on the mortal realm. Angels were beaten until they submitted to Lucifer's will. He unleashed his vile minions upon the earth, which were slaughtering everything. He was purposely trying to destroy everything their father held dear. Lucifer was surprised to see his father return, but he clearly didn't anticipate Katrianna's arrival.

"Katrianna!" he snarled. "you've come back. How lovely indeed."

Lucifer's soul was as black as his wings. She slowly unsheathed her sword and pointed it at him. It was the first time she saw real fear creep into his eyes, but it wouldn't be the last. Lucifer disappeared in a flash, taking all his demons with him. Zavier eventually purged the negativity from the realm, but it took an extensive amount of work. The realm had fallen almost entirely into darkness. The remaining human's and angels awoke from the nightmare to find their lives returned to somewhat normality.

"I'm sorry I didn't leave you in charge," Zavier apologized, shaking his head in sadness. "I've made many mistakes over the years, but this was one of the worst."

"Why didn't you, father? I never would have allowed this to happen."

"I didn't want to take you away from your training. Many will depend on you to defend them."

Katrianna grudgingly accepted his apology, and her father made her commander of the Red Wing warrior angels. Lucifer, on the other hand, was sent to another part of the kingdom until he could learn the error of his ways. He didn't learn, however. He unleashed a vast army, hoping to reclaim the Earth. Zavier knew Lucifer wasn't strong enough to conjure such a mass by himself. Lucifer made a deal with another evil force to acquire it. He released his

Crawlers and a plague of destruction.

Riding FireWind, Katrianna met him on the battlefield with her army of dragons and angels behind her. She used both magic and her sword to fight against them. She sliced through his army like butter. In the end, nothing remained of Lucifer's army, but a few wounded demons and some of the Crawlers. Lucifer slithered on the ground like a worm ready to be squashed. He screamed when her sword sliced his face. She was posed to take his head when Zavier stopped her. He separated his children, but not before Lucifer was able to whisper in her ear.

"Ah, my dear sister," he laughed, "you aren't allowed to kill me. I must say it gives me great pleasure to tell you I am responsible for taking away who you loved."

"WHAT!" she screamed, shaking him like a ragdoll.

"ENOUGH!" Zavier shouted, pulling her from him. "he will face a tribunal."

"But father …," she tried arguing.

"No! I won't hear another word about it."

It was at Lucifer's trial that Zavier banished him to an evil place called Hell. Zavier forbade Katrianna from pursuing her brother. She screamed in fury, determined to take Lucifer's head. She was thoroughly enraged her victory was stolen. Zavier thought his daughter would calm herself in time, but he was wrong. Katrianna was not so easily deterred … or placated. When her father was away on another realm, she took her sword and slipped into Hell. Lucifer seemed to know she was coming and made a grand spectacle of welcoming her to his home, which only infuriated her further.

"I'm *not* here for your hospitality. I demand to know what you meant … and I'm here for your head," she snarled.

"I'm just overwhelmed a creature as powerful as you would grace me with your presence. You're deliberately disobeying father … such a naughty girl," Lucifer mocked.

"Tell me now!" she hissed.

"What more can you do to me? You already marred my perfect face," he laughed.

She placed the tip of the blade at his throat.

"If you had spent more time learning about our parents, instead of playing with your stupid dragons, you might have known what I was up too," he sneered. "as you know, mother was a Dragon Angel. Funny fact about Dragon Angels … they hold onto their hearts for a very long time until they have found their soulmates. When they give their heart, they give it fully and never love another. That's what she did with father, but it wasn't hard to convince her, he had fallen for someone else. Ultimately, to break a Dragon Angels heart is to condemn her to death."

"What!" Katrianna gasped. "father loved mother to the ends of time, and she knew it!"

"She did know it … until I put a seed of doubt in her little mind. Every time she saw him with another female angel, she became more and more depressed. It wasn't long before she lost her will to live."

"WHY! Why would you do that to our mother! She loved us!" Katrianna screamed.

"Correction … she loved you. Everyone always preferred pretty little Katrianna to her brother. And you!" he snarled. "you rubbed it in my face! You were closest to our parents, you were chosen by the dragons, and you were put in command of the Red Wings! I have sat in your shadow long enough, dear sister."

"I will have your head for your treachery!" she screamed, raising her sword to strike.

"KATRIANNA STOP!" Zavier's voice echoed.

Zavier ordered her to return home. Katrianna protested, but Zavier wouldn't budge. He came close to removing her from command that day and looking back he wished he had. She knew she couldn't tell her father what Lucifer had done. It would have hurt him beyond measure, and she didn't want to take her revenge that way.

Zavier ordered her to the confinement of Eineitha, but she refused his command. The lust for vengeance was pounding in her ears. She gave up the authority of the Red Wings and called her army of dragons to her. Consumed by rage, she fled the realm and released her anger on any evil creature she found. Realm after realm fell into darkness as she swept over them killing everything … evil and good. Nothing could satiate her thirst for blood. In her blind rage, she tipped the balance of countless realms to evil and faced the punishment of the Old Ones. She became known as Katrianna the Reaper, and her command would be remembered for eternity.

She always felt the pulsing call of Rivaclore, but she could never touch it, and without her gifts, she felt empty. With only her anger as company, Katrianna raged against her father, her brother, and … herself. She wandered the darkness alone. The Old Ones told her she would only return when she could accept responsibility for the damage she caused under her command. That was ten thousand years ago.

Energy Unleashed
Chapter Thirteen

Nadia was mesmerized by the story. So many parts of it touched her soul, but it also raised a lot of questions. She eyed her aunt warily, wondering who she really was and how she knew so much.

"Let's begin your training," Lillya said after finishing a cup of coffee.

"Wait, wait, wait," Nadia protested, "you can't leave me hangin' like that."

"What else do you want to know?"

"Uh, for starters, where did you even here such a wild story? I've never even heard of this," Nadia asked, waving her hands in the air.

"So, because you haven't heard of something that makes it unreal?" Lillya asked, amused. "I suspect there's a lot you don't know."

"No, that's not it. I just … well, how do you even know this?"

"There are things from our past which remain hidden from us until it is time to remember," Lillya answered vaguely.

"How is it that God has kids? I mean Lucifer is God's son? How is that even possible?" Nadia protested.

"Zavier. His name is Zavier," Lillya corrected her.

"OK, Zavier. How …,"

"Nadia, do you really think people know everything there

is to know about the ruler of this realm? It boggles my mind when people assume they know everything and proceed to tell everyone how much they know. It's ridiculous! Why people think they're so bloody wonderful, they deserve to know everything is beyond me!" Lillya barked.

"I …," Nadia tried to speak, but her aunt continued her outburst.

"People like to put everything in a little box, stuff it away, and claim it's the truth just because they say so! Anyone who believes differently from them is considered a threat or simply stupid. It really burns me up!"

"I can see that Lillya," Nadia said. "I didn't mean to offend you. I just have trouble wrapping my mind around it."

"Don't overanalyze. Trust your instincts, and I know this story to be true because … I remember."

"You remember being told?"

"We need to get back to training," her aunt said, changing the subject. "I want to teach you how to throw your energy."

The finality of her aunt's tone told her not to push any further.

"OK," Nadia sighed.

A month into her training, Nadia could easily pull the energy from the earth. She used the same technique to draw energy from the universe. All it took was simply imagining the energy from the heavens coming down, bathing her in white light. The first time she did it, her whole body shook and buckled. It felt different than the energy from the earth … powerful yet refined. Eventually, she pulled energy from both places, which was almost overpowering.

230

More importantly, she learned how to control the energy she took, and stop the flow before it overwhelmed her. Every session exhausted her however, and it usually took several hours to recuperate. Nadia felt like she was learning how to walk all over again. Somehow, Nadia knew she always had the ability to tap into the energy streams, but her past negativity prevented her from reaching the light.

Nadia had an epiphany one day as she was brushing Gabriel. Her aunt had purposely waited to teach her magic until her anger and hatred had dissolved. It was a smart move on Lillya's behalf. If Nadia had known she was capable of working magic when she was in her dark place, she would have hurt everyone around her. It would have been disastrous for her karma. Nadia would have become a corrupt soul, stuck in a never-ending cycle of pain.

Lillya was an excellent teacher. She always explained how to work with energy and demonstrated several times before allowing her to try. Once Nadia got the hang of things, it didn't take her long to learn new tasks. As always, before they began a lesson, Lillya had her close her eyes and center herself. It was far easier to work with energy when one was calm.

For this particular lesson, Nadia called the energy and pulled it towards her hands. The idea was for Nadia to hold it like she was holding a ball. The energy collected between her fingertips would form into a sphere. Most people wouldn't be able to see the energy, but they would feel the effects. The goal of this task was to gather the energy and toss it to her aunt. The energy was mostly clear, however magic users could produce a color, by merely willing it.

Lillya's color was usually green, but for this lesson she chose yellow.

When Lillya demonstrated the technique, Nadia could see a glowing yellow ball between her fingertips. Nadia chose blue because she liked the color. She could easily form a sphere but had great difficulty throwing it. Whenever she tried, the energy seemed to dissipate.

"ARHHHHH!" she yelled in frustration.

"Relax, or you will never be able to do it," Lilly instructed.

"But I can't do this! I can't concentrate enough to keep it in a ball shape," Nadia complained.

"You can, Nadia," Lilly encouraged her. "search deep within yourself."

"Easier said than done," Nadia grumbled.

She closed her eyes, feeling the energy around her. Nadia liked to call it 'powering up', even though her aunt told her countless times she wasn't in a video game. The energy always made her feel powerful and a little giddy. Nadia slowly called it into her hands and delved deep into herself. Strange images suddenly surfaced into her consciousness. She lost track of time as these images came into focus. Nadia saw dragons of all shapes and colors flying across the sky. There were so many they blotted out the sun. They roared in unison as they continued their journey.

"Where are they going?" she wondered to herself.

Abruptly she saw an image of a hideous demon. It snarled at her with a mouthful of teeth. She screamed at the top of her lungs and launched a ball of energy, completely forgetting she was traveling internally. The energy flew from her hands and straight into the side garage door, narrowly missing the Jeep. A massive boom echoed throughout the small space as her energy ripped through the door, shredding it to pieces. Shards of wood and glass exploded outwards. Nadia was shocked when she opened her eyes. She tried apologizing to Lillya, but she began to lose consciousness. Her aunt caught her before she hit the ground. Nadia briefly heard her speak before she fell into darkness.

"Oh well. I needed a new door anyway," Lillya chuckled.

When Nadia opened her eyes, she found herself in a strange room. The walls were made entirely of moss with an old, gnarled tree in the middle. She stood up, feeling a little like Alice in Wonderland. Her hands stroked the walls, letting the soft moss caress her fingertips. Nadia inhaled deeply, enjoying the earthy fragrance. A sudden flutter in the tree caught her attention. A little blue dragon plopped from the leaves, landing at her feet.

"RORT!" she exclaimed, scooping the dragon up in her arms.

Rort? Nadia knew that name.

"It's so good to see you again!" he purred excitedly.

"You have changed a bit little one," Nadia said in that silky voice, which wasn't her own.

"Where are we?" Rort asked.

"How the hell should I know?" Nadia wanted to answer.

"This is a room I used when I needed peace. I came here

a lot," she laughed. "Come, let us walk."

Nadia pushed a branch on the tree. A doorway opened inside, which led to a dark hallway. The little dragon fluttered to her shoulders and nestled next to her collar. His tail circled her neck like an ornate necklace. He settled himself and began purring.

"Are we going to the door?" Rort asked.

"What door?" Nadia's internal voice asked.

"Yes. I can feel it. It's getting stronger," she said.

"I have felt it too," Rort agreed.

"What are you talking about!" Nadia shouted but no one answered.

Nadia walked a long way until she came to a stone door. She gently placed her right hand on it, desperately wanting what was on the other side.

"When will the door open?" Rort asked.

"When it is time I suppose," she answered slowly.

"When what is time? Why is everyone always talking about time!" Nadia yelled.

"What will you do when you have it?" Rort pondered.

"Go to Disneyworld?" Nadia answered.

"Attempt to correct my wrongs. There is a great deal of unfinished business between my family and me. I made horrible mistakes in the past. I have hurt so many because of my selfish behavior."

"Well, I still love you," Rort admitted, emitting a puff a smoke.

She burst out laughing.

"Thanks, Rort. I love you too."

She reached up and scratched the dragon's head. It wiggled trying to get closer to her.

A strange pungent odor took her away from everything. She blinked her eyes and coughed before realizing she was lying on the floor in her aunt's arms. Lillya was running something vile under her nose.

"I'm OK," Nadia gasped, pushing the ammonia capsule away.

"Welcome back. That was quite a surge of power."

"I'm sorry about your door," Nadia mumbled.

"It's fine. What happened exactly? How were you able to finally collect your energy?" Lillya asked.

Nadia rubbed her head, trying to remember. When the memories returned, she told Lillya about seeing the flying dragons. The vision of the demon sent her energy exploding from her.

"Ahhhhh, I understand now. That makes sense."

"It does?" Nadia asked.

"Yes. Interesting enough, you have discovered another talent … remote viewing. It's the ability to see things far away as clearly as you can see them in front of you. Think of it as creating a portal. It's difficult to learn, and most cannot see anything, but sporadic pictures. Once a person has mastered it, he or she can see things anywhere on any realm. Very few people are that powerful, though."

"Really? Can you do it?"

"Of course," Lillya chuckled. "when my sister and I were very young, we used to play hide and seek and use our talents to find each other. After a while, the game lost its appeal because we always knew where the other was hiding."

"That's cool."

"When we played hide and seek with the neighborhood children, we made them uncomfortable because we found everyone quickly. It wasn't our fault. We just closed our eyes and saw them. Our friends began shunning us. After a while, your mother's gifts made her feel like a freak."

"I think it's cool. It makes me feel like a mutant," Nadia gushed.

Nadia jumped into the air, giving her best Wolverine impression. Her talent was utterly wasted on her aunt, who simply chuckled and shook her head.

"You know… mutants from X-Men?"

Lillya just shrugged her shoulders.

"So, I saw actual dragons flying?" Nadia finally asked.

"Yes."

"And the demon?" Nadia pushed, curling her lip.

"Yes again," Lillya repeated.

"So, what happened to it?"

Her aunt closed her eyes, placed her hands together, and touched her forehead. She appeared to be in deep thought. Nadia wondered what she was doing and impatiently waited for her to speak.

"You destroyed it," Lillya said, finally opening her eyes.

236

"Really?" Nadia asked, surprised.

"Yes. Although the majority of your energy found my door, a portion of it went through your portal and hit the demon. It shattered into a million pieces. So, thanks to you there is one less demon in the world torturing people."

"YES! Nadia screamed. "I AM A DEMON SLAYER! Uh-huh, uh-huh."

She strutted around the garage like Mick Jagger. When she saw her aunt scowling, she stopped in her tracks.

"Killing one demon hardly makes you a demon slayer, young lady and you have to be careful with that."

"What? Why? What's wrong?"

"Remember the balance? If you go around destroying demons, then you could tip the balance," Lillya explained.

"So what? The world would be better off if we tipped it towards good anyway," Nadia protested.

"Oh, really? How are you so sure? Are you now the master of all knowledge? There are reasons for everything. This is beyond you, dear … beyond me."

"I don't understand," Nadia said, shaking her head in confusion.

"Often, bad things happen to people to help them learn from their mistakes. If the balance were tipped to good, no one would need to improve. They would become slovenly and self-serving creatures, which ultimately would make them evil. This has happened in the past on other realms. Many times, bad things happen to people because people themselves cause it. They think horrible negative thoughts, so negativity is what's returned to them. When they hurt people, they damage their own karma, and it comes around to hurt themselves. Demons are sometimes used to test us, but we aren't alone in the fight."

"Are you saying I deserved what happened to me?" Nadia asked, her voice rising.

"Someone must have thought so, or they wouldn't have been there."

"WHAT! I didn't do anything. I was a little kid when these demons started fuckin' with me. And what about my family! What did they do to deserve it?" Nadia yelled.

"Your family knew what was going on, especially your mother. As much as they didn't want to admit it, they saw the demons too. They just didn't see them as you saw them. They could have fought against them, but they chose to suffer instead."

"Why! Why would they choose that?" Nadia screeched.

"I don't know, but many people choose suffering over fighting," Lillya said, calmly. "Sometimes, it's easier."

"Easier! It sure as hell wasn't easier for me! Why did I have to suffer!" Nadia demanded.

"Perhaps to learn a lesson … a lesson in this life or another. One has to know darkness before they can step into the light."

Nadia wanted to scream. She could feel her energy building, she was calling it to her without even thinking. The air began to sizzle and pop. She wanted to fling her energy and blow the garage roof from the rafters. She probably would have … if her aunt hadn't stop her. Lillya put her hand gently on Nadia's forehead. Strange voices filled Nadia's mind. They were in a language she couldn't fully understand, but they touched her, nonetheless. They robbed her of anger, and a great calm overtook her.

"I'm sorry," Nadia mumbled, feeling weary.

"It's fine. You should go to sleep. Tomorrow we shall take a little trip."

Nadia fell into bed and slept without dreaming. When she awoke, she felt refreshed and positive. The cats, which now slept with her every night, meowed when they saw she was awake. She petted them, attempting to give each one ample attention. When they were satisfied, they jumped off the bed and ran out of the room. She yawned, feeling sore from the previous day's events. She dressed quickly, the smell of food driving her into the kitchen.

Lillya made her delicious crepes for breakfast and afterward took her to a 'special place'. Nadia pestered her about it, but all she would say was, 'you'll see'. They drove for 30 minutes before coming to a gate. The sign, BADLANDS NATIONAL PARK was next to a gate. Lillya paid an astronomically high price to get inside. The moment they drove through, Nadia was hit with an energy surge.

"Whoa! You feel that?" Nadia asked, rubbing her temples.

"I do. The earth here holds a great amount of energy. It's my favorite place in South Dakota."

"Because of the energy?"

"No. Because of the beauty," Lillya said.

The park was filled with tourists running everywhere snapping pictures. Nadia did her best to ignore them and focus on the energy surrounding her. It was so intense it gave her a headache. A long winding road took them deep into the park.

Nadia had never seen such a strange landscape. It looked like something on an alien planet. The earth was dry, cracked, but mostly stable to walk on. Sharp clay formations jutted out wildly, before round and square mounds. From a distance, she could see pointed peaks everywhere. There were thousands of acres of scarred and broken earth and the colors … the colors were breathtakingly beautiful. Lines of brown, red, and green were etched in the earth. In a few areas, the mounds were completely yellow or pink.

It was unreal and certainly different from anything she had seen in the Northeast. Nadia thumbed through the brochure they received at the front gate. According to it, there were thousands of fossils in the dirt, including Saber Tooth Tiger bones. She vaguely remembered reading something a while ago about a little girl who found a Saber Tooth Tiger skeleton while visiting the park with her parents.

"Hey, if I find a dinosaur bone, can I keep it?" Nadia asked suddenly.

"No. You are not allowed to take anything from the park. If you find a dinosaur bone, you must report it," Lillya explained.

"Lame!" Nadia protested.

As they drove deeper into the park, Nadia became nauseous. The energy from the ground was intensifying. Everything seemed to pulse with a heartbeat. She wondered what happened to the earth to make it so powerful. Her

240

aunt pulled over to the side and told her to get out of the car. Nadia could barely move. The constant pounding of energy gave her a migraine. She looked around the area. It was full of tourists leaping from one mound to the next. They were seemingly unaffected by it.

Nadia followed Lillya to an overlook. There were no guard rails or fences anywhere. If anyone stepped too close to the edge, it would be a disaster. The fall to the bottom was at least seventy-five feet. There were mean looking cacti at the bottom of the ravine. The ground was so dry, it was like stepping on powder. One wrong move would send a person sliding. Nadia stepped carefully, but her aunt seemed to almost float from one knoll to the next. She led her far away from the tourists.

The view was incredible. The mounds and peaks filled the vast valley before them. Far off in the distance, Nadia could see a mountainous ridge. The sight filled her with a sense of nostalgia, but she didn't know why. The energy's source seemed to emanate from this place. The air was thick as the sun beat down upon them. Nadia squinted and let the waves of power wash over her. It made her insanely tired. She wanted to curl up in a ball and fall asleep.

"Wha ... what happened here?" Nadia stammered.

Her voice sounded faint as if she were speaking through a cloth.

"A great battle," Lillya said slowly.

Nadia glanced behind them and saw more families pouring into the parking area. They were snapping pictures as their children played.

"Why can't they feel it? The energy from this place is insane. I can barely move because it makes me so tired," Nadia puffed.

"Most of them are young souls and have no connections with their inner selves. They live in the now, and their only concerns are material possessions. Some of them can feel it, though. Over by the railing … see that little boy who's clutching his head? He feels it. He just doesn't know what he's feeling."

"The brochure said this place was underwater and that's what caused the landscape. When did this battle happen?" Nadia asked.

"Eons ago … on an entirely different realm. It was so powerful it bled through many realms, tainting the very ground."

"You talk about realms all the time Lillya. What is a realm? Like a kingdom or something?" Nadia slurred.

The energy seemed to pulse.

"Somewhat. A realm is a different plane of existence," Lillya explained. "have you ever seen something out of the corner of your eye, but when you turned to look at it, nothing was there?"

"Yea, but I just thought it was a ghost or something."

"Sometimes it is, and sometimes you are simply seeing something on a different realm. Think of it as layers on top of each other, occupying the same space, but a different time," Lillya answered.

"How many realms are there?"

"Trillions. Too many to count," Lillya explained.

242

"Wow, that's nuts! And all these realms have people on them?" Nadia asked.

"Not hardly. There are different types of life forms in every realm. Realms are clustered into Chains or groups much like planets are to galaxies. This realm is called Meifilar, and we live on Parium. There are many other planets in this realm which sustain life, but I don't know all their names. Meifilar is part of the Delaphina Chain which has several hundred realms in it, each having their own ruler."

"Does the Delaphina Chain have a ruler?" Nadia asked.

"Long ago it did. Supposedly the Delaphina Chain was much larger. Something happened and the Chain imploded, killing the ruler. Now it's too small for an overseer. This realm has an identical sister realm located in the Nanalder Chain. That Chain contains millions of kingdoms and is ruled by Arcen, who certainly does consider himself a God."

"Who rules the twin realm?" Nadia probed, growing more confused.

"Zavier's twin brother, Shivet," Lillya said.

"Twin realms ruled by twin brothers? That's nuts! Who runs the whole thing?"

"That would be the council of the Old Ones."

"So, there's another Earth too?" Nadia guessed.

"Yes. It's identical to ours in many ways."

"Does that mean there is another Nadia and Lillya on the other Earth?" Nadia asked.

"No. Although the planets are similar, the souls are different," Lillya replied.

Nadia was totally confused by her aunt's explanation of the realms. She decided to change the subject.

"Weird. A battle caused all this?"

"Yes. There was once a young peasant man named Rexeral, who was tricked into serving the evil ruler, Gimindorf. Rexeral knew how to wield his energy but had no idea how powerful he was. Gimindorf promised him his daughter if he supported his army against his enemies. Rexeral agreed since Gimindorf's daughter was considered the most beautiful woman in the land."

"Typical man!" Nadia snorted. "never mind if she has a brain. It's all about how she looks!"

"Yes well, when Rexeral was on the battlefield, he siphoned energy from the heavens and poured it into the ground to create a barrier. It was so powerful when the initial opposing forces charged, their flesh was ripped from their bodies. Rexeral finally realized his true strength and became mad with power. He began summoning cosmic amounts of energy to engulf the entire opposing army. He dispensed so much energy the earth began to buckle. Chasms opened swallowing both sides. Rexeral saw the carnage he was unleashing but didn't stop driving the energy into the earth. Some say he couldn't stop."

"So, what happened?" Nadia asked.

"His energy laid waste to the entire kingdom. Gimindorf's castle exploded into splinters, killing both him and his beautiful daughter. Wave after wave punished the earth and spread into other realms. Rexeral laughed wildly when the castle fell. He relished his power, pushing himself to destroy everything in his sight," Lillya continued.

244

"What a douche bag! How did it end?"

"Very badly. The heavens decided they gave enough of their energy and terminated the flow ... permanently. The Old Ones stripped him of his powers and cursed him to wander the land for millions of years as a shadow ... never able to touch anyone again. When he realized what he had done, he was shattered. He wanted nothing more than death, but the Old Ones were not so merciful to grant him a quick end. He lost everything, including his soul. Today, he wanders his own kingdom as a wraith, overcome with anguish. His howls of torment are even heard in other realms."

"Wow," Nadia said quietly.

"I brought you here for a reason. This place serves as a reminder to what can happen if our gifts claim us. Rexeral was a kind young man, and it didn't take long for a taste of power to corrupt him entirely. This incident happened long ago on an entirely different realm, and yet we still feel the effects of it today."

"I understand," Nadia said.

"Good," Lillya chuckled. "now let's get out of here."

Nadia stumbled to the car, losing her balance several times. She was more than happy to leave the park. It was beautiful and yet foreboding at the same time. She thought about her aunt's explanation of the realms. Once again, Nadia was amazed by the amount of information Lillya knew.

Redemption
Chapter Fourteen

Lucifer was growing impatient. He found being forced to wait insulting. He arrived at Galvadar only to be told the council was in session. He demanded to be seen at once, but a large male centaur refused to let him in, mocking him. Lucifer tried using magic but failed miserably. As part of his punishment, he was restricted to the places he could travel. Lucifer rarely left Hell anyway, preferring the stench of corruption above anything else. Galvadar was far too peaceful for him. He felt uncomfortable and was eager to leave. A centaur guarded the entrance to the Old One's chamber. The beast was less than helpful.

"No, I will not interrupt the council just so you can speak with them. They are busy," the centaur asserted, stomping his hoof.

"You INGRATE! Do you know who I am!" Lucifer bellowed.

"No. Should I?" the centaur asked, laughing.

"I AM LUCIFER!"

"Who? Is that name supposed to mean something to me?"

"I would certainly think so, you filthy mare!"

"Insulting me will not get you into the council any quicker," the centaur smirked. "I suggest you take a seat and wait. When the council is finished, I'll inform them they have a visitor. Of course, they may choose not to see you. I suggest you try a little humility … fallen one."

Lucifer stewed in the corner, his wings flexing every few moments. He couldn't sit still for very long. He got up and paced around the room, much to the amusement of the centaur. After weeks of waiting, the guard finally told him he could see the Old Ones, but not before he explained the rules of conduct. Lucifer didn't want to hear any rules however, claiming he was above them. He stormed into the chamber and addressed the council without waiting to be acknowledged. They quickly put him in his place.

"I DEMAND TO KNOW WHAT'S GOING ON!" Lucifer screamed, his wings trembling with fury.

The council paused before speaking.

"You will adjust your tone and address us properly, son of Zavier or you will be removed from here … forever," the council said, speaking in unison.

Lucifer choked down his anger and bowed, waiting to be addressed.

"That is much better, youngling," they chimed together. "now tell us what vexes you so."

"I have heard," Lucifer began, choosing his words carefully, "that my father has brought Katrianna back."

"Your father is not capable of such a feat."

"But …," Lucifer paused, calming himself, "that is not what I have been told."

"Then you have been told a lie."

"Could it be that you're wrong?" Lucifer asked, his teeth clenched.

"No, youngling." The council answered. "we know all that

248

is happening, and all that will happen. We know everyone's fate, including your own. Now if that is all, we really have other things to attend to."

"That is not all … please. I have a question."

They patiently waited for him to continue. They knew he was having trouble containing his anger. They telepathically communicated among themselves as he paused. Lucifer was just like many other younglings, selfish and self-centered, refusing to learn any lessons no matter how long they were punished. Lucifer managed to fool himself into believing he was happy with his position and his actions, but the Old Ones knew better. They knew he was miserable, which was the reason he had difficulty controlling his anger. Anger was usually a byproduct of something greater, and in Lucifer's case, it was despair.

Lucifer was not only a disappointment to his father, but to the Old Ones as well. The coupling of Zavier and his Dragon Angel bride produced two of the most beautiful and powerful children in all the realms. Unfortunately, they both were headstrong. Lucifer and Katrianna gave into their selfishness and anger. He was almost beyond redemption, but his sister was not. She would only return after being tested.

During her banishment, she spent the first thousand years consumed by anger and fury. Unable to use her powers, she fell into a black abyss. Katrianna wanted nothing more than to be unmade and begged for it, screaming to the heavens. She lost her mind in the darkness. After several thousand years, she finally began to realize why she had been punished.

Zavier pleaded for Katrianna to be reborn as a human to finish her life lessons. He made an interesting point and swayed them. They didn't want Zavier to know exactly who she was, lest he be tempted to help her. They were sure he suspected the body her soul occupied. Only as a human could she understand what humans went through every single day of their lives. Being mortal was never easy. Most times, humans repeated the same mistakes, causing them to be continually reborn. Their trials and tribulations were epic compared to most creatures in other realms. They had such high capacity for kindness … and destruction.

Lucifer closed his eyes, fighting to regain his composure.

"Yes?" they asked weary of his stalling.

"Is it true my father cannot directly interfere with his realm?" he asked, eager to know the answer.

"That we cannot tell you," they insisted.

"Cannot or will not?" Lucifer hissed.

"Both. If you really want to know, I suggest you ask your father. Now … leave us."

Lucifer had reached his boiling point. He spun on his heels and headed for the door. His feet stopped before leaving the chamber. Quaking with fury, he turned and screamed at them.

"YOU ARE WORTHLESS CREATURES UNWORTHY OF YOUR POWER!"

"You are dismissed youngling," the council concluded, shaking their heads.

He returned to Hell, feeling defeated and furious. He

should have known they wouldn't tell him anything. They sat upon their thrones, doing nothing. Lucifer wanted to unleash the Crawlers upon them, but first, he would have to deal with his father … and his sister. It was unfortunate he didn't realize they knew everything he was planning.

Nezatel slipped into Hell via the secret gate. He knew immediately Lucifer wasn't there. The air always felt lighter when Lucifer wasn't in Hell. The demon was relieved. It would be easier to carry on his task without his master's presence. He searched for Yarish and found him supervising a group of demons torturing fresh souls. Yarish liked to be the first one who greeted the fresh meat. It gave him great pleasure to take their hope away. Yarish was a vile, deplorable creature and Nezatel couldn't wait to be done with him … and Hell for that matter. He sauntered up to Yarish and addressed him.

"Doing some work for a change, Yarish?" Nezatel snorted.

"Nezatel!" Yarish barked as he spun around. "where have ye been? Lucifer has been lookin' fer ye. He has a task fer ye."

"Ah but Lucifer isn't here, is he?"

"Never mind! Don't ye be disappearin'. When he gets back, he be wantin' to see ye."

"Of course," Nezatel simpered, giving Yarish a quick salute.

Yarish scowled at Nezatel and returned to his victims, but Nezatel wasn't quite finished with him.

"I certainly can understand why you are so angry, Yarish. I would be angry too if I knew I was going to be replaced … by an angel nonetheless."

Yarish turned his head, his eyes bulging.

"Wha' did ye say?" Yarish hissed.

"Your position … I would be mad too if it were promised to someone else. You must be doing a terrible job if Lucifer thought an angel could do better," Nezatel laughed.

Yarish grabbed Nezatel roughly and led him away from everyone.

"Ye worm! Ye better tell me what ye be barkin' on about!"

"Well, you see, Lucifer promised your job to Firthel. Of course, that was before the disastrous battle that never happened. Still, it would upset me greatly to know my work mattered so little to my boss, he should replace me with an angel … someone who didn't even earn the title of demon."

"YE LIE!" Yarish screeched.

"Well yes, I am a demon, after all. We demons aren't known for our honesty. I am telling the truth, however."

Yarish grabbed Nezatel by his neck and pulled him to his face. He wanted to rip Nezatel's head off.

"Ask him if you don't believe me," Nezatel said, smirking. "let's see if he can convince you."

Yarish threw Nezatel down and began pacing.

"Why are ye tellin' me this!" Yarish growled.

"I don't like you Yarish, but you are far more competent than the previous head demons," Nezatel said, smoothly. "I would want to know if my job was in jeopardy. Ask him

252

when he returns."

"I will!" Yarish roared.

Nezatel skipped away from Yarish and happily headed for the secret gate, knowing his last task in Hell was complete. He wished he could have stayed and seen the chaos unfold, but it was better to disappear before Lucifer returned. He stepped through the gate, eager to begin his life anew and amend his wrongs. Zavier was waiting for him with a smile on his face. He shook his head with laughter when Nezatel told him what he had done.

"It is time Renuphen. Close your eyes," Zavier instructed.

Nezatel did as he was told and felt Zavier's hands upon his head. A warm feeling of peace overcame him as Zavier began chanting in an ancient language. Suddenly, a white light pierced his skull, and he felt pain course through him. Within moments his whole body felt like it was aflame. He began screaming in agony. Nezatel didn't know how long the transformation would take, but it felt like the pain continued for hours. When he opened his eyes, everything was blurry. He tried to walk, but his legs failed him, and he crumpled to the floor.

Every few moments, a spasm of agony carved through his body, making him writhe in misery. His back hurt the worst. It felt like someone was slicing him open with a filet knife. His eyes rolled back into his head as he squirmed and convulsed, wanting nothing more than death at the moment. Death wouldn't come, however. Through his closed eyes, he saw every victim he had ever hurt and the results of his influence. Nezatel cried as waves of guilt encased him. Of all the different types of pain he had experienced during his transformation, this was by far the worst.

Memory after memory assaulted him until he thought he would lose his mind. After an immeasurable amount of time, the memories ceased. It took him some time to realize his ordeal was over. He stood up slowly, his face wet from tears. He looked at his hands and didn't recognize them. They were smooth and blue. He raced to a nearby mirror and was astonished to see his reflection. It had been such a long time since he saw himself as an angel. He touched his face, unbelieving. He was no longer hideous and appeared just as he remembered … blue flesh, broad face, and milky white eyes. He flexed his beautiful white wings and enjoyed the sound of feather's rustling.

"Tha … thank you," he said to Zavier, falling to his knees.

"Welcome home Renuphen!" Zavier announced.

"Tell me about my mother," Nadia asked.

"What do you want to know?"

"Well, mostly her childhood. She never talked about it, even though I asked her many times."

"And for good reason," Lillya clucked. "we were six when we discovered we were different. There were always ghosts around us, wanting to chat. At first, we were scared, but in time, we got used to seeing them. We began playing games with them. After a while, we discovered some of our other gifts, and that's when things became scary."

"Really?" Nadia gaped.

254

"When someone manipulates energy without protection, they can attract all kinds of nasty things … dark things."

"Like demons?"

"Yes, as well as other creatures. It just so happened we enticed a demon, your mother eventually named Roy. In the beginning, he pretended to be our friend, appearing as a small boy. I knew there was something wrong with him, though."

"Demons can appear as something else? Mine never did," Nadia admitted.

"It all depends on the strength of the demon. Your demons were trying to scare you, so they appeared as their true form. It takes an enormous amount of energy for them to manifest. That's why the air often feels cold when a demon or a spirit appears. They take it from the air."

"Yea! I didn't think about it at the time, but our house was always cold, especially the cellar!" Nadia exclaimed.

"Well, as soon as 'Roy' entered the picture, your mother began to change. She became angry when he was around. Roy whispered in her ear, and she would giggle cruelly. He tore a rift between us. After we turned twelve, Roy convinced your mother to push a girl down the escalator at the mall. Our parents took us there to shop for school clothes. I saw Roy whisper in her ear. I will never forget the look in her eyes right before she shoved that little girl."

"Oh, my god! What happened?"

"The girl fell and tumbled all the way to the bottom. Everyone started screaming at once. My sister just stared like she couldn't believe what happened. That's when I knew what Roy was … and I think your mother did too."

"Did the girl die?"

"No, the girl lived, but she was paralyzed from the waist down. No one blamed your mother. They assumed it was an accident. That was when your mother refused to believe in her gifts. She was depressed and scared for a long time. When she finally emerged from her sadness, she acted like the incident never happened."

"What happened to Roy?" Nadia asked, reeling from this news.

"Ultimately, I was able to drive him from the house. I fully accepted my gifts after my little stint in the mental hospital. My powers grew, and I drove anything dark from my home. I protected the family, even though I couldn't figure out how to stop them from invading my dreams for a long time. I used to have horrific nightmares," Lillya said, shuddering.

"What about the girl my mother pushed?"

"She's still alive and made something of her life. She's a brilliant painter," Lillya chimed.

"Wow," Nadia breathed. did my mom ever apologize to her?"

"No. Whenever I brought it up, she told me it never happened."

The story about her mother was very enlightening and sad. It explained why her mother was punished by Nadia's demons years later. It made Nadia hate them even more.

Lucifer immediately called a meeting with his generals when he returned. He was in a foul mood as usual, and everyone tiptoed around him … everyone except Yarish. The head demon slammed his fist onto the table, drawing immediate attention to himself. He sat stewing, ready to explode.

"You wish to address the council, Yarish?" Lucifer growled.

"No! I will address ye in private!"

"I don't have time to listen to your petty issues. We have a problem."

"Ye be right! We do have a problem, Lucifer!" Yarish hollered.

The rest of the council looked at each other warily, unsure of what was going on. The situation made them highly uncomfortable.

"Perhaps we should discuss what the Old Ones told you," Mortoc interjected, hoping to ease the tension.

"I BE NOT FINISHED SPEAKIN'!" Yarish shouted.

"Yarish, you have two seconds to get whatever it is off your chest before I punish you in unspeakable ways," Lucifer snarled, barely containing his anger.

"Have I not bin a faithful servant to ye? Have I not done everythin' ye asked for?" Yarish sneered.

"Yes. I don't know where this is …,"

"Then WHY," Yarish interrupted, "would ye promise my job … to … an … angel! To that scumbag Firthel!"

Lucifer's eyes widened. No one could have known that.

He didn't know what upset him more, being addressed so disrespectfully or Yarish knowing the truth. He was more concerned with how Yarish discovered the information. The council leaned forward in their chairs, unsure of what was happening. Lucifer knew he had to take control of the situation and fast.

"Who told you that?" Lucifer asked.

"Never ye mind who told me! Tis true. I can see it in ye eyes!" Yarish shouted.

The council glared at Lucifer. They knew he often made shady deals but making a closed-door pact with a traitor made them all feel betrayed.

"I hardly think it is …," Lucifer tried to say before Yarish bellowed.

"How could ye be offerin' my job to Firthel! Ye didn't even know him. He was a liar and ye put your faith into him. Sometimes I wonder what goes on in ye head to make such stupid decisions! YE be the one who should be replaced, not me!"

Yarish knew he crossed the line, but he didn't care. He was well beyond rage. The council held their breaths because they knew what was coming.

"HOW DARE YOU SPEAK TO ME IN SUCH A MANNER!" Lucifer screeched.

He grabbed Yarish by his arm, wrenching him to his feet. He reached inside the body of his head demon and took hold of his soul. Without hesitation, he ripped Yarish's soul from his body and threw the remains to the ground like garbage. Lucifer then broke the soul in half, forever destroying it. He slammed his fist onto the new table. The force of his blow sent the council flying in all directions. His eyes were blazing, echoing a murderous rage inside. None of the council spoke, for fear they would be the next victim.

"NOW IF THERE ARE NO MORE INTERRUPTIONS, WE CAN START THE MEETING!" Lucifer screamed, eyeing each demon in the room.

No one spoke. They held their eyes downward and waited for him to continue.

"The Old Ones refused to tell me anything. Even after all his crimes, they still insist on protecting my father," Lucifer huffed.

"What would you have us to do?" Elistax asked tentatively.

"I am finished with waiting! Now it is time for action. I don't know if Firthel was telling the truth, but I'll force my father from hiding. He will either meet me on the battlefield or allow me to ravage his realm. Katrianna is still banished and therefore, not a threat."

"YES!" Mortoc shouted, ready to begin the war.

"Once I am certain my father cannot interfere, I will release the Varafe to scourge the Earth," Lucifer continued, "but they will be the last to leave. I want to see if my father tries to stop me first."

Lucifer knew he would have to send the Varafe in waves. As soon as their power began diminishing, the next band would depart Hell. This way, he would always have a fresh batch ready for battle. He would use the Waru to do much of the fighting. When the balance was tipped, he would launch an attack on his father.

"Finally, we can shed some blood!" Elistax proclaimed.

"I cannot afford to lose any of you. Return as soon as you feel your power lessening," Lucifer ordered.

"Yes, my lord!" she shouted.

"I want every demon available to fight. I want them to influence, possess, manipulate, and I want them ready in seven days. Do I make myself clear!" Lucifer commanded.

"YES!" They cried in unison.

"Now, leave me. I have many things to prepare, and someone find me Nezatel."

The council left in a hurry. They were eager to begin the preparations. Finally, they could amass the upper surface in thousands. Nothing would stand in their way … not even the Red Wings.

Aiding the Defenseless
Chapter Fifteen

Lillya insisted Nadia take the last month of summer off. She thought Nadia was pushing herself too hard. It was taking her longer and longer to recover. As a diversion, they went hiking in the Black Hills almost daily. At first, Nadia couldn't hike for long, but in time, she grew strong and lean. Lillya explained how everything has energy which can be used … but never misused. One of the most significant sources of living energy was the trees. Trees were interconnected with each other through their roots. If you took energy from one, the others would share as well. Lillya liked helping the trees by pushing her energy into them. Nadia watched her aunt heal many dying plants with just her touch.

Rocks held a great amount of energy as well. Like trees, a person could put their energy into rocks. Lillya called it 'charging'. Rocks maintained whatever energy they received for a long time. Lillya often gave charged rocks to people who were depressed and needed a boost. It always seemed to help them. Her aunt despised people who put negativity into them to hurt people. She would rant about it for hours.

Nadia loved it when her aunt went on her tirades. Lillya used words like 'rubbish' and 'poppycock' which was amusing. Sometimes Nadia would ask her aunt questions just to listen to her heated lectures. Lillya hated people who 'dabbled' with magic. She called them fools.

"People who experiment with energy without putting

hard work into it are completely ignorant," Lillya criticized. "these people don't want to learn anything except how to cast spells. Stupid fools!"

Nadia smiled. Her aunt always sounded British when she used the word 'fools'.

"These morons do so much damage. They don't realize they draw dark entities to them by playing with energy. Then they become puppets, hurting people as they play. Everyone has gifts to some degree, but there are some ... like us who can actually do real magic, not that rubbish you see in the movies."

"What about witches?" Nadia asked, purposely egging on her aunt. "can they do real magic?

"HA!" Lillya snarled. "witches! I have known many wiccans and other spiritualists who run around, claiming they are grandmasters or high priestesses. It's all about their personal glory and attention. I prefer those in Earth-based religions who do their best to help others. Unfortunately, there are many who simply interfere with the natural flow of things. Morons! Never dabble with what you don't understand, Nadia. It will only bring you hardship."

The jarring ring of the telephone stopped her aunt's speech. Nadia laughed when she saw Lillya's phone for the first time. Most people didn't have a land line anymore or a phone with a cord still attached to it. It was garish yellow with a huge receiver and was mounted on the kitchen wall. Lillya didn't even own a computer, deeming them a distraction. When she first arrived, Nadia hated being without the internet, but in time she got used to it. There were other things in life to enjoy besides social media.

262

"I see," Lillya said into the phone, "we shall be there shortly."

"What's going on?" Nadia asked when her aunt hung up the phone.

"Get in the car. We're going on another field trip," Lillya replied.

Nadia was used to her aunt's cryptic answers, so she raced out to the car. She knew Lillya would eventually tell her. They drove in silence as Nadia gave her aunt curious looks every few moments. Lillya was tight-lipped and wouldn't say a word. After thirty minutes of driving, she turned onto a dirt road. There was nothing but rolling prairie for several miles. Finally, Nadia spied a brown house tucked behind some huge cottonwood trees. It was a relatively new house and seemed in good shape. As Lillya turned off the engine, Nadia felt a strange sensation coming from the house. It was something she hadn't felt in a while.

"There's a demon in that house," Nadia said flatly.

"Yes. The people who called me got my number from a friend of mine. Their son has been acting strange lately."

"Like strange how?"

"Speaking in tongues, throwing things, vomiting all over the place," Lillya answered.

"Is he possessed?"

"Yes, and I'm going to make the demon leave."

"AWESOME!" Nadia shouted, hungry to get into a fight.

"Now before we go in there, there is something you should know," Lillya cautioned. "*I* am going to handle this.

You may look at it, but don't speak."

"Damn," Nadia said disappointed. "do you think he will be crawling on the ceiling?"

"What? That is more Hollywood rubbish! A demon can only make a person do things a human body is capable of. Humans don't crawl on walls or spin their heads around, therefore a demon cannot make them do that … not without killing its host. They are extraordinarily strong, however. They do puke, but its normal human vomit and they will twist and contort."

The front door opened, ending their conversation. A tall, thin woman stood in the doorway, pale and visibly shaken. Lillya entered the house with Nadia trailing close behind her.

"Are you Lillya?" the woman asked.

"Yes. Take me to him."

"Thank you so much for coming. He's in his room. We had to …," the woman faltered.

"What is it?" Lillya asked.

"We had to tie him to the bed. He tried to choke his father and almost killed him. It took five grown men to hold him down. We didn't know what to do," the woman sobbed.

"It's all right," Lillya said calmly. "I will take care of it. Just show me to his room and stay in the kitchen. It won't take long."

The woman led them into the house. She walked past the kitchen and into a hallway. A man with a bandage around his head gave them a quick wave. He looked defeated and scared. The closer they got to the boy's room, the heavier and darker the energy became. Nadia instantly became angry and had to fight to control her temper. The woman pointed to the door and hurried away from them.

"Calm yourself," Lillya whispered. "remember, this is not your battle. You will have plenty of chances for that later."

They opened the door to a typical fifteen-year-old boy's room. Dirty clothes were scattered across the floor, half-eaten food was left on his desk, and posters of rock bands adorned the walls. The boy was lying strapped to the bed. He was pale and sweating profusely. His shirt, encrusted with dried vomit, saturated the entire room with a putrid stench. His eyes were open but unfocused as he stared at the ceiling. Nadia blinked and rubbed her eyes. She could see the dark form within the boy.

The boy suddenly wrenched his head towards them. His eyes widened with fear as he locked eyes with Lillya. He began howling loudly, desperately trying to free himself from the binds.

"SHUT UP!" Lillya snarled at the demon.

"Areshka nersha arey suru kataya," the demon hissed in some strange language.

His neck bulged as he strained against the ropes.

Nadia thought the language sounded familiar. She almost understood it. It was an ancient language, one long forgotten by anyone on this realm. She didn't know how she knew this. The thought just came to her. She shifted her body weight, drawing the attention from Lillya onto her. He howled even louder.

"Why … are … you … here!" the boy growled in a demonic voice, spittle flying from his lips.

"Leave! Now!" Lillya ordered.

Nadia could feel her aunt summoning energy from everywhere. The air seemed to crackle as the light overhead grew brighter. The demon made haste to exit the boy, but it wasn't quite fast enough to escape Lillya's grasp. She caught it with the energy in her hands. It struggled and fought against her superior strength, but it couldn't free itself.

"Goodbye," Lillya said softly.

She pushed so much energy into the demon, it shattered before it could utter a scream. With the demon gone, Lillya turned her attention to the boy. He slowly became aware of his surroundings and acted as if he was emerging from a deep sleep.

"Wha … what happened?" the boy mumbled.

"You had a demon inside of you. What have you been playing with?" Lillya asked, releasing his binds.

"Nothing … well, I had a Ouija Board, but I didn't summon any demons. I was talking with … something friendly."

"Nadia, tell the family they can come in now. Everything is all right."

The boy continued to look around confused.

"Now listen to me, young man. That board brought a demon out. The spirit you were conversing with was a liar. You invited it into your body. Give me that board so I can destroy it."

266

"K," the boy said weakly, pointing to the desk drawer.

"You have learned a valuable lesson. Don't dabble with things you don't understand," Lillya insisted.

The family rushed through the door, elated to have their boy back. The mother hugged him tightly even though he smelled like old vomit.

"He will be fine now, but he will need to rest for a few days. I'm taking this board with me so I can destroy it. It is the tool he used to bring the demon into him," Lillya said.

"Thank you," the father breathed, tears streaming down his cheeks.

Lillya told them it was her pleasure and scooted Nadia out to the car. Nadia kept eyeballing the Ouija board in the back seat. She had seen them before and heard they weren't anything to play around with. She picked it up and examined it. It seemed harmless, just a bunch of letters and numbers with Yes, No and Goodbye on it. She wondered how it could communicate with spirits. It appeared so innocuous.

"I've seen these at Hot Topic," Nadia said.

"Yes, I know. That's exactly what makes them so dangerous. They are sold as a toy. It's been around since the 1800's. It's actually more popular than the Monopoly game. It was invented to speak with spirits ... but often, other things answer. That young man accidentally opened a portal using it. Honestly, one doesn't need it to summon demons. They will come if a person wants one bad enough."

"What are you going to do with it?" Nadia asked, curious.

"You are going to destroy it," Lillya informed.

"Me? What? How?" Nadia asked, shaking her head.

"I'm sure you can figure out a way. Anyone who can blow my garage door into smithereens is capable of destroying a little piece of cardboard."

"I guess," Nadia said, not entirely confident in herself.

When they got home, Lillya led Nadia far away from the house and into the prairie. There was an area on top of a small hill that had splotchy dirt and little grass. Nadia learned much in the last few months, but on occasion, she still let her power escape her. Lillya didn't want to replace any more items on her property, nor did she want an uncontrollable wildfire. Nadia walked a short distance from Lillya and paused to think. She closed her eyes and fell into a meditative state. In the distance, she could hear Gabriel whinnying. It was almost as if the horse was cheering her on.

Nadia had an idea, but she wasn't sure if it would work. She picked up the board and concentrated as she placed her hands on the top and bottom of it. The board pulsed faintly as if it had a heartbeat. She could hear a voice coming from it, tempting her to use it. Nadia was disgusted by the object in her hands.

She called upon her energy and pressed it into the board. She heard a sharp scream inside her head as the energy pushed through the board and into the portal it opened. Abruptly, the board burst into flames. Nadia was startled and dropped it. Lillya grabbed some dirt to put around it. The flames licked it greedily. Nadia swore she saw … something in the flames. They watched it burn for a long time until nothing remained but ashes. Lillya covered it with dirt and smiled at Nadia.

"Well ... that was interesting. Did I make it burn?" Nadia asked, breaking the silence.

"Yes. Somehow you instinctively knew how to transform your energy into fire."

"I heard something scream."

"I did as well. You first closed the portal, and then you destroyed the board. Your energy touched whatever was on the other side, no doubt hurting it. A device which opens a portal can only be closed by fire ... fire that comes from energy," Lillya explained.

"How the hell did I know how to do that?" Nadia asked.

"It's in your blood, my dear."

"How? I don't understand," she groaned.

"You will ... in time," Lillya said, smiling.

They walked back to the house, each lost in their own thoughts. Nadia wished her aunt would tell her how she knew so much information. They washed their hands in the sink, eager to be rid of the filth.

"What was your life like when you were in your twenties?" Nadia asked.

Lillya sighed before answering. She turned her back to Nadia and looked out the kitchen window as she spoke.

"Difficult ... and I deserved it too. In my previous life, I wasn't a kind soul. I did unspeakable things to others. I was reborn in this life with a chance to redeem myself. If I had walked the right path I would have had a good life, but naturally, I chose the selfish one. I married a man who was … well, let's just say he wasn't pleasant. I wasn't in love with him, but I convinced myself that I was. This man was a gas lighting manipulator and a control freak. He was like a child and always wanted his way no matter what. He constantly tried to make me do things I didn't want to do," Lillya reflected.

She paused a moment to collect her thoughts.

"When I didn't do what he wanted," she continued, "he got mad and took his anger out on me. One time he grabbed my favorite radio and smashed it because I wouldn't turn a blind eye to his affairs anymore. There was nothing he wouldn't do when he was angry. The last straw was when he punched me in the stomach while I was doing yard work. I had finally taken enough of his abuse, and I smashed a brick into his head. He was bleeding and dazed when he launched himself at me, but I had already armed myself with a rake … the kind with heavy tines."

"Holy crap! You could have killed him," Nadia blurted.

"Yes, and there were many times I wish I had. He saw the rake in my hands and fled like a coward. I emptied the bank accounts that day and filed for divorce. I hated the house we bought, so I rented an apartment in town. It took a long time, but we were divorced after three years."

"Geesh! Why did it take so long?"

"Because he went to jail … for murder," Lillya said, looking directly in Nadia's eyes.

"Murder? Who did he kill?"

"Our unborn son."

It took a few moments for the information to register with Nadia. Then everything made sense. Her aunt was pregnant when he punched her in the stomach. That was why she finally snapped.

"You were gonna have a baby," Nadia said sadly.

"Yes, and he took him from me. The loss was horrible, and it took me many years to get over it, but I did. When he was released from prison, the first thing he did was look for me, but I wasn't the same person he remembered. I trained in various forms of martial arts. When he tried to attack me, I cleaned his clock and sent him back to prison. He was released after a few more years, but he never bothered me again. I broke him."

"You had such a hard life," Nadia sighed sadly.

"No harder than yours, my dear. I have learned my lesson. Our type is meant to help others, not use them for our own selfish desires."

"I must have been a selfish bastard in my other lives," Nadia laughed. "it was so hard. I don't know how I survived."

"You survived because you're strong. I can tell you are much happier now."

"Way, way happier. You saved my life," Nadia admitted, her eyes welling up with tears.

"We have a …," Lillya paused and cocked her head, "wait … do you feel that?" she asked.

Nadia closed her eyes and felt a strange flow of energy. It was everywhere and impossible to pinpoint. Suddenly her aunt screamed, clutching her head as she fell to the ground. Nadia's sight began to dim. She slowly sank to the kitchen floor and pulled herself into a sitting position. Nadia put her head between her knees. In the far distance, she could hear screams of agony, but it wasn't coming from her aunt. It was from somewhere else … somewhere else in the world.

When she opened her eyes, she was in the forest. FireWind was nudging her with his head.

"What has happened?" her voice asked.

"Lucifer has sent his armies onto your land. When enough of them arrive, they will wage war upon your people. He is only sending a few at a time because he is waiting to see how Zavier reacts."

"Bastard!"

"He plans on upsetting the balance," FireWind said sadly.

"The fool! Does he realize how many people he will destroy with his selfish actions?"

"Yes. Lucifer's counting on it."

"How do you know this, my friend?"

"There are whispers on the wind," the dragon puffed.

FireWind and the forest began to slowly disappear. She felt hands shaking her. Nadia rubbed her face to clear the fogginess. Her aunt was speaking to her, but it took a bit to register what she was saying.

"Nadia! Wake up!" Lillya pleaded urgently.

"I'm awake, I'm awake. Wha' happened?"

"There's been a disruption in the balance," Lillya said. "the smell of battle is in the air."

272

"Yea, I remember FireWind telling me something like that," Nadia mumbled. "what should we do?"

"Change of plans. Next week is when school starts again. I'm only going to teach you what you need to know to pass. The rest of the day will be spent perfecting your sword fighting skills and learning magic."

"Awesome!" Nadia shouted happily.

"You are not going to think it's so awesome. We are going to train harder and longer. You have much to learn yet."

Lillya was true to her word. She woke Nadia up at five AM. Nadia refused to get out of bed, so Lillya roused her cats. They crawled around Nadia's head, purring loudly into her ears. Since it was impossible to sleep, Nadia arose, yawning and protesting. She ate quickly, trying to pay attention to what Lillya was teaching. After a week, Nadia adapted the routine of waking up early.

The days continued into fall and Lillya pushed Nadia to learn her courses quickly. Nadia absorbed everything like a sponge. As the days began to turn cold, Lillya submitted Nadia's paperwork to graduate. Nadia felt relieved her schooling was over so she could spend the rest of her time concentrating on what truly mattered. During Nadia's breaks, Lillya scoured the newspaper looking troubled. She even relented and bought a computer so she could surf the web. Things were getting much worse in the world, and Lillya knew why.

There were always murders happening, but things were getting out of hand, even in their small town. It wasn't just the crime that had Lillya so concerned. Everywhere crops were withering, either by too little or too much rain.

Animals were becoming ill for no apparent reason, and so were the children. Lillya was receiving a lot more calls concerning possessed people. They weren't possessed with weak demons either. Lillya destroyed every single one she extracted. She didn't want any running back to Lucifer informing him of her presence.

For additional protection, Lillya increased the shield around her place so dark creatures couldn't even see into it. One thing she knew for sure, was that things were going to get worse … a lot worse. That's why Lillya felt it was so important to train Nadia. She knew this day would happen, but she felt unprepared. Once Lucifer sent the Varafe … life would be increasingly horrible for everyone. If he sent the Crawlers, it was game over for mankind. Lillya was determined to push Nadia because Lillya knew her niece was capable of so much more.

The garage became their primary training arena. Every day was the same for Nadia. Sword fighting was until one PM, and the rest of the day was devoted to magic. Nadia learned all the finer aspects of wielding a blade. She would leap in the air while clashing her sword with her aunt's. It didn't take her long to learn how to disarm. The more Nadia learned, the more she became hungry for it. She dreamed of sword fighting as she slept. It became second nature to her.

Magic now came easy to her as well. After she mastered the finer aspects of summoning energy, Lillya taught her how to shield herself. Lillya instructed her to imagine a green shield surrounding herself as solid as steel. When Nadia felt it was perfect, Lillya began throwing energy spells at her. Nadia quickly found out her shield was weak. The energy found a way through her defenses and struck her full force. It felt like her head was hit with a hammer. She dropped to the ground, screaming.

"Clear your mind, and we shall try it again," Lillya instructed.

For days they practiced until Nadia was forced to stop. The influx of energy gave her a migraine. She stayed in bed with the curtains drawn. Every little noise brought her a fresh wave of agony. After sleeping for almost three days, she was ready to try again.

"Why can't I do it?" Nadia whined, feeling frustrated.

"You are fighting against yourself. Magic should flow naturally. Relax and let it come from your soul."

Nadia closed her eyes and felt the energy come to her. She forced herself to relax. Within moments, a strange sense of peace overcame her. She imagined herself surrounded by green light.

"Good," Lillya said, startling her.

Nadia didn't realize, her aunt had been hurling energy at her the entire time her eyes were closed. Nadia finally learned how to shield herself. Lillya made her do it repeatedly until she created her shield instantly.

"I did it!" Nadia exclaimed excitedly.

"Yes, I'm proud of you," Lillya said, hugging her.

Nadia looked outside the window. She could see a green glow far off in the distance. It was everywhere she looked.

"Holy crap!" Nadia shouted. "there's a shield around this

place. It stretches for miles."

Nadia peered up and down.

"Wow! It's even above and below us. We're in a bubble."

"Yes," Lillya replied.

"Why didn't I see it before?"

"Because you weren't ready to see it. Now that you have delved into that hidden part of yourself, you will be able to see energy everywhere ... when you choose to see it. It will be far easier to spot someone in need or those immersed in evil by the energy they produce," her aunt explained.

"Kind of like an aura?"

"Exactly. The energy human's produce can vary in colors due to their moods, but the underlying energy is always either positive or negative ... and sometimes even darker if they have a demon nearby."

"Cool. What am I going to learn next?" Nadia asked eagerly.

"I'm going to teach you how to move objects with your energy."

"AWESOME!" Nadia shouted.

Lillya couldn't help but smile at Nadia's constant display of exuberance. Her niece had grown so much during the short time she lived with her. Nadia found her joy again, and that in itself was a huge accomplishment.

"Dear, do you remember when I told you magic has a price?"

"Yes, Rumpelstiltskin," Nadia giggled.

"Well," she said, ignoring Nadia's joke, "your hair is turning white."

Unlocking the Magic Within
Chapter Sixteen

Zavier called an important meeting for the Red Wing angels. He had given them new orders to redirect their efforts. He received word from his spies, Lucifer was emptying Hell. There was no way to know if Lucifer finally believed Firthel or was simply testing him. Either way, Zavier couldn't intercede. It worried him because he knew Lucifer would try to tip the balance. He was scared for his people and for his son. If Lucifer angered the Old Ones, they would undoubtedly take matters into their own hands, and it wouldn't bode well for Lucifer. Even though Lucifer was corrupt, he was still his son, and he loved him.

Zavier sometimes blamed himself for Lucifer's fall from grace. Perhaps if he gave him more attention when he was younger, Lucifer wouldn't have turned out so badly. He shook his head. His wife would have chastised him for thinking such a thing. Even his banishment wasn't as bad as living without his beautiful wife. Although he couldn't prove it, he suspected his son had something to do with her death.

"Red Wings," Zavier began, "I have a new mission for you."

A murmur echoed around the room. They were expecting this. They had seen the increased demon activity and were all equally concerned.

"There is something I have kept from you for fear it would reach Lucifer's ears," Zavier began.

For the next hour, he told them about his punishment and how Lucifer received the secret information. A stunned silence covered the room.

"I know many of you have questioned my methods in the past, but I need your full support in this dangerous new war."

"And you shall have it Zavier," a tall angel sitting next to him spoke. "I just wished we had known sooner."

"Alas, it was too dangerous to reveal my secret," Zavier said.

"What would you have us do?" a Red Wing asked.

"We are running out of time. I need all of you to fight every strong demon that arrives on Earth. I will send the rest of my angels to fight the weaker demons and give people hope. The only Red Wings who are excused from battle are the ones who have been reborn in human form. Only Katrianna can call them to her and sadly she's not with us."

The group immediately disbursed and armed themselves. They hungered for another battle, but they would have their hands full. It saddened him to see this day come. He always knew it would happen, and so did his people. They called it Armageddon. Now, all he could do was watch events unfold and guide his angels. He hated watching his people suffer, especially when it wasn't their fault.

Zavier left the meeting and sought Renuphen. As usual, he was meditating by his tree. His return brought much gossip among the angels, and he wasn't entirely accepted. Since the other angels didn't want him, he spent most of

280

his time sitting by the tree instead. He found peace there … peace from his guilt and regret. His experience as a demon changed him. When he was an angel before, he was impatient and angry. He couldn't understand why humans meant so much to Zavier, but he understood now.

Zavier quietly sat near him and waited for him to finish his meditation. Renuphen roused after a few moments, opened his eyes, and smiled.

"Hello, Zavier. I knew you were here," Renuphen greeted him.

"Oh?"

"Yes. You smell like cherries."

"There is still a touch of melancholy about you Renuphen. You should feel bliss."

"I know," Renuphen said quietly. "and I do. It's just … I still feel remorse for my actions. The others, even my former friends, don't like me."

"It will take them time, and you as well. I wanted you to know Lucifer has unleashed his armies."

"I guess he believed Firthel after all," Renuphen pondered, shaking his head sadly.

"It doesn't matter. I have faith things will turn out."

"Do you think Katrianna will come?"

"I'm not sure. Only time will tell," Zavier admitted.

"What would you have me do?" Renuphen asked.

"I have a special task for you, but the time isn't right to reveal what it is. In the meantime, you are free to find yourself again. Stay here if you wish it."

"Thank you, Zavier. You have been more than generous. I owe you a great deal for your kindness."

"Think nothing of it," Zavier said, dismissing his debt.

Zavier left Renuphen to his meditation. He went to his house so he could watch the battle unfold on Earth. His Red Wings tore through the Waru like paper, but Zavier knew that would soon change. Soon Lucifer would send the Varafe.

"Concentrate Nadia!" Lillya barked.

"I am!" Nadia shouted back.

Lillya had been teaching Nadia to move objects and thus far, it was her most challenging lesson to learn. She was able to move anything, even a tree from the ground. Controlling her energy was always the issue for her. She began with smaller things like cups. Nadia could easily make the cup rise in the air … and keep rising. Lillya lost over fifteen cups because Nadia sent them into the atmosphere. As far as she knew the cups were circling the Earth in orbit. Lillya couldn't wait to see the headlines in the paper: ALIENS ENGAGED IN TEA PARTY. CUPS FOUND IN SPACE.

After several days Nadia was able to reel back her energy before it went into the sky, but she couldn't gently set it down. The cups always came crashing down. It was all or nothing with Nadia. Lillya finally had enough of losing her cups and sent Nadia to meditate in her room. Nadia seemed to find her inner calm whenever she meditated. Usually, her meditation ended with her falling asleep. Lillya hoped it would help her control her power.

When Nadia emerged from her bedroom, she was ready to try again. Lillya had to give her credit. Her niece rarely complained about anything Lillya made her do. After several more attempts, Nadia was finally able to control her energy enough to bring a cup back down ... gently. That task alone seemed to be very difficult for her, and she was exhausted. Sweat was dripping down her face. She had to practice it many times before Lillya was satisfied. Nadia was so tired from her lessons, she fell asleep at the kitchen table. Lillya guided Nadia to her bedroom, where she fell into bed fully clothed.

Nadia learned the hard way about the price of magic. She was furious the first time she saw the white streaks in her hair. The more she practiced magic, the whiter her hair became, and soon it would turn all white. In the end, the price was worth the cost. Lillya knew Nadia was more embarrassed than anything with her white hair. She was young, not even eighteen and people stared at her when they went shopping. Luckily, it was winter, so her hair was always covered with a hat. The first thing she bought at the store was hair dye and lots of it. Nadia dyed her hair red. It wasn't just a little red. It was the color of a stop sign, but the color suited her.

It was important for Nadia to learn control because soon she would be learning how to transform her energy into fire, ice, and lightning. If she didn't learn how to manage her energy, things could become deadly very quickly. Lillya accidentally set her school on fire one day while playing with her energy. She didn't even realize she was transforming energy until the walls of the bathroom blew apart in flames. No one blamed her, but everyone wondered if she had anything to do with it since she was seen in the bathroom earlier. The entire school almost burned to the ground.

Lillya had led an interesting life, but thankfully, she was finally at peace with herself. Helping Nadia was a vital task she had to do in this life. She wished someone like herself helped her when she was Nadia's age. Things don't always work out to plan, and often it's because of past deeds. No one can escape their karma. It would always catch up to a person. One way or another, the circle would become whole.

In the morning, Nadia was ready to start again. She was beginning to renew her energy at an extraordinary rate. Most people would stay asleep for days after one training session. Lillya assumed it was because of her youth. Lillya once again tested her niece's ability to control the objects she lifted. Nadia performed better than Lillya could have hoped. She finally had full control of her power, instead of the other way around.

"OK, so now what am I gonna learn?" Nadia asked, setting Lillya's jeep down gently.

"Next I want to teach you how to transform your energy into an element," Lillya lectured.

"That sounds cool. Are you teaching me all this stuff cuz you knew I was gonna have to battle demons?"

"I knew a war was inevitable. It's been brewing for a long time. I didn't want you falling to the evil path. They would have used you like a puppet."

"Yea ...," Nadia said slowly, "I'm glad you came along

284

when you did. If I had known, I could do these things when I was so unhappy, I would've fucked up anyone who pissed me off.

"I know. You have great power, Nadia."

"And great power means I have a duty to help others. I think I finally understand."

"I am very proud of you," Lillya said, smiling. "now enough goofing off. This is your next task. Pull the energy and keep it in your hands. Remember how you set the Ouija Board on fire? This will be similar to that. Eventually, the energy you pull will gather heat and turn into a flame. This may take you a little while to learn, but please for heaven's sakes don't burn down my garage!

Lillya demonstrated before she allowed Nadia to try. Nadia could see the energy between her aunt's hands. Within moments the energy burst into flames. Lillya twisted the fire around in her hands like a ball.

"See, that's how you do it," Lillya explained.

"Will I get burned at all?" Nadia asked, warily.

"Of course not, silly," Lillya laughed. "anything that comes from you will not harm you. You could shroud yourself in flames, and it wouldn't hurt a bit."

"Wow, that's amazing!"

"But make no mistake about it, the fire you create is quite lethal to anyone else. Now it's your turn."

Nadia closed her eyes and concentrated. It seemed easy enough for her to learn. It took her only a few moments to bring fire to her hands. Before the flames rose too high, she took the energy away extinguishing it.

"Wow, that was easy," Nadia declared, "and I don't feel tired at all. Will other people be able to see the fire I make?"

"Yes. They cannot see the clear energy itself, but anytime you transform energy, it becomes visible."

"Wow! I am a fire bender!" Nadia shouted.

"A what?"

"It's from a cartoon called the Avatar. They called it bending. This kid could bend fire, water, air, and earth."

"Ah. I remember that cartoon. You are far more powerful than a cartoon character."

"Well, yea. That's a cartoon," Nadia giggled.

"What I mean is, even if the cartoon were real, you would be still more powerful," Lillya revealed.

"Really? What else can I do?"

"In time you will be able to shapeshift, transform objects, travel through time, teleport to different realms, summon vast armies and manipulate energy as a weapon. In addition, you are very good with a sword."

"Holy crap! I can do all that?" Nadia asked, stunned.

"In time, you will."

"Awesome!"

Lillya shook her head and laughed. 'Awesome' seemed to be Nadia's response for everything she taught her. She was so excited to learn.

"Next you will learn to transform energy into ice," Lillya began. "ice can be useful for freezing your opponents but transforming energy into ice isn't the same as fire. All energy has some degree of heat to it, but instead of adding heat, you're going to pull it away until there's nothing left but a ball of liquid ice. I'm going to do something extreme, but I want you to shield yourself before I do it."

Nadia was extremely interested with the new spell. Lillya never asked her to shield herself before she did magic. The danger element was exciting.

Lillya summoned a massive ball of energy. As it got bigger, the air became colder. A few moments later, the entire ball was a light blue color. Then Lillya did something Nadia didn't expect. She smashed the ball of ice into the garage floor, freezing the floor instantly. Seconds later, the walls inside the garage and everything else was covered with a thick layer of ice. The air was so cold it was difficult to breathe.

"Wow! That was awesome!" Nadia squealed.

"Thank you. If you had not shielded yourself, you would be a solid block of ice," Lillya laughed. "now it's your turn."

"It's freezing in here! Can we try this outside?"

No, this place is already frozen. It's the best place to work with ice energy," her aunt insisted.

Pulling her thin jacket closer to her body, Nadia summoned the energy to her hands. She found this spell just as easy as the fire spell. Her hands held a blue orb within seconds. Nadia wanted to smash it to the ground like her aunt, but Lillya wouldn't let her. She instructed her to add heat to the ball and return it to its former state. Nadia was of course, disappointed, but did as she was told.

When the energy dissipated, Lillya wanted to return to the house and let the garage thaw. Nadia suggested they create fire, but Lillya didn't want her to waste the energy. The only heat Lillya allowed her to produce was just enough to melt the door. Nadia worked her hands along the edges and gently pushed her energy into it. In no time at all, the door began to melt, and before long she was standing in a pool of cold water. Her body shivered, eager to leave the garage. Out of the corner of her eye, she noticed her aunt was unaffected by the cold.

"Aren't you cold?" Nadia asked, her teeth chattering.

"Not really. I raised my internal temperature. I don't want to teach you that, however. If you raise it too high, you could injure yourself."

"I'm freezing!"

"Well then melt the door quicker, but do not set it on fire," Lillya warned.

Nadia poured just enough energy to get the door open. The chilly winter air felt warm compared to the meat locker garage. She sprinted into the house, warming her hands by the fireplace.

"Aunt Lillya, why do you even use a fireplace if you can raise your internal temperature?"

"I have cats, dear. They would freeze. Besides, it isn't good for a house to stay cold. Pipes would burst and so on."

"Well … why do you wear a coat when we go outside?"

"Because I don't use my energy unless I have too," Lillya explained.

288

"But you can do magic without paying a price," Nadia pointed out.

"True, but I paid my price a long time ago," Lillya said softly. "remember what I told you. Just because you can do something doesn't mean you should."

"I suppose your right," Nadia sighed.

"While you are warming up, I want you to think about how you might transform your energy into lightning. I will be right back. Do not try the spell without me. Is that clear?"

"Yup," Nadia giggled, rolling her eyes.

Nadia sat down and stared into the flames. She thought heat and ice were basically rudimentary spells. She was either adding heat or taking it away. Lightning was electricity and entirely different. To create lightning, she would have to completely transform her energy into something else. She had no idea how to do that.

"Unless," she thought, "I have to pull the positive energy atoms from molecules."

The more she thought about it, the more it made sense. Positive molecules were in everything. All she had to do was harness their energy. It seemed simple enough. She decided to give it a whirl. Nadia looked around for her aunt but couldn't see her anywhere. Slowly, she created a tiny ball of energy. She pulled as much positive energy as she could muster from the air and combined it with the energy in her hands. The small ball began to spark and sizzle. Suddenly she began coughing violently and let the spell disintegrate.

"I thought I told you not to try the spell without me," Lillya chastised her from behind.

"I … I'm sorry. I just had to try," Nadia apologized, giving her a sheepish grin.

"You are so stubborn! When are you going to listen! You're just like your father," Lillya reprimanded her.

"My dad was stubborn?" Nadia thought to herself. "well, perhaps a little."

"I figured I had to pull protons from molecules," Nadia said to her aunt.

"Correct. This is a very dangerous spell, which is why I didn't want you to try it on your own, young lady. When you pull protons from molecules, they are left with electrons and neutrons. It will change the air around you into something not breathable."

"Oh. I didn't think about that," Nadia admitted, realizing why she coughed so suddenly.

"Uh huh," Lillya said, glaring at her.

"I won't do it again."

"See to it you don't. That being said … I'm very pleased you figured it out so quickly," Lillya praised, her tone softening.

"Thanks," Nadia beamed.

"Are you feeling all right?"

"Yup. A little pooped, but otherwise I'm OK."

"Feel like going back in the garage for more training?" Lillya asked.

"Are you kidding? I'm not gonna train in that ice box," Nadia protested.

"It's fine. I melted the ice."

Nadia ran out to the garage expecting to see the frozen walls, but everything had disappeared. Even the floor was dry. It was as if her aunt hadn't even used the spell. She stared at Lillya in wonder.

"What?" Lillya asked.

"How … how did you do that?"

"It wasn't hard dear. You just have to know how much energy to summon, so the place doesn't catch on fire."

Nadia created lightning until long after nightfall. Lillya first instructed her niece to shield herself so the rancid air wouldn't hurt her lungs. They frequently moved around in the garage. Lillya concluded the lesson and told her she would take care of the animals so Nadia could rest. Feeling grateful, Nadia returned to her room to think.

Questions barged into her mind. She wondered why her aunt knew so much information, but more importantly, how she could perform magic so well.

"Surely she didn't learn all of this on her own. I wonder who trained her?" Nadia asked softly to herself.

Nadia thought about Lillya for a long time when an idea entered her mind. She rushed from her room to confront her aunt. Lillya was relaxing by the fireplace.

"I know now!" Nadia shouted, startling Lillya.

"You scared me," Lillya exclaimed, "know what, exactly?"

"I know how you know so much information, why you

are so powerful and why demons are scared of you," Nadia blurted.

"Oh? And why is that dear?" Lillya asked, amused by Nadia's enthusiasm.

"You are KATRIANNA!"

"What?" Lillya asked.

"Katrianna! You are her reborn in this life."

Lillya brought her head back and laughed.

"I most certainly am not Katrianna," Lillya clucked.

"What? But … you're not?" Nadia asked, puzzled.

"No dear heart. You are."

To Thine own Self be True
Chapter Sixteen

"It is time!" Lucifer ordered. "send the Varafe. My father has done nothing to intervene except send his pathetic warriors. Now they can face my finest soldiers. The Varafe will not stop until everything is covered with blood! I wish to destroy Parium first. I want my father's humans to be the first to die. Inform the Varafe to begin fighting the weaker nations."

"Yes sire," said Lucifer's newest head demon, Kereshus, "but wouldn't it be wiser to have them destroy the stronger nations first?"

Lucifer growled at Kereshus. Again, he was being questioned. It made his blood boil.

"How dare you question me! I can see I shall have to train you properly. I'll answer you this one time, but unless I ask for your input, never question me again!"

"Ye … yes, my lord. I apologize."

"If I send my armies to the stronger areas first, the entire realm will fold too quickly. My poor Varafe have not been out of Hell in a long time. I seek to cause optimum bloodshed. The people of the stronger nations will turn on each other as news of the apocalypse reaches them. It will be magnificent!" Lucifer chimed, raising his arms to the heavens. "once the balance has been tipped … I will enter the fray."

"I understand," Kereshus gulped.

"But that carnage is nothing compared to what will happen when I conjure the Crawlers."

"I am sincerely sorry for questioning your methods," Kereshus apologized again.

"Never mind. Where is Nezatel? I sent for him ages ago!" Lucifer demanded.

"No one can find him, sire," the head demon gulped.

"What do you mean no one can find him! He's a demon. Track him using his signature."

All living creatures had an energy signature ... even demons. Once a signature was known, it was easy to find the owner.

"We tried sire," Kereshus said quickly, "but he has disappeared."

"What do you mean ...,"

A sharp knock on the door interrupted their conversation.

"ENTER!" Lucifer barked.

Araphel peeked his head inside, seemingly amused.

"My lord ... a Kerbal has discovered something most interesting."

Lucifer waved his hand, beckoning the lowly demon to enter. The Kerbal was clearly afraid, having never been so close to Lucifer. Quaking in fear, he stood before his master bowing deeply.

"Well?" Lucifer asked expectantly. "don't keep me waiting."

"Master ... M ... M...," he stammered. "me clean torture chambers. Me find room."

"AND!" Lucifer barked.

"Me go in for supplies. Me see hole in wall. Me look through. Meeting room on other side. Someone use room to spy."

"What! Are you certain?"

"Yes, me cer … cer… me, sure. Furniture put in front. Me find footprints."

"Show me," Lucifer said, gnashing his teeth.

The Kerbal was quick to stay in front of Lucifer and Kereshus. He could feel his master's angry eyes burning into his back. He didn't want to be the one to deliver the message, but Araphel refused to relay it. He opened the door so Lucifer could enter the room.

"Hole behind furniture," the Kerbal said, pointing.

Lucifer pushed the heavy cabinet to the side with one arm. It careened into the wall, splintering into pieces. He bent over and looked through the hole. Anger welled up within him. Someone had been using this room to spy on him. He knew exactly who it was too.

"This reeks of Nezatel!" he shouted, standing up. "now I know how Yarish knew of the deal. Nezatel told him."

The little Kerbal quickly got out of the way as Lucifer stormed from the room.

"What is your name, Kerbal?" Lucifer asked.

"Me name is Jereasho, master."

"You have done me a great service today Jereasho. I will repay your act in time."

"Jereasho thanks master!" the Kerbal said, beaming.

"Now go!"

Jereasho ran as fast as his little legs would carry him, grateful to still be alive.

"I wonder," Kereshus began, "what that dark shadow is over there?"

Lucifer charged over to the hall cloaked in darkness. To his dismay, he found the hidden gate at the end.

"WHO PUT A GATE HERE! I DIDN'T AUTHORIZE THIS!" Lucifer screeched.

"It had to be Nezatel, sire. The shadow holds a faint signature of his," Kereshus advised cautiously.

"I don't care where you have to search. I don't care how many realms you must enter. I don't care what you must do. Find me that fucker!"

"What do you mean, I'm Katrianna?" Nadia asked. "you're the one with the powers, not me."

"Think about it, Nadia. Remember how that demon reacted when I brought you along to see that possessed boy? The demon wasn't scared of me ... well, it was a little scared, but mostly it was terrified of you. There is such a light that burns within you now. All creatures can see it unless I shield it."

"But I ... but ... I can't be. I'm no one!" she protested.

"Hah! You are far from no one," Lillya laughed.

"NO!" Nadia shouted. "if I am this woman then I am a murderer! I won't believe it! I WON'T!"

"It doesn't matter if you believe it or not, my dear. You are her," Lillya said calmly. "I'm sorry I couldn't wait for you to realize it on your own, but evil is swarming the land and you are needed."

Nadia wanted to run away. She looked around the room as if it were a prison.

"The woman I saw in my dreams. The one with red hair …,"

"Is you," Lillya finished.

"And FireWind …,"

"Is your dragon," Lillya finished again.

Nadia plopped onto a chair and covered her face with her hands. She didn't want to believe it, and more importantly, she didn't want to accept it. Some things, however, were beginning to make sense. She ran into her room and picked up the plastic dragon that reminded her so much of FireWind. It would explain her fascination with dragons. She shoved the dragon into her pocket and returned to Lillya.

"Did the demons who lived with me know who I was?" Nadia asked, tears falling from her eyes.

"No. Your father placed a shield on you when you entered banishment. Lucifer suspected you were a Red Wing which is why he sent them. The more warriors he can corrupt, the weaker Zavier's army becomes. He had no idea, but the one he was most afraid of was right under his nose," Lillya explained.

"Lucifer is my brother?" Nadia asked.

"Yes, and Zavier is your father. Your mother was a Dragon Angel and you, my dear, are one of the last of your kind."

Nadia paused to think. The wind was beginning to howl outside, kicking up snow on the ground. Although it was only eight PM, the sky was pitch black. The cats, sensing her emotions, began rubbing furiously on her legs. Shortly, the bottom of her pants was entirely covered in hair. She didn't care, though. Nadia stared at her aunt who was watching her intently.

"If I am Katrianna, who are you?" she asked.

"Still, you do not recognize me? I am an old friend of yours."

"Who?"

"I am Alastar," Lillya announced.

"But …,"

"After I left you," Lillya interrupted, "I traveled to my home. Word of your bloodshed reached everyone on my realm. Instead of shunning me, they praised me as the man who trained the greatest warrior in all the realms. I became arrogant and hungry for more power. I made a deal with a magic user who promised me powers if I trained his young son with a blade. I never should have made that deal," she said, shaking her head.

"What happened to you?" Nadia asked.

"His son grew up to be villainous and ruled his kingdom with a cruel fist. His people suffered terribly.

"So, were you punished for training his kid?"

"No. I punished myself for that later. I was punished

298

for how I treated people after I knew magic. I became incredibly selfish and self-centered. I treated people like they didn't matter and took whatever I wanted. Women, in general, didn't matter to me. I deemed them weak and hurt as many of them as I could. I savored the pain I disbursed. I was a vicious bastard."

"Oh man," was all Nadia could say.

"My ruler sent me to Zavier who thought it fitting I be reborn as a woman. I had a difficult childhood and a terrible marriage. I've only found real happiness in the last five years of my life. Things had to play out as they did so we could learn … we serve something greater than ourselves. We are meant to help others, not hurt them."

"Lillya or Alastar or whoever you are … this is too much for me to handle right now. I'm gonna go outside for a walk."

"It's freezing and dark. Wear the proper attire, take a flashlight, and don't be outside for long," Lillya said sternly.

Nadia grabbed a heavy coat with a hood and some gloves. She took the Maglite in the closet, but she didn't turn it on. She didn't want any external light. The light from the moon was bright enough. She wandered around the yard, unsure of where she was going. In the distance, she could hear the animals in the barn. She wanted to be near them, so she slipped into the barn and turned on the light. The inside exploded into a ruckus as the animals came to life around her. The chickens began clucking, leaving their perches for hopes of food. The goats now grown leaned their heads over the railing, bleating for her attention.

She patted them on the head and continued to Gabriel stall. He softly nickered at her approach. Nadia wrapped her arms around his thick neck and took comfort being near him.

"Oh Gabriel," she said, rubbing his neck. "what am I going to do? I can't possibly be Katrianna, can I?"

He pulled away from her and began prancing around his stall, whinnying loudly. The sound echoed throughout the barn. Gabriel raised his left hoof and began stomping wildly.

"What is it, boy?" Nadia asked, worried about the horse's behavior.

He came over to her and stared into her eyes.

"Oh ...," she breathed.

As the horse locked eyes with her, memories flooded her consciousness ... memories of battle and death. She remembered everything about who she truly was and what she had done. Tears ran down her face as she was overcome with remorse. She earned the nickname 'The Reaper', a name she now despised. Nadia didn't know how long she stayed there, her eyes glued to Gabriel's, but he finally moved and broke their connection.

"Wow!" she said softly.

Nadia kissed him on the nose and ran back to the house, glancing at the clock inside. She had been outside for over two hours.

"Sorry I was gone for so long," Nadia apologized.

"I knew where you went. I followed you. I knew you were

300

safe, so I just let you be."

"Oh."

"So, my dear, do you feel any better?" Lillya asked.

"I feel … different. Out in the barn … I remembered things … things I shouldn't have known."

"Memories of your past I suspect," Lillya suggested.

"I killed so many people," Nadia bawled.

"Yes … you did. You succumbed to your anger and let it rule you."

"Why!" Why didn't I listen to my father?" Nadia wailed.

"What child listens to their parents? When children reach a certain age, they think they know everything. Your father tried to make you understand, but you refused to listen. You had to learn the hard way."

"I've been gone a long time," Nadia said wistfully. "I was alone in my banishment. I was like a ghost."

"Yes, well, you couldn't have returned at a better time. Lucifer has unleashed the Varafe, and the balance is shifting."

"He has what!" Nadia shouted.

"They are led by Elistax."

Nadia's posture immediately changed. She stood up taller, her eyes blazing.

"I have precious little time. I need to meditate and leave my body. Will you fight with me, Alastar?"

"Always, Katrianna."

"Thank you. I will see you shortly," Nadia said.

Nadia didn't want to believe she was Katrianna. She wanted to run away and hide, however, that was just not possible. There was only the option of accepting who she was, taking responsibility for her actions, and fighting for those who couldn't. It was her destiny, and it was time she claimed it.

She sat in the lotus position on her bed, closed her eyes, and left her body. When she opened them, she was in the forest. She sniffed the air and faintly remembered these woods. It was another one of her special places. She came here a lot when her mother disappeared. A small pool of water was near the largest tree in the center of the forest. She kneeled and peered at herself. A familiar face looked back at her. Her fiery red hair surrounded her face. Radiant hazel eyes looked back at her. Her skin was flawless and almost seemed to glow. Katrianna hadn't seen her reflection in a long time. She had forgotten how beautiful she was.

"Admiring yourself?" a familiar voice asked behind her.

"Alastar!" Katrianna shouted, spinning around.

"In the flesh."

Alastar looked exactly as she remembered him, except for his eyes. His eyes held pain in them.

"Welcome my brother," Katrianna said, hugging him fiercely.

"What's the plan?" he asked.

Katrianna whistled sharply. Alastar raised his eyebrows and looked skeptical. Within moments they heard the beating of wings ... large wings. FireWind and a black dragon circled the forest, before landing gently next to them.

"FireWind!" Katrianna shouted, hugging his thick neck.

"Nice to see you, FireWind," Alastar greeted, smiling.

"Alastar, this is your steed," she said, pointing to the other dragon. "she's an ice dragon, and her name is CrystalMoon."

"Interesting name. Shall I call you Crystal or Moon or CrystalMoon?" he asked, smiling.

She didn't think his joke was so amusing and blew snow into his face.

"Ahhh!" he shouted, brushing the freezing slush away.

"There, there, CrystalMoon. You will have to forgive him. He thinks he's a lot funnier than he really is," Katrianna laughed.

Alastar examined his dragon. Now that he knew she was a female, he could easily distinguish between them. FireWind, who was a male had a heavy neck and head. He was small, but he also looked a little clumsy. CrystalMoon, on the other hand, had a long, slender neck with almost a snake-like head. She was five times larger than FireWind and lean. She looked like she could fly circles around him.

"I humbly apologize, my lady," he said, bowing to the dragon.

She seemed to accept his apology and lowered herself so he could climb on top. Alastar scrambled most ungracefully onto her back.

"How the hell do you ride one of these?" he asked, feeling very uncomfortable.

"Just hang on!" Katrianna responded as they rose in the

air. "we're going to the armory. I have to get my armor … and my sword."

Katrianna grabbed ahold of FireWind's fleshy spikes, tucked in her knees, and laid her body close to his. Alastar, who had never ridden a dragon before, wasn't nearly as comfortable as Katrianna. He initially buried his face into the dragon's neck. After a while, he brought his head up and began enjoying the passing scenery. He glanced over to Katrianna. She had an expression of extreme joy.

The ground grew smaller as they climbed higher. The dragons slipped through several different Chains until they entered the dragon realm. Alastar could see a tall stone building rising in the distance. He couldn't think of a better place to hide a sword than one guarded by dragons. As they flew closer, the dragons began to dive. Alastar hung on for dear life as CrystalMoon headed straight for the ground. She knew he was a novice and took great enjoyment scaring him. Just before she slammed into the ground, she brought her body up, flapping wildly. She unexpectedly landed very gently. He jumped off and kissed the ground.

"Did you enjoy the ride?" Katrianna laughed, hopping down from FireWind.

"No offense to CrystalMoon, but that wasn't my favorite," Alastar returned.

Katrianna chuckled and headed to the building. The door to the armory would only open to two individuals, and luckily, she was one of them. Her father was the other. As they entered, torches on either side burst into flames.

"How very medieval," Alastar commented.

"Yes, my father has a flair for creating a proper armory atmosphere."

Inside there were rows and rows of swords, but she was only interested in one. Her sword was in the rear, furthest away from the door. There were several rooms on the left which held suits of armor. It was easy to find her own. It was hung on the wall by itself, and it was the only armor that glowed.

"Choose what you want to wear, Alastar. Anything you need is in here. Armor is in the next three rooms. Swords are along the wall. Saddles are in several rooms on the left."

"Saddles?" he asked.

"For the dragons, silly. You can't expect to fight bareback."

"I guess I didn't think about it," Alastar laughed.

Katrianna smiled and walked towards the rear. The stone door at the end sealed her sword inside. She stood before the door and gently placed her hand on it.

"I know my actions have proved me unworthy of wielding you. I hardly think I am worthy now, but if you open the door, I promise to do right by you."

The door stayed tightly sealed for a few moments, making her heart sink. The seconds dragged into minutes until slowly, the door began to creak and groan. Inch by inch the stone door opened, revealing the shining blade inside. Tears of joy filled her eyes as she grasped the hilt and pulled the sword from its prison. She grabbed the scabbard and a belt made of dragon scales, racing to don her armor. She finally felt complete again. It had been such a long time since she held Rivaclore, but she always felt its presence.

She found Alastar outside, attempting to saddle his dragon without much success. She couldn't help but laugh.

"It's a lot harder than it looks," he said embarrassed.

"Soon Alastar, this entire valley will be filled with dragons. They have heard the call of Rivaclore."

"Ah! You have reclaimed your sword. That is great news," Alastar cheered.

"Yes, it is. I'll be back shortly. I must see my father. I suggest you make nice with your dragon because when I return, we shall head straight into battle."

"Your father, huh? I suspect he will be happy to see your return."

"As *I* will be happy to see him," Katrianna said. "besides … I'm about to wage war upon his realm, and I need his permission."

She disappeared before his eyes.

The Battle
Chapter Seventeen

Zavier was observing another planet in his realm when the heavens exploded into pandemonium. Angels erupted into shouts of joy as Katrianna searched for her father. They rushed from all corners, happy to see her. She smiled and told them she would talk to them later. At the moment, she was only interested in finding her father. When she first arrived, she thought he might be in his house, but it was empty. She finally saw him as he was exiting a wooden doorway, searching for the source of the commotion. He was astonished to see her, especially when she strode up to him and kneeled.

"Father, I've … well, I've been an asshole. I'm sorry for bringing shame upon our family. Please forgive me," she pleaded.

"Katrianna!" Zavier exclaimed, lifting her up. "you are my daughter. Of course, I forgive you. I forgave you a long time ago."

She wrapped her arms around him, hugging him happily.

"Come walk with me. We have much to discuss," Zavier said, as he guided her away from the throng of angels.

Katrianna gazed at her home. It had changed so much since she was last here. One thing was obvious, her father found peace at last. He certainly deserved it after what he had been through.

"I always knew you would return someday, my daughter. I knew where you were, but the Old Ones told me I couldn't contact you until you discovered your true nature."

"Well, a friend of mine told me I was as stubborn as my father," she said, winking.

Zavier laughed and hugged her again.

"It's so good to have you home again," Zavier said grinning

"Father, I cannot stay long. A little bird told me my brother has unleashed the Varafe."

"I'm afraid it's true. Your return couldn't have come at a better time. Lucifer has tipped the balance and escaped his prison. He is leading his army here. Any time now he will conjure the Crawlers."

"That FOOL! My dragon army stands ready. I ask your permission to bring war to your realm."

"War is already here. Do what you must to destroy the evil upon the land and protect the innocent, before the Old Ones interfere."

"I will, father."

"One more thing daughter," Zavier said softly, "I know you hate your brother for what he did to your mother, but …,"

"You knew about that?" Katrianna interrupted.

"I suspected as much. While I was banished, I put the puzzle pieces together. I wish I had known how corrupt Lucifer was at the time or I never would have put him in charge of the realm. Still, I can't blame him entirely. I'm to blame as well."

"Don't you hate him?" she asked.

"No. I gave up hating him a long time ago. It's not healthy

to hold onto hatred."

"Tell me about it!" Katrianna chuckled. "father … am I truly the last of the Dragon Angels?"

"No, there is another and she is on Parium. You should seek her out when you can. It's sad to see such a powerful race of women die out."

"Who were they?" Katrianna asked, trying to remember.

"All Dragon Angels can trace their lineage to one woman, Kellia. Kellia was the product of a human mother and a dragon father.

"Um … that must have been painful," Katrianna surmised.

"He was a shapeshifter," Zavier laughed. "he came to Kellia's mother as a man. Kellia was the start of the magnificent race of females."

"So, there has never been any male Dragon Angels?" Katrianna pondered. "sorry for the questions. I have forgotten much during my stint as a human. It's taking a bit to reclaim all my memories."

"No worries, daughter. Dragon Angels are only female, and they preferred it that way. Males were highly unpopular and were usually put to death immediately following their birth. The few boys who were allowed to live didn't have any special abilities. The traits were only passed on to the females. In their heyday, there were over fifty thousand of them, but over time, their race began to die out."

"Why?"

"Many died in battle with warring clans. Others waited too long to give their hearts, and others like your mother were betrayed. When I met your mother, she was only one of four left. Two of them were too old to have children. When you and the other die, the last of a great race will disappear from existence."

"So, my brother doesn't have any of our mother's genes?" Katrianna asked.

"No. Only you. Another reason he is jealous of you."

"I won't kill him, father. I'll send him back and right the balance," she said fiercely.

"Thank you. Your brother is infuriating, but he does serve a purpose. Don't be tempted to travel to Hell and slaughter the remaining demons. Once they quit fighting, the war is over."

Katrianna sighed. Her father must have read her mind. She would have loved to eradicate every single demon, but her father wouldn't let her.

"But father, shouldn't they be punished?"

"It's not your job to decide punishment. That is my responsibility. Besides, you wouldn't want the Old Ones to intercede again, would you?"

"No. I don't ever want to be banished again," Katrianna said softly.

"All of the Red Wings are already in battle. You must call upon the others in human form. Lucifer will probably run the moment he sees you."

"He is a coward!" she growled.

"He's weak and refuses to change. He only wishes to control and manipulate others. He cannot see anything but himself and therefore denies himself happiness. Your brother will never know the simple joy of a beautiful flower or … the love of another. Come, my dear. Before you leave, there is someone I want you to meet."

Zavier guided Katrianna to the tree with pink flowers. Renuphen nervously waited for them. He kept wringing his hands as if he didn't know what to do with them.

"Katrianna, this is Renuphen, and he is a very special angel."

She somehow knew him. There was something very familiar about him. She was stunned when he fell to his knees before her.

"I don't expect you to accept my apology, but I swear to you I'll spend the rest of my life trying to make it up to you," Renuphen wept.

"W … who are you?" she asked cautiously.

"I was an angel who was tricked into falling and became a demon. I was the one who took everything from you. I was the demon who lived in your house. You called me Moe."

"YOU! You're that bastard! I remember you now. I should take your head as payment," Katrianna snarled.

"Take it, if you wish," Renuphen murmured, his eyes filling with tears.

"Katrianna," her father interjected, "he realizes he was wrong. He's trying to make amends with you."

"Amends! How can he possibly fix what he has done!"

"If you are going to be mad at him, you might as well be mad at me too. I allowed it to happen. I knew what was happening, but you needed to learn what it felt like to have everything stripped away from you. He is the reason I knew about Firthel. Renuphen's information gave you time. I trust him."

Renuphen took out his sword, put one hand on the hilt and the other on the blade. He bowed and held the blade to her.

"I hereby pledge my sword to you," he said solemnly.

"Paa! You are not a Red Wing, and I don't need a servant. I should feed you to my dragon. At least then you would be useful."

Katrianna walked a few steps away and began to pace. She didn't know what to do. She could clearly see he was sorry for his actions, but she didn't trust him either. He betrayed one master after another to get what he wanted. After a few moments, Katrianna grabbed Renuphen by his neck and hoisted him to his feet. She put her face inches from his and snarled.

"It would be wise if you listened to me now. I will allow you to fight with me. I will even give you a dragon to ride, but if you betray me … I will slice you to pieces beginning at your feet. Now tell me the names of the two demons who helped you. I won't destroy you … yet, but I make no promises to save your friends."

"Tyrient and Ieckisht, and they are no friends of mine. Thank you, Katrianna, and I will not betray you," he said calmly. "all I ask is for a chance to earn your forgiveness."

She released him and turned her attention towards Zavier.

"Father, time is running short. My army waits for me."

312

She hugged her father and left him with tears in his eyes. Her wings unfurled as she silently called to the reborn Red Wings to meet her on the Meinashar. They answered her call and shed their flesh suits like snakes. Katrianna greeted everyone once she arrived with Renuphen.

The dragons filled the valley, roaring in unison. They welcomed her, knowing she would finally restore order. Even the old king Rivaclore, now weary with age, was waiting for her. Alastar had mastered the art of saddling a dragon, saddling FireWind for her.

"Thank you, Alastar. Now, I want to put your saddling talents to good use."

"Oh?"

"Yes, this betrayer," she said, pointing to Renuphen, "wants to fight with us. Could you please saddle that brown sand dragon over there?"

"Geesh! Anything else you want? Some toast, perhaps?"

Alastar could see she wasn't in the mood for jesting and climbed down from CrystalMoon. Katrianna stroked the sand dragon and whispered quietly to him. After some coaxing, he allowed Renuphen to ride him. She beckoned to the angel.

"Renuphen, this is DustWing. He will be your mount."

"Thank you," Renuphen replied, becoming weepy.

"Listen to me!" she barked at Renuphen, "I need a warrior! We're going into battle, and lives will be lost. I need you to put your melancholy away and bring out your fighter. If you truly want to fight with me, then find your inner strength, or you will be dead in minutes. Do you understand?"

"Yes."

She turned away, disgusted by his behavior. She vaulted upon FireWind's back, raising her sword to the heavens. A thunderous response greeted her ears as thousands of wings beat the air. Suddenly everyone shrieked their battle cries. Katrianna roared above the din.

"Dragons!" she shouted. "you've followed me into battle before, and I betrayed your trust. I brought dishonor to the dragon clan. Today is the day I return your honor. Today we right the wrongs we were meant to right. Today we fulfill our destiny! WILL YOU FIGHT BESIDE ME!"

The dragons roared and stomped their feet so noisily, the trees began to shake and collapse. FireWind launched himself into the air with Alastar and the rest of the dragons following closely behind. They positioned themselves in a V-formation with Alastar on her immediate right and Renuphen on her left. The Red Wings trailed behind the dragons. Alastar gave her a quick smile and patted CrystalMoon's neck. Only the strongest and fiercest dragons were in her army, comprised of fire, ice, poison, sand, and shadow dragons.

As she entered the human realm, she saw a sight that greatly disturbed her. More than half of realm was engulfed in flames as millions of demons ravaged the land. The Varafe and the Waru were systematically destroying every living thing on the planet. Since most people couldn't see demons, they didn't know what was happening. They only knew people were dying in sprays of blood around them.

Those who *could* see the monsters lost their minds in fear. A small number attempted to fight back but were

314

mostly unsuccessful. Demons with wings made a game of hoisting people high into the air and tossing their victims to one another. When they became bored with their game, they either let their prey fall to the ground, or tore them to shreds. They grabbed a man wearing a red shirt by his feet and smashed his head into a pile of rocks. By the second hit, he stopped screaming, and by the third, his brains were no longer in his skull.

Her fellow Red Wings were greatly outnumbered. They found themselves in a tight circle fighting for their lives. Many of them were slain. It sickened her to see what was happening. She spied her brother at the edge of the fray, murdering those who sought to escape. She thought it was typical of her brother to hide behind his army. He was too much of a coward to lead. Those he killed were already injured. Unfortunately, it wouldn't be long before the entire realm was devastated.

Katrianna screamed ferociously and charged into battle. The demons on the ground stopped momentarily unsure of what to do. After a few moments, they resumed their assault. The remaining Red Wings regrouped and joined her army. Katrianna's dragons split into different groups and attacked. Since most demons weren't bothered by fire or ice, those types predominantly used their teeth and talons as weapons. They flew into the air, seizing as many flying demons as they could and carved them apart. Several dragons, however, were ambushed by hundreds of demons. They covered them like a blanket of ticks, sticking their swords into any vulnerable areas they could find.

The poison, sand and lightning dragons were on the

ground slithering through the army, choking and shocking their enemies. The shadow dragons used their talents to the fullest. As a demon charged, the shadow dragons would turn back time long enough to slip behind. When time resumed, the demon would find the dragon had disappeared and reappeared behind him. This game of cat and mouse was effective in slaughtering the majority of the ground armies.

The exhausted Red Wings rejoiced as their numbers increased and fought with renewed hope. Their swords sliced into the air, cleaving demon heads and other body parts. Before long, the Waru found themselves severely outnumbered and looked to Lucifer for some kind of leadership. He was nowhere to be found near the action. When Lucifer saw his sister enter the realm, he became instantly terrified. He looked for a place to hide, but there was no hiding from Katrianna. She spotted him and made a beeline towards him. Flanked by her companions, she landed with a thud in front of him. She slid from FireWind's back, signaling for Alastar and Renuphen to do the same. Lucifer kept looking between Katrianna and Renuphen. Finally, it dawned on him why he couldn't find Nezatel. His demon had betrayed him. His face colored in anger.

"You will pay for what you have done, brother!" Katrianna yelled.

Lucifer raised his sword and screamed in fury. Instead of rushing towards her, he ran in the opposite direction putting as much distance between him and his sister that he could. Katrianna charged after him, hacking and slashing through the throng of demons standing in her way. Renuphen followed her, killing any who sought to injure her from behind. She cast a spell and destroyed the multitudes around her, but she couldn't use magic often, or it might accidentally kill her allies in the process. She whistled for FireWind, quickly climbing to his back. They circled in the air, looking everywhere for Lucifer. Katrianna instead saw Elistax and her Varafe hacking one of her ice dragons to pieces.

Infuriated, Katrianna brought FireWind to the ground and jumped down. With one mighty swing of Rivaclore, she decapitated Elistax, smiling as the head rolled in the dirt. Katrianna grabbed the head and pierced it on her blade, holding it high so the others could see. The Varafe were shocked that their leader was destroyed so easily.

Alastar and Renuphen steeled themselves. They knew the Varafe would never retreat and both were injured. Alastar had a deep gash across his chest, as well as an arrow in the shoulder. Renuphen had a cut on his forehead, but it was his wings that suffered the most. Sadly, he would never fly again with his twisted and mangled wings. He never left Katrianna's side, vowing to stay with her to the end. Katrianna had her own share of injuries, the worst being a slash in her right leg. Luckily, as a Dragon Angel, she healed fast and wouldn't even have a scar.

"COME ON!" Katrianna screamed at the Varafe. "DO YOU NEED AN INVITATION!"

She motioned for Renuphen to stay back. She knew he would only get in the way. Within moments hundreds of Varafe rushed them. Katrianna spun in a wide arc, her blade biting into flesh. Their blood sprayed over her as she

317

slew one after another. Rivaclore glowed brightly as it sang through the air. The bodies were piled in a heap at her feet. Katrianna screamed, with bloodlust pounding in her ears. It had been a long time since she had so much fun.

As Katrianna finished the last of them, she saw Mortoc and Alastar engaged in a vicious battle. She wanted to help, but she knew Alastar could take care of himself. Mortoc outweighed Alastar by at least a hundred pounds and used his brute strength to overcome his foes. Alastar was far quicker, and Mortoc had great difficulty connecting any of his blows.

"Stand still so I can cleave your head in two," Mortoc growled, raising his massive, spiked club.

"Yes," Alastar laughed, "that is the only way you will ever hit me."

"Damn you! The day I cannot defeat a dark elf is the day I resign."

"Well then, I accept your resignation," Alastar taunted.

Alastar knew if Mortoc connected with his club, he would be dead in an instant, so he did his best to keep out of its way. Mortoc was becoming tired. His labored breathing drowned out the battle around them. Alastar leaped into the air and over Mortoc's head, slicing his shoulder. The infuriated demon screamed in pain. As a general, he was expected to best any opponent. He hadn't seen his blood in a long time. He raised his club and began swinging wildly, trying to smash Alastar. Alastar crouched and dodged, landing his own strikes in between. Mortoc shrieked in frustration as Alastar sliced him across his chest. Bleeding profusely, he tried in vain to strike Alastar, but fell to his knees.

"Wait!" Mortoc begged. "let me go."

Alastar didn't bother replying. Instead, he grabbed his blade and shoved it into Mortoc's throat. Mortoc gurgled as blood sprayed from his lips. Alastar grasped the demon's head and forced him to gaze into his eyes. He smiled as the life dimmed from the demon. Alastar ripped the blade from Mortoc's throat and returned to the battle. Katrianna was pleased he had lived through his encounter and clapped him on the back. Together they continued forward hacking and slashing as they ran.

Screams of death echoed as her dragons chewed through the demon army. The Red Wings around her were mopping up the residual Waru. One after another, the demons fell. With the deaths of the Varafe, the balance began to tip towards neutral. Out of the millions of demons, there were only several thousand remaining. Now leaderless, they scattered in all directions.

Out of the corner of her eye, Katrianna spied one remaining Varafe lying next to a pile of dead. She was covered in blood and gasping for air. Her strength was ebbing. Katrianna summoned her energy and encompassed the female demon in a white shield. The demon screamed in pain. She clawed the ground as she writhed in agony.

"Where is my brother!" Katrianna demanded.

"He has returned to Hell and sealed the portal so none of us can return. Release me, I beg you," she screeched.

Katrianna placed Rivaclore's edge on the demon's chest

plate.

"Today is your lucky day. I shall grant you your wish and release you," Katrianna snarled.

She raised Rivaclore. In one fluid motion, she spun the blade and rammed the tip into the demon's chest. The fallen Varafe died before she could utter a scream, black blood pouring from her wound. Within moments, the last of Lucifer's mighty warriors were dead.

"Do you wish for us to hunt down the rest of them?" Alastar asked.

"No. My brother's army is broken, and the balance has shifted. Renuphen ... care to take a little trip with me?"

"I will follow you anywhere," he said.

Renuphen winced in pain, but she didn't have time to baby him. Instead, she turned her attention to her dragon.

"FireWind, I'm sure my father already knows we won. Please, let him know I will return to him shortly. I must speak with my brother first. Tell father, I promise not to take his head."

"Be careful," he grunted.

"Ain't I always," she laughed.

It was quite easy for her to get into Hell. She uttered a few ancient phrases under her breath and instantly teleported. Like Zavier, she could enter anywhere on the realm. Renuphen was shaken by his return to Hell. He rubbed his temples and scowled. Hell seemed largely empty of demons, and those who saw her, scattered. Katrianna strode into the castle with her sword sheathed. She wouldn't need it since she could easily use magic to control him if necessary. She found him standing in front of his throne. It took her a moment to realize it was FlameEater. She stopped in her tracks and stared. Katrianna always wondered what happened to him. Many dragons had searched for him.

"Well, well, well," he sneered as she approached. "how lovely that you have bothered to visit me in my home and with a traitor in tow."

"FlameEater?" she breathed.

"Yes," Lucifer laughed. "he was in so much pain when I broke his bones to make my chair."

Katrianna trembled, fighting to control her rage. She wanted to slit his throat. Her poor dragon didn't deserve what happened to him. As her anger disappeared, she was filled with great sadness. At least she had some closure now.

"What do you want? Are you here for my head?" he growled.

"No."

"How interesting you chose a traitor as your personal servant," Lucifer mocked. "what else does he do for you … wash your back, or perhaps he simply fucks you?"

"I'm here to tell you I forgive you," Katrianna said, ignoring his questions.

"What?" he asked, unbelieving what he had just heard.

"I forgive you," she repeated. "for mother's death, for all the pain you caused me … for FlameEater and everything else.

"I DON'T NEED YOUR FORGIVENESS!" he screamed.

321

She shook her head in sadness. She was once obtuse like her brother. He had no idea she was forgiving him for herself, not him.

"Nonetheless, you shall have it. Now bring me those two demons who tortured my family."

"I WILL NOT! I DON'T HAVE TO LISTEN TO YOU."

Katrianna closed her eyes and searched for them. They didn't fight in the battle, or she would have sensed them. They were somewhere in Hell, and she would find them soon enough.

"That's OK, I will find them myself."

"DO NOT DARE! This is my home," he screeched.

"Oh? And who's going to stop me?" she asked, smiling. "look brother, I didn't come down here to pick a fight with you. I simply came to give you forgiveness and to have a little chat with those two demons."

Lucifer immediately switched gears, hoping to manipulate her.

"You have to excuse my temper, dear sister. I tend to get grumpy when things don't go according to plan."

"Wow, you must be grumpy a lot then," Katrianna snorted.

Lucifer wanted to scream but kept his teeth clenched shut.

"Well, I must be off now, brother. Don't worry, I won't kill your little watchers."

"Katrianna wait. Join me. Together we can rule everything," Lucifer said sweetly. "I will even allow Renuphen to rejoin my ranks."

"You must have bonked your head when you ran away

from the battle," she laughed. "why on earth would I want to join you? So, I can be a miserable cunt who takes advantage of everyone? You are stuck in a vicious cycle, and I rather feel sorry for you, but I can't be manipulated … not anymore. I have stepped into the light, and that is where I shall stay."

"I am not interested in rejoining your ranks, Lucifer," Renuphen said, boldly. "I too, have stepped into the light."

"Goody for you Renuphen. You are pathetic!"

"I AM NOT PATHETIC!" Renuphen bellowed. "you are the one who chooses to live in darkness, to be unhappy. If anyone is pathetic, it's you!"

"All that power wasted!" Lucifer snarled. "I swear to you I will have that head of yours dear sister, one way or another."

Renuphen drew his sword and took a step towards Lucifer. Katrianna gently put her hand on his shoulder. Subtle energy coursed through him, calming him. Renuphen sharply returned his sword to its scabbard.

"Goodbye, brother," Katrianna said, smiling, "but before I leave …," she said, sending a stream of energy into his throne.

FlameEater's corpse burst into scarlet flames sending remains everywhere. Lucifer stared at her enraged.

"Y … you destroyed my throne!" he shrieked.

"FlameEater deserved better. At least now his bones will be purified," she said, smiling. "remember unlike father, I can see into Hell and … I will be watching."

Katrianna left her sibling stewing with rage and searched

for the miscreants. She wanted to leave as soon as possible. The air reeked of unhappiness. The only light in the place was her and Renuphen. Punished souls and their tormentors shied away from them as they walked around. She sensed her prey near the wall that divided the sections of Hell. They were playing a game of some sorts and weren't paying attention to her.

"Hey, boys! Deal me in," she said loudly.

They surged to their feet and spun around. Horror crossed their faces as they tried to run away. She caught them by their arms and wrenched them closer, before sealing them in a ball of energy. They recognized Renuphen but were confused to find him an angel.

"Now, now boys, how rude of you to try and run away like that. After all, you were so intent on getting close to my family and me."

"Please, please! We didn't know it was you," the shorter one squealed.

"What does that matter?" she asked dangerously. "I was a human, and you caused me great pain. Therefore, the question is what should I do to you?"

"Let us go," they wailed.

"That is one option, or I could show you my dicing skills with my sword. I can assure you my weapon is so sharp it can split a hair. I could make your pain last for an eternity."

"NOOOOOOOO! Please! We're sorry. We won't do it again ... not to you or anyone else."

"Ah, now there you are correct. You won't."

324

She promised her father she wouldn't destroy the demons in Hell. Instead, she opened her heart and poured love into her hands. She gave her light to the struggling demons. They wailed … but only for a few moments. Their hearts opened, purifying them. They would never be welcome in Hell again. When she released them, they were confused, unsure of who they were.

"Now gentlemen … you will find my human family and take them to Zavier. Do you understand?" she asked, glaring at them.

"Y … yes," Tyrient sputtered. "we know where they are. We can take them away without anyone noticing. Hell is in chaos."

"Good. Snap to it then," she growled.

Katrianna took Renuphen's hand and returned to her army. A thunderous applause greeted her when they arrived.

"Renuphen, I still distrust you, but thank you. You fought well today," she praised.

It amused her when he tried to defend her from Lucifer.

"You are welcome. It was the least I could do."

"Come, we have some celebrating to do," Katrianna proclaimed, grinning.

Epilogue

When Katrianna returned to her army, shouts of happiness greeted her ears. Everyone rushed around her, rejoicing in their success. She asked for a moment of silence to honor the dead … who fought so bravely and gave their lives. She thanked the dragons for their help and ordered them to return home. Saying goodbye to FireWind was the worst. She wrapped her arms around his meaty neck.

"I shall miss you, my friend," Katrianna choked, trying not to sob.

"Are you going somewhere? I thought you were back for good," the dragon grunted.

"There is something I have to do first, but I shall try to visit you as often as I can."

"I'll miss you, youngling. Your father knows we were victorious. He wishes you to return to him as soon as you can."

"Well then, I had better leave," she said, kissing the dragon on the nose.

Katrianna said her goodbyes and teleported to her father's realm, taking Renuphen, Alastar, and the remaining Red Wings with her. The angels cheered her arrival. She stepped to the side and gave the praise to her army, clapping furiously and cheering for them. Zavier motioned to her, so she left the army and embraced her father.

"You were hurt," he said, pointing to her leg.

"Phaa. I heal quickly," she said, smiling. "and I won't even have a scar."

Zavier offered to repair Renuphen's wing, but he refused. Renuphen thought his wounds were a badge of honor. It had been a long time since he felt any kind of honor.

Zavier led his daughter away from the crowd.

"Come my daughter, let's talk somewhere quieter."

She gave her fighters a quick wave and followed Zavier into his house. They surveyed the damage from the arcane orb. Almost half of Parium was still aflame. He immediately created a massive raincloud. He knew if he didn't do something quickly, the remaining people would suffocate. Once the fires were squelched, he would ensure the weather stayed favorable so the earth could heal.

Since nature was such a powerful force, it would take no time at all to replenish itself. The people, on the other hand, were a different story. Those who survived Lucifer's assault would be scarred for life. People who walked the evil path got to see what evil truly was. It would be interesting to see the choices his people made … whether to keep their old habits or reject them and become something better.

"It looks so bad from up here," Katrianna commented.

"Yes," Zavier said sadly.

Lucifer's carnage began in what humans called Africa and spread both to Europe, Asia, South America, and Mexico. They continued their extermination traveling to the western part of the United States decimating California, Oregon, and Washington. There were entire islands like Hawaii under water. It would take years for humanity to recover, but they *would* recover. There was something else that was troubling Zavier, and Katrianna knew it.

"Father, what's wrong?"

Zavier sighed.

"It's my brother. I sense he's in danger and I fear the worst. Something dark is brewing in the Nanalder Chain,"

"Do you want me to check it out?"

"Not yet. I must find out what's going on first. I'm sure the Old Ones will be watching you like a hawk for a while. You are, after all, on probation."

"Father, I have to ask you for a favor."

"What is it, my daughter?"

"When Lucifer sealed the portal, it left many demons stranded on the realm. There is no doubt they will impede the realm's progress," she insisted. "Lucifer will use them to create chaos.

"Katrianna, I cannot let you wage war. The Old Ones agreed your return would be to defend the realm. Your banishment ended because they deemed you worthy ... and more importantly, you found yourself worthy. You have learned much, but there is still some concern as to your control."

"I don't wish to wage war. I wish to return to my human form ... and hunt them as Nadia."

"Really?"

"Father, there are so many things I need to learn, and I can only learn them as a human. I can do more things for people as Nadia than I can as Katrianna. I'll send the demons back to Hell, but I will be more effective because I can teach people how to defend themselves."

Zavier kissed her on the forehead.

"You are becoming the person you were meant to become," he said proudly.

"Not yet, but I'll get there," she said, smiling.

Zavier gave her his blessing, and she bid everyone a fond farewell. Renuphen swore he would continue his quest to protect her and elected to become her guardian angel. She disappeared and headed home.

Nadia woke from her meditation, feeling sore all over. Nadia left her room to find Lillya already awake. Her aunt was sitting in the living room, staring out the window.

"That was some dream," Nadia said, winking.

Lillya held up the paper for her to see. The title read: END OF DAYS! We survived!

"I'm glad they didn't destroy everything," Lillya sighed.

"Yea, but now there are tons of demons loose to fuck with humans."

Lillya couldn't help but smile at Nadia's directness.

"What will you do?" Lillya asked, cocking her head to the side.

"I'm going to hunt them down," Nadia said softly.

"Oh?"

"I was once called The Reaper," Nadia revealed, "so let the reaping begin!"

The Awakening
Book 2 of the Gods and Guardians Chronicles

"UGH! I hate this. I don't understand why I can't do anything anymore. My gifts are gone!" Nadia complained to her aunt, Lillya.

"They aren't gone. Nobody ever loses their gifts. They are just hidden from you again. You will have to find them," Lillya explained patiently.

"But why? Why am I suddenly having this problem?" Nadia whined.

"Honestly … I don't know."

"Gee, that's helpful," Nadia snapped.

So far Nadia's eighteenth birthday was a complete bust. The day started out promising but quickly fell apart. Her aunt insisted on making a 'healthy' cake, which consisted of wheat germ, apple sauce, and dark chocolate. Nadia tried it and wanted to vomit but choked down a few bites just to satisfy her aunt's steely gaze. Then one of her aunt's goats, a brown Nubian named Walter, jumped from a barrel, and landed on her back. He knocked the wind out of her as she fell into a steaming pile of crap.

To top everything off, six months after returning from the war, her powers seemed to disappear. Nadia knew something was off for quite some time. She tried to pretend it wasn't happening, but by her birthday she couldn't even create a ball of energy. She was ready to scream obscenities at the top of her lungs. It was frustrating beyond belief.

Nadia had grown tall in the last year thanks to her aunt's 'healthy' food. She was lean and strong. Working on her aunt's farm gave her the ability to throw hay bales effortlessly. She continued to dye her hair red because she hated the natural white color ... the price of using magic she didn't expect. She liked the color red. It suited her hazel eyes. She was stunning, but she didn't really see herself as such. She was a warrior, and that's all that mattered.

She had been the 'chosen' one ... the daughter of a god. She led millions into battle but now was reduced to nothing. There were times she still dreamed of the battle where she saved humanity. She fought in her true form, a mighty soldier with burning long hair named Katrianna. Her name struck fear into the hearts of all evil creatures. Now she was just Nadia, the small and useless. Why she ever chose to return to her human form was beyond her. She should have remained as Katrianna and stayed with her father.

"I need a break!" Nadia snarled and stormed out the door.

Lillya shook her head. Just when she thought her niece was learning patience, Nadia would throw a temper tantrum. Lillya guessed it wasn't easy for her. Everything was a tad surreal. The war caused so much death and destruction it would take the Earth years to recover ... if it ever did.

The United States only received a fraction of the damage ... comparatively. California, Oregon, and Washington were utterly wiped clean. No movies came out of Hollywood anymore because it didn't exist. Hawaii disappeared from the face of the earth. It sank to the depths ... or rather it was sunk by a vile legion of demons known as the Varafe.

Everyone living on the islands perished as volcanos erupted instantly.

The worst damage was done to Europe and Africa. Lillya had been to Europe once, a long time ago. She wanted to cry when she thought of how it was altered. Africa and Europe were now one big country and a vile one at that. Not many survived, and those who did weren't the best sort of people. A few nefarious leaders rose up, and the entire nation became a dictatorship where women were traded like cattle.

The United States was unfortunately weakened and could do nothing about it. Women in the other countries were slaves and beaten into submission. A man's worth wasn't in how much money or property he had, it was in the number of women he had in his stable. Riots eventually broke out among the women as they refused to be treated like vermin. They formed large gangs, murdering those who chose to chain them. It was a huge mess.

Lillya sighed and reached down to pet her troop of cats demanding her attention. They mewed in unison. She had all sorts of different cats, but one ginger named Rocky was the most peculiar of the bunch. He would pee on his rear feet like a man using a urinal, and he loved to have his belly rubbed. His most unusual feature were his eyes. He would gaze into a person as if he could understand their needs. Rocky was the most intuitive of her cats.

A line of worry crossed her forehead. Lillya was an old soul, like Nadia. Her soul wasn't female, either. There were lessons to learn in this life, so she was reborn as a woman. Lillya appeared as an elderly teacher, her grey hair wound tightly in a bun. She seemed old and frail but was far from it. A mugger learned that painful lesson once. He pulled a knife on her and tried to take her purse. Before he knew what happened, he was dumped in a puddle of his own blood. She had broken his nose and kicked him so hard, he would never have children. She knew how to push her energy into every movement, and that included kicks to the groin.

Her home was in South Dakota, and it was relatively safe, but scumbags lived everywhere. They saved humanity from Lucifer's war. When he was beaten, he ran away like a coward, slamming the gates on his army. Ironically, with the state of things, it seemed he had won anyway. Nadia was a non-issue now because she couldn't unleash her gifts. The remaining demons ran amuck, unchecked, and angry. Lillya had no idea why Nadia was blocked, but it concerned her greatly.

It wasn't just Nadia's gifts which were hidden, but also her ability to travel the astral plane. Even though her niece never mentioned it, Lillya knew she missed her father, Zavier … the god of the realm. She couldn't even converse with her dragons. After the battle, Nadia surprised everyone by choosing to return to her human form rather than remain as Katrianna. Lillya decided to follow her and return as well. She wondered if they made the right choice.

"Perhaps Nadia returned because she thought it would be different," Lillya muttered softly to her cats.

Still … it did worry Lillya somewhat that Nadia was completely shut off from her abilities. It was almost as if she was blocked rather than simply forgetting her powers.

334

The question was … who or what was blocking her?

Lillya knew Nadia was frustrated. Before her gifts began disappearing, Nadia was adamant on hunting her brother's loose demons. She only was able to find a few, but she taught them the meaning of true suffering. Nadia tore their souls to shreds. After the fifth demon, they did their best to hide from her. It was around that time Nadia noticed she wasn't as strong as usual. It all went downhill from there.

Lillya glanced out of the window. Her niece was sitting under a willow tree by the creek. It was her favorite place to contemplate, and lately, Nadia spent a lot of time under it. It seemed to bring her some measure of peace. Lillya understood why, even if Nadia didn't. The willow was believed to be the 'first' tree ever created. It had powers few could comprehend, including fantastic medicinal properties. In fact, the main ingredient in aspirin was willow bark.

Lillya used to have terrible headaches, but she hated taking pills for anything. She discovered quite by accident that simply sitting under the willow tree alleviated her pain within twenty minutes. Whenever she had one now, she simply made a visit to her tree. Lillya tried explaining her natural healing methods to Nadia, but her niece was too frustrated at the moment to pay attention.

Lillya watched for a few moments before she noticed Nadia was not alone. An angel figure loomed over her.

"Renuphen!" she snarled.

Lillya didn't know why but she couldn't stand Renuphen. She didn't trust him, but who could blame her? Renuphen was an angel who betrayed Zavier and became a demon for

Lucifer. Then he betrayed Lucifer, begging for a chance to prove himself to Zavier. He caused Nadia great pain when he was a demon, but supposedly Zavier forgave him. He pledged his allegiance to Nadia and even fought by her side during the war. He earned Nadia's trust, but Lillya still didn't like him.

He was always around Nadia … when she was alone. He seemed to sense Lillya didn't like him. He was always giving Nadia huge cow eyes, but her niece was completely oblivious to the fact the angel was hopelessly in love with her. He doted on her like she was his reason for living. It was quite sickening to watch. Nadia seemed to be able to take him in small doses. He annoyed her, however, when he fawned over her.

Lillya scowled and turned away from the window. In her heart she could sense … something was wrong.

About the Author

Alana Wells is a fantasy writer and the author of The Reaping. Born in Milwaukee, Wisconsin she spent twenty-four years traveling the world in the United States Air Force. After falling for the haunting beauty of the Black Hills, she retired to South Dakota with her family and 6 pets.

She spends her free time writing, hiking, hanging out with her daughter and playing video games.

Alana's love of writing began as a child. She would often write short stories to entertain her parents and friends. Her work on the Gods and Guardians Chronicles began thirty years ago and is the passion that fills her soul.